LOST *before you*

A HEART'S COMPASS
BOOK TWO

USA TODAY BESTSELLING AUTHOR
BROOKE O'BRIEN

LOST BEFORE YOU

My life was turned upside down the night I walked in on my boyfriend with another woman.

The look on his face when he saw me standing in the doorway will forever be ingrained in my memory. I would've given anything to escape the pain of my broken heart.

Like all the times before, when my world was left shaken, Mason was always there to pick me up when I fell.

He's a notorious ladies man and no stranger to chasing away his problems with alcohol and one night stands.

When I asked him for one night to help me forget, I begged him to promise me nothing would change between us. I hated the thought of losing him too.

I wish someone would've warned me about the risks of falling in love with your best friend.

Now our friendship will never be the same...

Thank you for reading **LOST BEFORE YOU**! I hope you love Mason and Brea's story as much as I do.

You can join my Facebook group, Brooke O'Brien's Rebel Reader Group, to discuss the series and get sneak peeks on future releases. Sign up for my newsletter to find out more about my new releases. To join, visit at: www.author-brookeobrien.com/follow

Enjoy their story!

dedication

This book is dedicated to my boys. You're my reminder to never give up on my dreams.

I love you!

BREA

A warm breeze flows through the window, causing my hair to whip around my face. My eyes squint from the sunlight as the music blares through the speakers, helping to drown out all my plaguing thoughts. Pressing down on the gas pedal, my eyes avoid the rearview mirror as I put miles between me and my problems.

I still remember the day I learned my parents were getting a divorce. Maybe my mom was just blind or clueless, but it came as a surprise to her, too. The day after my seventeenth birthday, my mom was served divorce papers. I guess my dad was tired of living a double life.

The life where two towns over he had another family with two children.

Somewhere along the way, things had changed. When you're busy focusing on your career and how the world views you, I guess it's easy to miss how the foundation of your life is crumbling beneath you.

I still hear the wails coming from my mother as she begged my father not to leave her. My heart still aches for the broken woman who was willing to turn a blind eye and share the man she loved than not have him at all.

I vowed never to become so dependent on another person that I lost myself.

Spending a week at home during spring break was at the bottom of my list of fun things to do. Nothing about the place I grew up feels like home anymore. Until my trip home, I hadn't seen or spoken to my dad since Christmas. I'm not surprised at how clueless he still seems, oblivious to the fact I want nothing to do with him anymore.

He called me the day before I left for Chicago, asking if I wanted to meet for lunch. I remember how my hand clenched my cell phone when he offered for me to come by his house. For a second I considered disconnecting the call, but I couldn't bring myself to do it.

Instead, I told him I wasn't ready, and it's the truth.

I'm not ready to see the family he chose over ours. I wasn't prepared to meet his other kids. I can't bring myself to accept what he's done to my mother or forgive him for the years of lies.

I'm still just not ready.

So, I keep driving with my foot heavy on the pedal, leaving everything I'm not ready to face behind me.

The soft vibration on my lap diverts me from my thoughts.

"Mase." I smile as I click the button on my steering wheel connecting the call. It's been almost a week since I've heard his voice. We've exchanged a few texts while I've been gone but texting is different.

Mason is my best friend. Along with my roommate, Lissa, he is one of the few people who knows about the drama with my parents. They are also the only two people I trust.

"Hey," he sighs. With just one word, I can sense something is off.

"How's the drive going?"

"Good. I'm about forty minutes or so out."

Running my hand through my hair, I perch my arm on the side of the door, holding the strands away from my face.

"How did the visit home go?"

Only Mason understands and knows how hard it is for me to go back. How every day I'm there sucks a little bit more out of me. While I know he is curious how I'm doing. I can tell he's hiding something bothering him, too. That's Mason for you. He's always more willing to be there for everyone else, but he doesn't focus on himself.

"As good as I expected it to be," I say, putting it as nicely as possible.

"That good, huh?"

"Yeah," I sigh. "Is everything okay? You sound like you're upset?"

"I'm alright. You want to stop by when you get home?" Mason asks.

I hesitate for a minute, thinking how I will be able to explain this to Kaleb. I haven't seen my boyfriend, Kaleb, since I went home to Cleveland. He doesn't exactly accept our friendship, but I know he knows how important Mason is to me.

"Uh, yeah, I can," I say, swallowing the guilt I feel. Mason needs me more right now, and I know if I called him, he'd come running to be here for me.

"Never mind," he mutters, picking up on the strain in my voice.

"No, don't," I say, hoping to reassure him. "It's okay. I just need to call Kaleb and let him know I'll be by a little later. Okay? I'll swing by as soon as I get in town."

We both say our goodbyes. I press my head against the headrest, thinking through how to tell Kaleb about the change in plans.

Sliding into my seat in the lecture hall, I leaned forward to retrieve my notebook and textbook. Waking up late, I barely had enough time to brush my teeth much less get ready for class. I was fresh-faced and dressed down in yoga pants and a t-shirt.

I couldn't help feeling like I was starting the year off on a bad foot.

Leaning back into my seat, I immediately recognized my mistake as I let out a string of curse words that would rival the mouth of a drunken sailor.

"Everything okay?" a smooth voice asked. I couldn't help the sudden inhale of breath when my eyes met the deep green irises staring at me. The dimple gracing his cheek would make my knees weak if I wasn't already sitting.

"I'm sorry?" I asked, forgetting what was said while letting my eyes roam over his face and chest.

"I couldn't help but overhear you. You seemed a little upset."

"I brought the wrong notebook and textbook," I said, holding up my integrated science book for him to see.

Running my hand across my forehead, I brushed away a few errant curls framing my face. I didn't have enough time to get ready, so I opted to toss my hair into a messy bun. My natural curly hair would never look good if I left it loose and untamed.

"Here," he said, flashing me his perfect smile as he handed me his. The dimple was back in full effect. Wrapping my hand around the edge of the textbook, I muttered out a thank you just as someone slipped in next to me bumping my shoulder.

"Good morning, beautiful."

Turning my head, I found Mason sitting next to me wearing his signature smirk. I felt my cheeks warm at the embarrassment. I was guessing he heard me talking to dimples and he was trying to ward him off.

"Knock it off and pay attention," I said, turning my head, trying to focus my attention as the professor started class.

"What, you're not going to tell me I look handsome?" He feigned hurt, pressing his hand against his chest. I couldn't help but roll my eyes.

"Like you didn't already tell yourself before you walked out of the house this morning." I wanted to laugh at my joke, but the chuckle sounding from next to me told me dimples heard it too.

"I always like to hear it from you," he whispered loud enough for those around us to hear, as he leaned in close to my neck. "I'm hurt." This time, for my ears only.

After class that day, Kaleb worked up the courage to ask me to dinner with Mason standing right there. Despite how many times I've told him Mason's antics that day was us joking, I know he doesn't believe it.

Even after I told him how much trust in a relationship means to me, after baring myself and sharing about my parents' divorce, he still throws our friendship in my face. I can't say I don't understand where he's coming from. My insecurities often get the best of me. I'm scared I could end up like my mom, giving my heart to someone only to have them crush it.

Kaleb has never given me any reason not to trust him, and I've worked hard to prove to him there is nothing to worry about where Mason is concerned.

Approaching my exit, I hit the turn signal as I veer my car toward the off ramp. Deciding it's time to bite the bullet, I reach for my cell just as it vibrates in my hand. Kaleb's name appears on the screen, and I smile as I swipe to accept the call.

"Hey, babe! I'm almost back. I am just pulling onto Washington Street now."

"Sounds good, baby. I can't wait to see you. I thought we could go grab dinner together."

"I miss you, too," I sigh. My heart warms as it hits me just how much. "I need to make a quick stop at Mason's house. He didn't say much, but I could tell something is going on. I'll call you when I'm leaving his place."

The line goes silent, and I hold the phone in front of me to check whether the call has disconnected.

"Are you there?" I mumble, already feeling terrible.

"Yup," he retorts. "Is it always going to be like this, Brea? Will I always come in second place?"

I blink back the tears filling the brim of my eyes.

"It's not like that, Kaleb, and you know it. Mason's my best friend, and he needs me right now."

"Yeah, well, I've spent the last week away from you and right now I need you, too. What about me, huh?"

I can't hold it in anymore. Tears fill my eyes making it hard to see as I maneuver my car onto the side of the road.

"I'm sorry," I choke. I don't know how to get Kaleb to believe me when I know I still struggle to trust him, too.

"Yeah, baby, I am, too." I hear the hoarse sound of his voice before the line clicks, disconnecting the call. I know he has every right to be upset with me. We had made these plans before I ever left town, knowing it would be a long week away from each other.

Looking in the rearview mirror, I run my fingers under my eyes wiping away the mascara streaking down my face. My hair is windblown and wild. Running my fingers through the strands, I attempt to calm the madness.

Checking the time on the dashboard, it's a little after five o'clock. I decide to try and keep the visit quick. There is still time for us to grab dinner. Letting out a deep breath, I pick up my phone and type out a message.

Brea: I promise I'll make it up to you. I love you. I'll call you as soon as I leave and we can meet for dinner.

Scrolling through my Spotify playlist, I click on Salt-N-Pepa before tossing my phone on the empty seat beside me. Adjusting the rearview mirror, I pull onto the road leaving my problems behind me for the second time today.

MASON

"Fuck, baby. That feels good," I groan, tilting her head back until her eyes meet mine.

Running my palm along her cheek, I grip my other hand around the base of my cock as I guide it into her mouth. Her tongue swipes the head as I tamp down a strangled groan.

"Mm," she moans as her tongue darts out, licking the bead of precum before her lips suction around my head.

The action causes lights to flash before my eyes as my vision turns blurry with my impending release.

"Shit, I'm gonna come," I grunt. "If you don't want me to come in your—"

At the same moment the words leave my mouth and her lips tighten around my dick, I hear a thunderous pounding on my bedroom door. I'm too far gone to care.

With my fingers laced in her long blond hair, I feel my body shake as I erupt down her throat. Feeling the aftershocks of my release, I lie back on the side of the bed and run my hand over my face as I take a deep breath, forcing air into my lungs.

The quietness is once again interrupted with the loud thumping on the door.

"You left your phone in the living room, and it's been ringing nonstop, man!" Graham shouts from the hallway.

I hear the annoyance laced in the deep baritone of his voice.

"Yeah, I heard you the first fucking time!" I yell. "I'll call them back, just give me a minute."

I run the tip of my finger along Sierra's bottom lip as I shoot her a wink. Flashing me a quick grin, she pats me on my thigh as she stands. My eyes follow her as she pulls on her bra and slides her tank top over her head.

Sierra is a beautiful woman, and this isn't the first time she's visited my bed. I always make it clear with the women I'm with that it is what it is. Sierra is the only one I've ever made an exception for a repeat. It's not because there is more there, in fact, it's the exact opposite. She knows the score and is only looking for someone to repay her the orgasms she is good at delving out, and I do in spades.

"I'm sorry. I'll call you later tonight," I say, feeling sorry for the interruption.

"No, you won't." She laughs, leaning forward to pull her pants over her slender hips, never taking her eyes off mine.

As I said, she knows how things are. Although we've exchanged numbers, I've never called her. We work together and run with the same crowd. Usually, we happen to bump into each other and one thing leads to another. Before we know any better, here we are.

"Yeah. I guess you're right," I grunt, pulling up my pants from where they sit around my ankles.

She smiles at me with her doe eyes, making her look far more innocent than I know her to be. Sauntering over to my nightstand, she collects her phone and slides it into the back pocket of her jeans that fit her like a glove. Pulling my t-shirt over my head, I watch as she makes her way over to the door.

"Until next time, Mason." She winks, turning the door-knob and sauntering down the hallway.

I hear Sierra's laugh and Graham's grunt, followed by our apartment door slamming shut. Running a hand over my chest, I ease the tension in my muscles as I meander to the living room.

"Sierra, huh?" Graham mumbles, crossing his arms over his chest.

"We ran into each other last night. She had a few too many drinks and I wanted to make sure she got home okay. Change of plans, she ended up stopping by."

"Change of plans alright," he says, shaking his head.

Graham is one of my best friends. We grew up together in Arbor Creek, Iowa. After graduation, we both decided to get out of the small town we call home, although our reasons for leaving were altogether different.

"Your phone rang ten times in the last hour. Someone named Mary Jo. I didn't answer, but it must be important," Graham says, tossing over my phone. The hangover I'm suffering delays my movement, as I fumble to catch it.

Clicking the call button, I don't bother to listen to the voice mails.

"Mary Jo," I say when she picks up, the words sounding more like a question. MJ has been my dad's assistant at his law office for years. I've grown to know her quite well over the years. She is like a grandmother to me.

"Mason, son. I'm sorry to bother you."

"It's okay. What's going on?"

I can't help but feel the panic rise in my chest. Running my hand along the back of my neck, I work to ease the tension.

"Your father was arrested earlier this morning. I got the call a little over an hour ago."

She doesn't tell me what happened because I already know. My dad has struggled with alcohol addiction most of my life. His problem is what led to my parents divorcing when I was five years old.

"Again?" I sigh, running my hand through my hair. The strands are longer than I like to keep them.

"This time it was for drinking and driving. I don't want you to worry, Mason," she reassures. It's hard not to though. "I'll take care of everything. Can you call Callum?"

Tilting my head up, my eyes meet Graham's, and I know he heard the other side of the conversation. With a single nod of his head, he stands and walks into the kitchen leaving me alone.

"Yeah, I'll get a hold of him."

The words are a lie. I know this is the last thing my brother would want to hear right now. In fact, this would serve to solidify the opinions he has of our father. I've grown up listening to Callum grunt and groan, calling him a deadbeat.

Yeah, he's made his share of mistakes, but I can't bring myself to cut him off like Callum has. He's still my dad.

I don't have the patience to listen to his shit right now.

"Alright, I'll let your dad know to call you when he's released."

We say our goodbyes, and I click end before taking a seat on the couch. With my elbows pressed against my knees, I clasp my hands over my head. Sometimes I feel like I resent my brother for the way he treats our father, leaving me to deal with this on my own.

I'm all he has now, and I can't bring myself to give up on him the way Callum did.

The sound of the fridge door has me turning my attention toward Graham. I hear his question without him uttering a word. He knows all too well the relationship dynamics among my father, my brother, and me. I also know his feelings toward all the drinking, both my father's and my own.

"I'm not even going to say it," he cuts through my thoughts.

"Well, that's a surprise."

"How about we talk about last night instead? I got home from Velvet around two-thirty, and you were still nowhere in sight. How did you get home?"

"We called an Uber. What are you now, my babysitter?" I scoff, running my fingers along my forehead.

"No, I'm your friend, and as your friend, I think I'm justified in warning you when I see the path you're headed. God, man, have you not learned from the people around you?"

Here we go.

"It's not like that, and you fucking know it."

"Yeah, isn't that what your dad said a few months ago when you got the same call asking if you'd bail him out of jail? Sounds familiar."

"What the fuck does that mean?" I spit, the words coming out with more force than I intended. I'm not sure if the anger laced in my tone is because I fear he's right or because I know he is.

"It means I see where you're headed. I've been down the same road. There's nothing for you down there. How do you think Brea would feel if she knew?"

My body tenses even at the mere mention of her name, narrowing my eyes and gritting my teeth.

"This has nothing to do with her. Don't you drag her into this," I grunt, reading between the lines. Graham's right though, and that's the problem.

I think I fell in love with Brea the moment I first met her. She's the only girl I've ever been friends with; I mean true friends. I'm not talking about the type of friendship I have with Sierra.

Brea isn't the kind of girl you fuck and forget. No, she's the kind of girl you marry. I'm the idiot who didn't realize what was right in front of him until it was too late. Now she's with someone else and she's happy. He makes her happy. I see it on her face when she's with him and when she talks about him.

Brea's friendship and keeping her trust mean more to me than anything. So, I've focused my energy into doing my best to move on. There are nights where I crave her and the relationship we used to have. Those are the nights I turn to the brown bottle to bury the pang of loneliness I feel in my chest.

With nothing left to say, Graham stands and treks toward the front door. His stomping feet pound on the hardwood floor before he opens the door, slamming it behind him.

Without thinking, I lean forward and snag the phone from the coffee table.

"Mase." The words float through the speaker. I've never liked nicknames, but something about the way she says it makes my heart beat faster. It's hard to hear, her words muffled by the sound of the wind blowing and music blaring in the background.

I can't help but smile as I picture Brea with her long hair whipping around her face, wearing her oversized sunglasses and a smile.

"Hey." I chuckle. At that moment, the ache I feel in my chest lifts. "How's the drive going?"

"Good, I'm about forty minutes or so out."

I hear her sigh as I picture her running her hand through her hair, brushing it out of her face like she often does.

"How was the visit home?"

"As good as I expected it to be," she mumbles.

"That good, huh?"

"Yeah. Is everything okay? You sound like you're upset?"

I should have known she would sense something bothering me. As much as I thought hearing her voice would help, I guess I should've known better.

"I'm alright. You want to stop by when you get home?"

She takes a moment before she responds and I feel like I'm counting the seconds tick by.

"Uh, yeah, I can." The hesitation in her voice has me regret asking.

"Never mind," I start before she cuts me off.

"No, don't. It's okay. I just need to call Kaleb and let him know I'll be by a little bit later. Okay? I'll swing by as soon as I get in town."

I want to feel guilty, especially since she has been out of the city for the past six days. I do for a second until I remind myself she's dating that douche bag, and I can't find it in me to care anymore.

"Alright," I say, "I'll see you in a bit."

I feel somewhat relieved knowing she will be here soon. Even when I can't make sense of my life, she's always here to keep me focused on what's important.

chapter three

BREA

Pulling into the parking lot outside of Mason's apartment, I quickly check my phone for any missed messages. A pang hits my chest when I find Kaleb hasn't returned my text, leaving me on edge. I hate feeling like I'm torn between the two of them. While they have never been more than cordial to each other, I've started to piece together moments from the past.

The way Kaleb would grumble when I would tell him I was meeting Mason for coffee, how he didn't understand why we planned study nights together, or how I can trust Mason when I don't trust people easily.

I understand Mason's history with women. He has grown to be quite the ladies' man over the years. Although he has told me he isn't looking for anything serious, I know he's a good person. The women he's with know that, too.

Shoving my phone into my purse, I step out of my station wagon and hit the lock button. Mason and his friend, Graham, live together in an apartment near campus. Living in downtown Chicago is not cheap, but neither is living in a dorm.

Hitting the button for his apartment, I hear Mason's voice filter through the speaker not even two seconds later.

"It took you long enough," he says. While joking, the laughter that is usually there is gone.

"Well, I'm here now. You going to let me in? It's chilly out here," I say, running my hands over goose-pimpled flesh on my arms.

The buzzer sounds, unlocking the door. Rounding the corner, I find Mason standing in the doorway to his apartment with a small smile on his face. When I get closer, he stretches his arms out to his sides, and I go to him immediately, wrapping my arms around his waist, accepting his warmth.

"Hi," I say, pressing my cheek against his heart.

"Hey," he sighs. I hear it in his voice. He's thanking me for coming by without even saying the words.

With a nod of my head, I lean back and flash him a smile of my own, ducking beneath his arm and walking inside.

Mason and Graham's apartment is nice for a college pad. I think a lot of it is due to Graham's personality. He has a need to keep things in order.

Slipping off my shoes, I waste no time crossing through the kitchen into the living room. Folding my legs beneath me, I curl up on the couch and pull the throw blanket over my lap. It always feels like an icebox in here.

Looking at Mason, I find he's still standing in the kitchen with his arms crossed and an odd look on his face.

"Talk to me," I say, cutting through the silence. I can see Mason subtly shake his head as if shaking himself from his thoughts. He seems more in his head today than normal.

Following my lead, he bounds into the living room and sits at the opposite end of the couch. With his forearm folding over his eyes, I can tell one of us is not going to like what's going to be said.

"You're freaking me out. Knock it off. Spit it out already," I say, smacking Mason's arm. It's things like this that make me paranoid and unable to focus. His uneasiness is putting me on edge.

"My dad has been arrested. This time he was pulled over for drinking and driving."

"Again?" I say, remembering the last time Mason called me after his dad got in a drunken altercation. Steven Reid is a defense attorney in Florida. From what Mason had told me, he had been out drinking after New Year's and apparently started fighting with some guy over whether the Patriots or Falcons would win the Super Bowl.

I could tell Mason was surprised it had escalated to that level. Mason felt guilty for spending the holidays with his mom and brother back in Iowa, rather than going to Florida. Especially now, knowing his drinking has grown even heavier.

I've never met Mason's dad, but I've heard a lot about him since we met. I know he's the reason why Mason is pursuing his Criminal Law degree. I can see the way Mason talks about his father, how he looks up to him. Although, sometimes, I'm not sure I understand why.

"Yeah," he says, rubbing his thumb and forefinger over his eyes. "I have mentioned to him a couple of times he should move home. Or even to Chicago—there are a lot of great opportunities for him here, but he won't hear it. The last couple of weeks has gotten progressively worse. I don't know why he wants to stay there. He has nothing there, no family, no friends. I just don't get it."

"Mason, we don't always understand why people do the things they do. It's not your job to spend your day feeling guilty over the mistakes he makes. I know you feel like if he were here, you could fix it. Take it from me—sometimes you don't see your world falling apart until it's already in shambles."

With his head tilted against the cushion of the couch, he rolls it until he's facing me.

"Are we still talking about me?" he asks, his eyebrows furrowed in question. I didn't mean to make this conversation about me. I meant what I said; I am leaving all those problems in Cleveland.

Right now, I'm here for my friend.

I don't answer his question, instead I nod my head. "How was your visit home?" he asks, reading between the lines. I should have known he would pick up on my attempt to evade this conversation.

Music starts blaring as I peer at the cell phone on the coffee table.

I'm thankful for the save.

Mason quickly leans over and mumbles out an apology.

"MJ, hey." Holding up his finger to me, he walks into the kitchen.

Leaning forward, I grab the remote and turn on the television. As I flip through the channels, I hear keys in the lock, just as Graham enters. A bag of takeout in one hand and a bottle of water in the other.

"Hey, Graham," I say, giving him a wave as I focus my attention on the TV.

"Brea," he replies with a nod of his head.

"Do you know how long they'll be holding him?" Mason asks. I turn my head toward him hearing the question, watching as he paces the small space, running his hand through his hair.

My eyes meet Graham's as he sets the container of Chinese on the table. I see the annoyance written on his face, as he shakes his head in frustration.

I decide to give Mason his privacy, turning to the TV and settling on a movie. The Blind Side is playing, and I use it as a distraction from the thick tension in the room.

Graham carries his food around the bar and takes a seat on the loveseat opposite of where I'm sitting.

"Did he tell you what's going on?" Graham asks, taking a bite of his sesame chicken. He is usually not one to go out of his way to make conversation, so the fact he's talking to me causes my ears to perk up.

"About his dad? Yeah, he told me."

Peering over at Graham, I see the worry he wears on his face. Whatever is going on with Mason is clearly bothering him. I get the feeling he wants to tell me, but he doesn't want to breach the guy code.

"Is there something more I don't know about?"

Running his hand over his face, he lets out a deep sigh, as if considering the next words to come out of his mouth.

"He just hasn't been himself lately. He's drinking heavier than I've ever seen him drink before. I got home late from Velvet last night, and he still hadn't been home. I woke up this morning to the sounds of him—let's just say he wasn't alone."

I feel like a boulder is weighing heavy on my chest at the thought of Mason with someone else. I know he's not seeing anyone; I've heard about his sexual escapades enough over the past few years. I just always hoped he would grow out of this phase of his life.

"I'm not telling you to make you worry, Brea. I'm just hoping you can talk to him," he urges, taking another bite—more like a shovel—of his food. Graham's a big guy. Hell, I'm pretty sure his arms are the size of my head and I mean it as a compliment.

"Yeah, I'll see if I can talk to him."

Just as the words leave my mouth, the sound of Mason's hand slamming against the side of the pantry door startles me from my thoughts.

"What the fuck, man?!" Graham grumbles, disliking his outburst no matter the cause. "Was that necessary?"

I don't know what to say as my eyes bounce back and forth between the two of them. I've never seen them talk to each other like this.

"What happened, Mase?" I ask, using the nickname I have for him, hoping it will help soften the approach.

"It's nothing you need to be worried about. I didn't mean to—" Mason stops, forcing a deep inhale through his nose. His frustration and anger are evident on his face, and his shoulders are tense. "I'm sorry, I didn't mean to get upset. I'm just frustrated."

I hear Graham let out an audible sigh as he turns his attention back to his meal.

"Brea, will you come to my room with me?"

Any other day, I wouldn't think anything of it. We hang out in his room all the time, but knowing he had brought some girl home just hours ago leaves me with an unsettled feeling in my stomach.

Not knowing what to say, my eyes find Graham's as if searching for a way to get out of this. As if reading my thoughts, I hear the frustrated exhale come from Mason as Graham moves to get up from his seat.

"Don't leave the room on my account. I need to get in the shower anyway. I have to be at Velvet soon."

I see the look on Graham's face, hoping he will save me from voicing my thoughts. "I'll see you there," Mason mumbles.

Mason, Graham, and Lissa work together at Velvet, a nightclub downtown. Mason and Lissa serve drinks and run the bar while Graham, along with their friend Dean, work security.

It makes sense though; the stocky build Graham and Dean carry around with them is enough to scare any fool who dares to step out of line.

As soon as Graham is out of the room and down the hall, Mason swings his legs over the couch, planting himself next to me.

I scoot closer to him and he lifts his arm, inviting me in. I wrap my arm around his waist, curling my body around him. We both stare at the TV screen, getting lost in the movie.

"My father won't stand before the judge until tomorrow morning," Mason says. "I guess he was so drunk they felt he needed to wear it off a little more before he could be released."

"There's not much you can do at this point. He's somewhere safe and is alive. I would focus on that for now."

He sighs, running his hand through his hair. "You never did tell me how your visit home was."

"I don't have a lot to say about it, honestly. My mom isn't the same person she once was, and it makes going back there even more difficult."

"I know what you mean," Mason says. "Did you talk to your dad? I mean, I know you don't want to, but I was curious if he reached out to you since he knew you were home."

"He did call and asked to meet up, but I couldn't bring myself to go. I know I shouldn't pick sides, but I'm still not over what he's done to our family. I can't accept the way he treated my mom. They weren't happy; I know that now. I'm just so fucking angry after hearing about all the lies. I feel like everything I've ever known is a lie."

I don't know how much time passes as we sit here like this, watching the TV screen. I can feel the stress of the day ease a little bit from the both of us, but neither of us move.

"Thank you for being here for me," Mason whispers against the side of my head.

Tilting my head back, I flash him a small smile. "You know if you ever need me, I'll always be here for you."

"I do know, and I thank God every day for you," he says. The emotion behind his words take me off guard, and I feel the tears fill my eyes for the second time tonight.

Turning my head toward the TV, I blink back the tears as Mason presses his lips against my temple, breathing me in.

I don't know what I would ever do if there came a day when Mason wasn't in my life and I don't want to find out.

chapter four

BREA

It's not until after six thirty when I finally leave Mason's house. He ended up ordering pizza, and we finished watching the movie. Thankfully, the conversation turned to happier topics, like our plans for the weekend. As crazy as it seems, we are only a month or so away from finishing our junior year of college. I decided to take the summer off to save some money. Since I'm avoiding my dad like the plague, the last thing I want to do is call him and admit I need help.

Hell fucking no!

Leaving Mason to get ready for another night at Velvet, I decide to head home in hopes I can still salvage what's left of my Friday night. Knowing Lissa will be leaving any minute now for her shift tonight, I send off a text to Kaleb in hopes he wants to stop over so we can have a night in together. After our fight and us not seeing each other for a week, I think a night alone is what we need.

Brea: On my way home. Have the apt to myself. Want to come over?

I watch as the notification on my end confirms it was delivered and subsequently read. I wait for the bubble to appear indicating Kaleb's texting a response, but it never comes. It takes me only a few minutes to get home, as Mason lives roughly five blocks away from my apartment.

Scrolling through my phone, I decide to give Kaleb a quick call.

"Yeah." His tone has an edge of irritation to it.

"Hi, hey. I'm sorry. I, um, I just got home. Are you doing anything? I thought maybe you could come over or I, um, I could come to you," I mutter, fumbling over my words, thrown off by his change in demeanor.

"Brea, listen. I'm just not in the mood for this tonight, okay? I'll talk to you later."

The boulder I felt sitting on my chest earlier is back. It feels heavier and heavier as each second of this call ticks by. Who is this person and what have they done with Kaleb? My Kaleb.

"You're not in the mood for this? What the hell is that supposed to mean?" I feel the rise of anger course through me as my hands start to shake.

"I'm not in the mood to deal with this between us right now. I'm getting ready to head out in a few minutes. You wanted the night to hang out with your friends and, look, that's what I'm giving to you."

"Are you shitting me? I told you something came up. Mason is my friend, and he needed me. I'm sorry, I know we had plans, and I feel terrible for bailing at the last minute. I miss you, and I want to see you. Are you saying you don't want to see me?"

"No, don't fucking put this on me. I want to see you; I wanted to see you. You bailed out on me for Mason—AGAIN! I'm sick of coming in second place to him," he says, raising his voice at the last part.

"What are you talking about? It's not like that between us, and I thought you could see it by now. He is nothing more than a friend, Kaleb. Mason is my fucking friend." I feel the tears pouring out of my eyes.

He knows how I feel about trust and the fact he's accusing me of choosing Mason over him makes me angry.

"Listen, I'm going to let you go. I'm getting ready to head out with the guys, and I don't want to do this right now. We can talk later."

Before I have a chance to respond, the sound of the line clicking in my ear forces another onslaught of tears streaming down my face.

"Okay," I whisper to myself, holding the phone in front of me. The screen illuminates, confirming the call has ended.

Leaning my head back, I scrub my hands over my face, wiping away the tears as I let out a deep breath. Shoving my phone into my purse, I get out of the car and walk around to grab my bags from the trunk.

A wave of guilt passes over me for a minute as I think about what Kaleb said. I know he doesn't always like how close Mason and I are, but have I made him feel like he comes in second place?

I always try to reassure him it isn't like that with Mason. Mason is my best friend. He will always be my best friend.

Pulling my suitcase out of the back hatch, I set it on the ground next to me and pull the handle. It's mid-April in Chicago and, as expected, it's windy outside, causing my hair to whip across my face.

I take the two flights of stairs to our third-floor apartment. Not bothering to unpack my week's worth of clothes, I immediately head toward the kitchen and pull out a pint of ice cream. I ate a piece of pizza at Mason's, not wanting to eat too much in hopes Kaleb would want to grab dinner.

The direction my day has gone, the only thing that will make me feel better is a bowl of delicious ice cream. Well, tacos would do, but ice cream is easier at this point.

Not bothering with a bowl, I swipe a spoon from the drawer and head into the living room. Looks like a night of Netflix and chilling by myself.

It's after two in the morning when I hear Lissa come in. Her loud yawn sounds more like a groan as I sit up peering over the side of the couch.

"Good morning to you."

"You're here? I thought you were going out with Kaleb. I expected you to be staying at his house tonight."

"Yeeeaah," I say, falling back against the pillow on the couch. "That's what I thought, too."

"Whaaaaat's going on?" Lissa asks, emphasizing the word as I did. "Matter-of-fact, hold that thought. I want to get these clothes off and the look of sin and sex off my face." She laughs, walking down the hall.

I stop myself from dozing off when I hear her clear her throat, in an attempt to wake me. Peeking one eye open, I see her stretched out on the loveseat in a tank top and yoga pants. Her long red hair is piled on top of her head and her face is clean.

"How was your trip?" she asks. I'm thankful for the reprieve.

"It wasn't bad," I say, not giving anything else away.

"Did you talk to your dad about next year?"

Before the divorce was ever brought up, my parents promised they would help me pay for school. Despite needing to ask my dad about tuition for next year, I couldn't even bring myself to utter the words. I would do just about anything before I give in and ask him for money.

"No."

"No, you didn't talk to him about next year, or no you didn't talk to him at all?"

"I didn't talk to him about it."

"That's what I thought," she sighs, shaking her head. She knows how I feel about asking for things, especially when it comes to having to talk to my dad.

"I think I'm just going to take the summer off and put some money into my savings. With my scholarship, I can do it on my own. It's only one year."

"If that's the case, you're going to need to find something better than working at The Coffee House. You're struggling enough as it is. You really should get a job working at Velvet. You'd make way more money and would only have to work half the hours."

Lissa only works Thursday, Friday, and Saturday and makes more than I do on tips alone. She has a point. The only problem is how would I explain to Kaleb I'm working there. I know when I bring it up to him, he'll immediately jump to Mason.

"I'll think about it."

"Alright. So, are you going to tell me what happened or are you going to continue to avoid the conversation?"

"We got into a fight," I sigh. "I'm not sure what's going on now."

Turning over on my side, I face her. I'm too tired to bother asking what's with the confused look she's throwing my way.

"What do you mean you don't know what's going on? You're still together, or dating, or whatever. Right?" she asks, waving her hands at me.

"We are still together, but he's not very happy with me right now."

"He's not happy with you?" She chuckles. "What the hell did you do?"

"I got a call from Mason on my way into town. He asked me to come over."

Her eyes glitter, as if piecing it all together as she nods her head.

Pursing my eyes at her, I feel the guilt I felt earlier settle in.

"Let me guess... you blew off your plans with him and met up with Mason?"

"Well, yeah... He has some stuff going on with his dad and he asked me to come by to talk. If you called me and told me you needed me, I would be there for you. You would do the same."

Nodding her head along with me, I am getting the sneaky suspicion that while she knows it's true, she's not buying it.

"What's with that?" I ask, waving at her.

"With what?"

"Your face. Why are you making that face at me?"

She twirls a loose strand of hair around her fingers. She normally does this when she's deep in thought. It's too late, or early, depending on how you look at it, for those thoughts.

"Brea, do you really believe what you're saying right now?" she asks, her face serious as she changes the subject.

I feel the anger rise as I swallow what I want to say. I want to tell Lissa she's full of shit and I'm over this conversation.

"Let me ask you something then. Have you ever thought about your relationship with Mason as being something more? Like, down the road when he grows the hell up?"

I would be lying if I said the thought hadn't crossed my mind, but not since Kaleb and I started dating. I would never do something like that to Kaleb, especially after witnessing the heartbreak my dad's actions had on my mom.

"Do you remember on New Year's Day when you and Kaleb had planned to go out to dinner?"

As soon as it's mentioned, I know where this conversation is going. Immediately, the guilt sits in my throat like a ball of cotton I can't swallow.

Mason had called me after he got the call his dad was in jail the first time. I could tell he was still sporting a hangover from the night before. As soon as I heard his voice, I knew the guilt he felt over leaving his dad alone during the holidays was too much for him.

I apologized to Kaleb profusely but ultimately left him to be at Mason's side.

"Will you stop?" I mutter.

"I'm going to head to bed, but I think you should think about it. Look at it from Kaleb's perspective. Every time Mason calls, you go running. You're always there for him. I think the question you need to ask yourself is if something happened to you and the only two people you had to turn to were Kaleb or Mason, who would you choose?"

She doesn't give me a chance to answer her question before she stands and walks out of the room.

I know what she's thinking. She feels like I should turn to Kaleb. After seven months, I should be able to trust him enough to open myself up to him.

The truth is, I would turn to Mason. He knows me better than probably anyone and I trust him.

Every time I would choose him.

chapter five

BREA

After the way things ended last night with Kaleb, I'm not surprised when I don't hear from him all day. Thankfully, I spent most of my time working at the coffee house on campus. Normally, it's so busy with back-to-back customers and college students who are cramming for a test and just trying to stay awake, but with everyone still gone on break, I felt like I was in my thoughts more often.

Checking my phone for the millionth time, I feel the pang of worry in my chest when I see I still haven't heard from him. Like any couple, we argue. This is different; we always make up shortly thereafter. This is the first time we've gone over twenty-four hours without talking.

Grabbing my purse from the locker in the back room, I slip the strap over my head.

"We're going to head out, Sam. I'm off tomorrow, so I'll see you next week," I shout toward the office. We closed a little over twenty minutes ago, and I know he's finishing the nightly deposits.

"Sounds good. Do you want me to walk you two out?" Sam yells. It's only Sara and me closing with him tonight. Looking at her, she shakes her head no before I shout down the hall.

"No, we're good. It's dead out here anyway."

After we say our goodbyes, we walk out the employee entrance located on the side. Waving goodbye to Sara, I jog over to my car. Most nights I don't bother driving to work. I'll catch a ride with Sara since she lives close by or I'll take the bus. Tonight is a little bit different. I had planned before I left town to hang out with Lissa. We were going to head over to our friend Dean's for a bonfire. I was already planning to meet Kaleb there, and I know since Dean is friends with Graham and Mason, they will be there, too.

Sliding into the front seat of my car, I slip my phone out of my pocket just as a text message comes through.

Mason: Ur still coming, right?

Brea: Yep, picking up Lissa now and heading your way.

Mason hasn't said anything more about my fight with Kaleb. We don't talk a lot about our relationships. He doesn't ask how things are going with Kaleb, and I don't mention the nameless women I know he brings to his apartment.

It is what it is, I guess.

A few minutes later, I'm pulling up in front of our apartment. Shifting into park, I shoot Lissa a text to let her know I'm here. Not even two seconds later, I see her strutting out the front of the door. Her long red hair is down, curled in waves. Dressed in her skinny black jeans and a gray burnout tee, she has her plaid flannel tied around her waist. She's carrying the shirt I asked to borrow over her arm.

"What up, babe?" Lissa smiles, climbing into the front seat.

"Here," she says, shoving the shirt at me. "You know, it probably would've been easier for you to come upstairs and change quick," she adds, watching me as I let my hair down from the messy bun I had going.

"What's the point? You know I don't care about going to these parties," I say, shaking my fingers through my hair. Whipping my work shirt over my head, I toss it onto the backseat of my car.

"You're right; only you would wear a cable knit sweater to a college party," Lissa smarts. Looking down at myself, I want to laugh because she's right. Dressed in a white tee, a blush colored sweater, and distressed jeans, I'm dressed more for comfort than anything.

"It's cooler outside tonight. I don't want to be cold."

With a laugh and roll of her eyes, she pulls the seat belt over, buckling herself in.

"Let's put the pedal to the metal then, Grandma," she cheers, smacking her hand against the dashboard, encouraging me to get moving

"Watch it!" I yell. "You love this station wagon, and you know it. I'll show you 'Grandma' alright."

Leaning over, I turn the volume up just as "North Carolina" blares through the speakers. I can't control my laughter when I see the look on Lissa's face as she shakes her head at me. She doesn't understand my love of old school rap and hip hop.

"Who am I? Petey Pab' motherfucker!" I sing, letting the beat of the music flow through me, pushing away the earlier thoughts of Kaleb and our fight.

It doesn't take long before I'm parking my car in front of Dean's on the outside of town. You can hear the music playing from inside as swarms of the party goers filter in and out of the house.

Closing the car door, I slide my cell phone into my pocket as I use the remote to open the back hatch to grab my Vans I shoved back there.

"Girl, I swear you could live in your car with as much shit as you keep stored in there."

I don't even bother to acknowledge her as we both make our way toward the front of the house. Spotting Mason and a couple of his friends, I climb the hill in the yard to where they are standing.

Wrapping his arm around my shoulders, he greets me with a hug. With my head tucked beneath his chin, I inhale his clean scent.

We stand here for a few seconds, and I enjoy the feel of his warmth. Peering over his shoulder, I can see Lissa looking at me with a strange look in her eyes like she's not sure what to make of it. Pointing over her shoulder, she nods her head to the door, signaling she's going to head inside. I assume to find Adam, her boyfriend.

Nodding my head, I give her a thumbs up behind Mason's back. Shaking her head, she turns on her heel and heads inside.

"How was work?" Mason asks, tilting his head to meet my eyes.

"It was work," I say, taking a step away from him. I would hate for Kaleb to come outside and make it out to be more than what it is.

Lifting my hand, I wave at the guys and mumble out a "hey."

Dean raises his beer to me with a nod of his head, and Graham grunts, what I assume is his way of saying hello. They are men of few words.

"Have you seen Kaleb since you got here?" I ask, surveying the yard, spotting his car parked along the curb down the street. The souped-up Mustang is not easy to miss.

"No, but I haven't quite made my way inside yet. We've been standing here waiting for you."

Normally I wouldn't think much of it, but usually Mason is the first to join the party. People flock to him, especially the women. They're like eager puppies, wanting his attention.

"Have you talked to him since last night?" he asks.

"He hasn't been responding to my calls or texts. I guess I'm not sure what's going on."

Nodding his head, he takes a long pull from his beer. The sound of a woman shouting Mason's name interrupts our conversation as he turns his head toward the sound.

"Mason, I didn't know you were here," croons the sugary sweet voice of none other than Veronica. Saddling up close to him, she wraps her arms around his neck. I don't miss the way his hands press against her lower back and I do my best to advert my eyes away from his.

See, I'm not different. Mason does this with everyone.

"I'm going to head inside and see if I can find him," I mutter. Mason looks at me, his eyebrows furrowing for a minute before nodding his head. I don't let myself over think the look on his face as I jog up the steps into the house.

The sound of the music and chatter inside is so loud it's almost deafening. The house is packed, making it difficult to get through the hordes of people. Spotting Dean's roommate, Seth, I reach my hand out and grab his forearm, trying to get his attention.

"Have you seen Kaleb?" I ask, enunciating the words, hoping he can read my lips. He doesn't bother trying to say anything, instead, uses his hand to point toward the stairs, signally he's up there.

He must read the confusion on my face. Furrowing my brows, he nods his head, reassuring me I understood him correctly. I can't ignore the dread and uneasiness that fills the pits of my stomach as thoughts race through my mind.

No one goes upstairs at these parties except for one reason, and it's not to use the bathroom. With a nod of my head, I continue to push my way through the crowd of people toward the stairs. Sweat is trickling down my face and neck, making me instantly regret my decision to wear a sweater.

Once I make it to the top of the stairs, I'm thankful when I find it much quieter. Having people pressed against me right now is putting me on the edge of a panic attack.

Taking a deep breath, I amble down the narrow hallway. Dean and Seth have always made it clear their rooms are off limits, so I don't even bother checking, knowing the doors will be locked.

Knocking on the door to the bathroom, I hear a woman's muffled shout that she'll be out in a minute. I don't bother waiting as I continue down the hallway, checking the doors as I go, finding each one locked. I'm one step away from turning on my heel and ceasing my search when a loud moan pierces the air, halting my movement.

"Harder, harder." I hear the words chanted through the sound of skin slapping causing my heart rate to pick up.

It's as if everything clicks into place and I know what's going to come. I press my back against the wall as I squeeze my eyes shut. My heart feels like it's about to pound its way out of my chest. The dread and fear seeps in.

The familiar sound of Kaleb's deep grunts spurs something inside me, lighting a fire, tamping down the foolishness I felt a moment ago. I feel the heat rise up my neck as I clench my fists.

With all my strength, I push the door open. The force behind it causes the wood to slam against the wall. Immediately, my eyes fall on Kaleb's as I clench my jaw. His eyes go wide with shock and surprise.

It's still not enough to stop him as he continues to thrust his body into the bleached blonde bent over the bed in front of him.

All this time Kaleb has promised me I could trust him, but it was nothing more than a lie.

"Brea." The sound of my name on his lips while he hands grip her hips cause bile to rise in my throat.

"What'd you just call me?" the blonde tramp asks, turning her head behind, her only to find his eyes firmly planted on me.

My feet are weighted, planted firmly on the floor. I can't move as much as I want to leave and erase the visual before me from my sight and my mind forever.

"You're a lying son of a bitch," I spit, feeling the anger rise in my throat. "I fucking hate you for doing this to me!" I shout. "I fucking hate you, you hear me? I won't ever forgive you! Don't you EVER talk to me again!"

My hands are shaking, and I feel like my throat is burning through the hoarse shouts of my hatred for him. Forcing myself to move, I bolt.

Once again, I'm reminded to be careful who you trust. Not everyone is who you believe them to be.

chapter six

BREA

As soon as I hit the bottom step, the dam breaks and I can't control the surge of tears. Searching through the hordes of people, I seek out Lissa in hopes I can find her, but it's no use. Darting across the kitchen toward the door leading to the patio, I keep my head lowered and make my way through the crowd.

For a moment, I consider heading toward the front door and running to my car. The urge to drown my sorrows in a pint of Ben & Jerry's is strong at that moment.

Swiping a bottle of whiskey from the counter, I open the sliding glass door and step onto the wrap-around wooden porch. With tears streaming down my face, all I want is to be alone.

Keeping my head trained on the ground, I race across the deck and down the stairs, headed for the walking trail that lines the property. Knowing my only path is through the crowd of people who also take the trail, I jog my way down the graveled path.

Once the people and music are far enough away, I slow to a steady walk. Sliding my phone from my pocket, I open the camera app to do a quick once-over of my face. I'm relieved to find while the tears left my face looking red and puffy, my waterproof mascara has done its job.

Letting out a slow breath, I stare into the night sky. The darkness has fallen, leaving the dimly lit path hard to navigate beneath the stars. The only light guiding me are the small solar lights lining the walkway.

The quietness surrounding me allows the swirl of my thoughts to invade my mind. I feel disgusting and embarrassed over what I just witnessed, as the fear of whether this is something he's done before fills my stomach. Taking a swig of the whiskey, I squeeze my eyes shut, focusing on the burn as I swallow the alcohol.

How can someone you've spent the past seven months of your life with, whom you've opened yourself up to about your goals, dreams, and fears only turn around and throw all those things in your face?

The one thing Kaleb knew he could do to hurt me was make me feel like I was living a lie. After what my father did to my mom, and what I just witnessed, the reality it has happened to me weighs heavily.

A small wooden pergola holding a table and chairs sits off to the side of the trail. The sound of gravel crunching beneath my feet fills the silence. I take another drink, this one much smoother. I already feel the warmth of the alcohol rushing through my bloodstream.

I take a seat at the patio table, letting out a huff as I fall back into the chair. The chair is surprisingly comfortable, and I think about hanging out here by myself until Lissa is ready to leave. At some point, I'm going to have to break it to her that it's up to her to drive us home.

Pulling up Facebook, I spend a few minutes checking my notifications and scrolling through my newsfeed. It's full of people enjoying their spring break, and I feel envious of how happy everyone looks in their photos.

So much for having a relaxing and fun weekend off. Opening my text messages, I decide to tell Lissa I'm ready to go home when I hear Mason's laugh filter through the air. It's the kind of throaty laugh I could spot anywhere.

I can tell he's close, but I'm unable to pinpoint where it's coming from, causing me to look around for the location of the sound.

"Brea." My name sounds more like a question, as if he's wondering what I'm doing here by myself. I can't help but wonder the same thing.

"Hey, what are you doing back here?" I ask.

His feet kick the loose gravel. By the looks of the beer bottle in his hand, he's likely a few beers past tipsy, although he looks like his usual self.

"The guys and I were out in the shed over there," he says, pointing with his thumb over his shoulder. "They wanted to set off some fireworks."

"Sounds like an accident waiting to happen," I joke.

Walking closer, he moves to take a seat on the bench next to me. The closer he gets, I see the question written on his face.

"Why are you here all by yourself? Everything okay?"

"I guess I just needed a little bit of time to myself. I'll be fine eventually."

"What's that supposed to mean?"

"I'm just learning not everyone is who they say they are, at least not to your face. If we were all honest with our feelings, to ourselves, and each other, maybe we'd save all the heartbreak. What's the point of going through life living a lie?"

He doesn't say anything right away, but I feel his eyes track my movement as I take another drink. Maybe he's not sure what to say. Instead, he only nods his head.

"Is this about something specific?"

The words come out hoarser than the last question. Mason picks up on the change in his tone of voice as he lets out a hoarse cough, as if clearing his throat before taking a drink of his beer.

"Kaleb was cheating on me," I spit, choosing a poor time to make the announcement. Mason works to swallow back his beer, but instead it sends him off in a string of coughs, choking on his drink.

What's the point of easing right into it? Honesty and all of that.

"Wait, what?" Mason asks. I feel the heat of his gaze as he turns to look at me, but I don't turn to face him.

"Yep," I say, enunciating the 'p' with a pop. "So much for thinking you know someone."

"What a fucking prick," Mason sneers, turning his head away and facing forward into the night sky.

"This is the universe's way of reminding me relationships are a joke. You've been doing it right all along, Mase," I sigh. "I've never been one to sleep around or have a night of meaningless sex, but why not? There's no need for trust or commitment when you're in it for the sole purpose of having someone fuck your brains out. Right?"

"You can't be serious right now," Mason says, wrapping his hand around my forearm. "Look at me, Brea."

I feel the hot tears welling up in my eyes, all my emotions rising to the surface. Breathing in through my nose, I force down the feelings raging through me. Maybe it's the alcohol, or maybe this is how I feel, but I don't want to see the look of pity on his face.

"This is not who you are," he commands, moving to take the bottle from my hand. "Don't settle for someone who doesn't deserve you, all because some piece of shit doesn't know what he had."

I roll my eyes. Shrugging my arm from Mason's hold, I let him take the bottle. He sets it down on the table as I stand, planning to head into the party.

"That's sweet of you and all, Mason. Still, it doesn't change how I feel about relationships. Maybe if I let myself get lost in someone else for a night, I will be able to ignore the disgusting feeling I have in the pit of my stomach."

By the sound of the gravel crunching behind me, I know he's not too far behind.

"Wait, Brea. Will you just stop and talk to me?"

"What more is there to talk about? I'm going to find someone to spend the rest of my night with," I say, turning to face him. "Unless, of course, you want to be that person? I know how skilled you are in the pleasuring women department. Maybe you can show me what it is about you that has all the women falling over themselves for a night with the illustrious Mason Reid." I laugh. "Maybe you can be the one to make me forget."

His arm wraps around my waist and pulls me into him. It happens so fast, I don't even realize what happened until his arm is pressed against my lower back. Using his hand beneath my chin, he tilts my head until my eyes find his.

"Is this really what you want?" he asks, his voice low. There's an edge to it I've never heard before.

"What?" I ask, looking at him beneath the soft glow of the lights lining the path. It's hard to read the expression on his face.

"You want to know what it's like to have one night with me?"

I nod my head. "I want to know what it feels like for one night to forget everything else and get lost in someone. You don't have to worry, Mason, I know what one night with you means. I promise it won't change our friendship, and I won't even make you cuddle with me when you're done." I laugh.

I see the curve of his lip tilt up in a smirk.

"C'mere," he says, tangling his hand in mine, leading me back to the pergola. He takes a seat in the middle of the bench. Peering up at me, I can see the cocky grin on his face.

He's so confident and sure of himself as he drags me into his lap. He runs his hand along the side of my face, pushing the strands of hair away. Tracing his thumb along the edge of my cheek, I watch with bated breath as his eyes consider my lips.

I silently beg for him to make the first move because as much as I said I wanted this, I can't be the one to initiate it.

Pulling me closer still, I feel the air sucked out of me when his lips connect with mine.

Clutching onto his shoulders, I let out a quiet whimper and feel my body relax into his touch. I don't let myself over think it. Instead, I focus on the way my body feels under his touch.

Sliding his hand over my chest, he cups my breast with his palm. I lean into his touch, letting him get a better feel. The movement causes his eyes to spark as the corners of his mouth curve up.

Sliding his hands down my arms, he pulls the sleeves of my sweater with them and tosses it on the chair next to us. The combination of the alcohol coursing through my system and his fingertips brushing along my skin has a warmth rushing through my bloodstream.

"Mase," I whisper. It must've been the way I said it by the look on his face as if he's scared I'll change my mind.

"Promise me," I whisper, swallowing my nervousness. "Promise me this won't change anything between us."

A look of hurt passes over his face, but before I can overthink it, it's gone.

"I promise you'll always be my best friend."

It's what I need to hear from him. Nodding my head, I let out a slow breath as I hold onto his hands clenching my waist.

Gathering the material from my t-shirt, I raise my arms as he pulls the material over my head. Sitting in front of him, with only the dimly lit lights around us and the stars shining in the sky, I see the desire gloss over his eyes and the way his throat moves as he swallows and his eyes roam over every inch of my chest.

Leaning forward, I press my mouth to the base of his throat, feeling his heartbeat against my lips. Running my fingers over his torso, I follow his lead and pull his t-shirt over his head, dropping it on top of my sweater.

"C'mere," he whispers, pulling me to straddle his lap.

I feel his cock harden beneath me where our bodies touch. Something about it spurs me on, pressing my pussy against him.

He lowers his head, pressing his mouth against my chest, leaving kisses along the swells of my breasts. My fingers slide into his hair as I hold him closer to me, earning me a groan.

"Brea," he grits out. Just one word, but hearing my name fall from his lips makes me want to hear it from him again.

I slide back on his knees and slip my hand between us. I thank God he isn't wearing a belt as I slip off the button and unzip his pants.

I see his head snap up, looking at me as if gauging my reaction.

We promised we wouldn't let tonight ruin anything between us. Slipping my fingers into Mason's underwear, I fist my hand around his thick length, rubbing my thumb over the velvety smooth tip. I feel the wetness beneath my finger as I let out a small whimper.

"Fuck me, Brea. You're gonna kill me with those noises alone," he groans.

Tightening my fist, I pump my hand up and down his hard length. I can't help the overwhelming sense of pride as I watch his eyelids lower and his head tilt back. His chest heaves with every forced breath and his nostrils flare as he works to stay calm.

"Your hand feels perfect. You're perfect," Mason groans, lowering his head to meet my stare. My mouth feels dry from each deep inhale. My tongue darts out, wetting my lips as he lets out a deep grunt.

Mason runs his palms up my thighs, wrapping his hands tightly at my waist. As soon as I feel his rough skin against mine, I feel my stomach quiver with anticipation.

"I want to feel you around me," Mason mutters. The words are coming out more pleading than I think he intended.

Standing, I ease the button undone and unzip my jeans. I watch as Mason reaches into his pocket for his wallet, slipping out a condom. He's quick, and for a second, I think about how experienced he is before I push it out of my mind just as fast.

If this is the only night we have together, I don't want to focus on thoughts of him with other women. Tonight, it's just the two of us and no one else.

Leaving my thong in place, I resume my position on his lap. The thought of completely baring myself to him out in the open feels too intimate. He doesn't say anything, and before I know it, his hands are back on me.

As soon as his thumb rubs against my pussy, I can't even hold in the moan I unleash.

"You're killing me, Brea," he says as I roll my head forward, looking him straight in the eye. When his thumb slips beneath the lace material, I hold onto his forearm to keep from collapsing on top of him.

"Please," I beg. Mason doesn't say anything, and I'm grateful. Easing myself up onto my knees, he holds his cock in his strong hand, positioning himself beneath me.

Keeping my hands firmly on his shoulders, I slowly ease my way down, feeling every inch of him fill me. My body craves the way he fits so perfectly inside me as I slam down in his lap.

"Brea," he sighs, squeezing my hips.

The sound of his voice and each moan he makes urge me to continue, as we both chase our release. My body shudders as we fall over the edge together.

I press my forehead against his shoulder as his strong hands slide up my spine, holding me against him. I feel his breath feather along my heated skin as he presses a soft kiss at the base of my neck.

It was wrong of me to ask Mason to promise me nothing would change between us because it was a lie. I think maybe he knew it, too. There is no going back, and that's what scares me the most. I don't want to ever lose him.

chapter seven

BREA

My thoughts are swirling as I stare up at the blades of the ceiling fan spinning around and around. It's been six days since I've seen or heard from Mason. With each day that passes by, I can't help but feel like I'm drifting further and further away from my best friend.

I think back to my conversation with Lissa after my fight with Kaleb. I had never given any thought to a relationship with Mason. For as long as I've known him, he's always been someone I could trust but I knew who he spent his nights with.

Remembering how it felt having his lips on mine has my heart rate picking up once again. I hear myself whimper, thinking about the gravelly tone in his voice as he said my name with each hurried thrust. He stole the breath right out of my lungs when he punished me with his kiss.

Two knocks sound on my door, as Lissa peeks her head into my bedroom.

"Hey, you're up!"

"I just woke up a few minutes ago actually."

"You nervous about your first night?" she asks, leaning against the doorway.

After Lissa suggested it to me, I gave it some thought and went in on Wednesday to talk to Craig, the owner of Velvet. He offered me the job on the spot. I never pictured myself working at a nightclub. There's nothing wrong with it, but I've always preferred working with kids. When I was a teenager, I spent my summers volunteering at a day camp with underprivileged kids. My focus now is on getting my degree to teach kindergarten.

"Just first night jitters. Nothing I won't soon get over."

It's only partially true. While on one hand I am nervous about the new job, I am more anxious about running into Mason. I don't want it to be awkward between us.

"How are you feeling about seeing Mason tonight?" Lissa asks, walking over and sitting on the edge of the bed. Pulling the blanket to my neck, I roll over on my side to face her, scooching back enough to give her some room.

I told Lissa about Mason the day after it happened, mostly because I needed to hear if I was just as bad as Kaleb for what I had done. I knew she wouldn't hold back in telling me the truth. In true Lissa fashion, she told Kaleb to fuck off and agreed finding him sleeping with some girl doesn't compare to me giving him the finger and spending the night with Mason.

I could sense she wanted to ask me if I had given any more thought to her questions about us being more than friends, but she never did. Maybe she saw it coming, and I wonder if Kaleb did, too.

"I'm fine. It's just Mason," I say, but even hearing it in my ears sounds like a lie. The way she raises her eyebrow at me confirms she thinks I'm feeding her a line of BS, too.

"Have you heard from Kaleb?"

I don't say anything, instead just shake my head. I'm not surprised he hasn't reached out to me and, honestly, I'm grateful. I don't know what I would say to him if he did.

"I'm gonna finish curling my hair and make something for dinner. We can drive over together; I don't mind showing up a little early."

Peering over at the side of the bed, I check the time on the clock and see it's four minutes after six. I have less than an hour until I have to leave for Velvet.

Craig had me stop by yesterday to show me a few things. Since tonight is my first night, Craig asked me to come a little bit earlier. It's loud in the club, making it hard to hear when it comes to training, and he wanted to ensure I felt prepared for my first night on my own.

"Well, you should probably get ready if you want to shower before we go," Lissa says, swatting me on my ass as she throws me a smirk, sauntering toward the door.

I'm so glad I have her coming along with me.

We're a little early when we arrive at Velvet. Parking off toward the side of the building, we enter through the employee entrance. I immediately notice how dim the lights are, giving the club more of a romantic ambiance. The ceiling is high, making the room look and feel twice as big.

In two of the corners, opposite each other, are the large wrap-around bars they refer to them as the West and East bars. There are tables lining the wall between them, leaving the middle of the club open for people to dance. Craig said he would start me off serving tables near the West bar where Mason works so I can stay close to Lissa. I was so relieved because I knew they would look out for me and help me through the first couple of nights. He assured me serving would be a good way to ease into things, as some of the tables are reserved for some of their more special guests.

We take the hallway near the West bar, leading toward the employee locker room. We quickly stash our purses and walk around the row of lockers toward the exit as Mason and Graham bound through the door. Mason has his head thrown back, laughing at something Graham apparently doesn't find funny. Although with Graham, it can be tough to tell with the permanent brooding look on his face.

"Brea," Mason says, "Craig told me he gave you a job working here. Are you feeling ready for your first night?"

Approaching me, he opens his arms, and without thinking, I immediately go to him returning his embrace. Pressing my cheek against his chest, I let the feel of his warmth spread through me, along with the relief I needed.

See, I tell myself. We are still us.

"Ready as I'll ever be," I mutter, plastering a fake smile on my face, causing him to chuckle.

The way his lip perks up as he smirks has me staring at the laugh lines on his face. His hair is longer than he normally keeps it. Usually it's neatly styled, but tonight it looks different. It has this wild look like he's ran his hands through it a hundred times.

"So, I heard about you and Kaleb. I'm sorry," he says, the words coming out hesitant, as if he's unsure how to approach the subject. The fact he's mentioning it like we haven't talked about it before sends off warning bells in my head.

"It's okay; it's not like it's your fault. I guess you don't always know people like you think you do."

"Yeah," he says, nodding his head as he shoves his hands in his pockets.

I feel my heart fall into the pit of my stomach. Does Mason not remember talking to me or us spending the night together? I mean, I know we had both been drinking, but I didn't think neither of us were to the point of forgetting.

Wrapping my arms around my midsection, I try to keep my hands busy or maybe I'm trying to hold myself together. I want so badly to ask Mason what the hell is going on.

Peering up, I see the confusion lining Graham's brow as he tries to piece together what we're saying, and for a moment I wonder if maybe he knows what happened. I don't remember seeing him before I left, but by the look on his face, I can tell he is catching on that something isn't adding up.

This is not at all how I envisioned this conversation going.

The sound of the locker room door opening and closing draws my attention over his shoulder as I see Sierra enter behind him. When my eyes fall on hers, I see her looking at Mason out of the corner of her eye, which causes my stomach to roll.

It's no secret she's frequented his bed. I just never thought it was anything serious, but the way she's looking at him, it's like their bodies are in tune with one another. I can't get out of the locker room quick enough.

"So, um, I'm just gonna head out. I have to talk to Craig quickly, and Lissa's going to show me a few things before the doors open."

I'm sure he can see the uneasiness on my face. I've never been good at hiding the way I'm feeling. I wear my emotions on my face like it's written there with a permanent marker, spelling it out for everyone to read. Mason knows me better than anyone.

"I'll catch up with you later," Mason says, smiling as he nods his head toward the door.

Not even bothering to respond, I turn to look over my shoulder, making sure Lissa's behind me as I walk around Mason and out the door.

"Well, that was awkward as fuck," Lissa mumbles loud enough for only me to hear.

"Did any of that bother you?" she asks, but I know she already knows the answer. She just wants me to admit what just happened out loud.

"I don't know, Lissa. I don't know what's going on."

It's the truth. Seeing Sierra was just another reminder of how allowing myself to feel anything more for Mason would be a grave mistake. The hardest part now is also accepting, despite what we both wanted, our night together has changed our friendship.

The first half of the evening flies by quickly. I'm so busy running all over, I don't have time to think about the conversation with Mason or how bad my feet hurt in these shoes.

Making a quick stop by the bar to grab a drink order, one of the bartenders, Farin, flags me over.

"I hate to ask this, but I'm getting slammed here. Can you grab me some ice from the cooler? Just a couple of bags will do."

"Yeah, of course. I'll be right back." I remember Craig showing me the cooler they keep stocked.

I pick up the pace, wanting to hurry to get back out to my tables. Focused on what I'm doing, I don't even see someone standing off to the side of the dimly lit hallway. A steady hand slips around my arm, catching me off guard.

"I didn't expect to see you here." The fiery look in his eyes tells me he isn't happy about it.

"Yeah, well, I was hoping I'd never see you again and what do you know," I say, sweeping my hand in front of me.

The snippy retort is causing Kaleb's lip to sneer.

"So, what, you're working here now? As if ditching me to spend time with your BFF wasn't enough, you had to go and get a job with him, too? Wow, a little desperate, don't you think?"

He moves in close, pressing both of his hands against either side of my head, not letting me leave.

"Let me go, Kaleb."

"You wanted to talk the other night, and I was a little busy. I'm ready now though, so let's talk."

"No, you know what, I have nothing left to say to you. I have to get back to work."

"So, what, you can forgive Mason for sleeping around, but it's not okay for me to do the same?"

I can tell he's angry as he clenches his teeth and his shoulders tense. It's a look I've never seen before and, for the first time since I've met Kaleb, I find myself unsure of what he will do next.

"Kaleb, seriously, I don't have time for this right now. I need to go."

"No, I want you to answer my question. What is it about your precious Mase that has you so willing to overlook his trail of countless women coming from his bedroom?"

"She told you to let her go. I suggest you do as she says unless you want me to help you out."

The sinister smile on Kaleb's face is back. With a shove, he pushes away from the wall as I move to stand closer to Mason. I feel Mason beside me, pressing his hand against my lower back. The move fuels the anger on Kaleb's face before Graham interrupts and tells him it's time for him to leave.

Easing his arm around my shoulder, Mason turns me so I'm facing him.

He looks over my shoulder, muttering to Graham to get him out of here, before turning his attention back to me.

"What the hell was that about?"

"He's upset about our fight from the other night is all. I'm fine though; it's not a big deal."

"Not a big deal, Brea? I walked around the corner and see this fucker intimidating you and the scared look on your face. I know you better than this, Brea. This isn't something little to be waved off like it's nothing. Has this happened before?"

Gritting my teeth, I force a stern look on my face. "No, he has never gotten angry like this. What the hell? Do you think I'd stay with him if he did?"

I hear the frustration rising in my throat in defense of his accusations. Does he seriously think I'd be with someone who would talk to me like that?

"I'm fine though, I swear. I'm upset of course, but I'll be okay. Now if you'll excuse me, I need to get ice from the cooler and check on my tables. I'm sure they're wondering where I'm at by now."

"Don't worry about the ice. I'll get it. If that asshole comes around again, I want you to tell me."

I can't help but want to roll my eyes knowing it would likely make the situation worse, but I accept it because it's not worth arguing over.

"Thank you," I quip as I turn to walk away.

The rest of the night doesn't go nearly as quick as I would've hoped. With so much that has happened tonight, I can't even wrap my head around it all.

Why is Mason acting like the other night never happened? Where did Kaleb get the idea I'd be open to forgiving him for cheating on me?

Above all, when did I become the woman who would let a man treat her any less than what she deserved?

chapter eight

MASON

Pulling the towel from my back pocket, I wipe my hands off. It has been a busy week, and my shift at Velvet tonight hasn't been any different. Thankfully, Dean has been helping Farin and I run the bar.

Running into Brea in the locker room was hard. We haven't spoken since our night together at Dean's, and when I saw her, all I wanted to do was pull her into my arms and kiss her. I've thought about reaching out to her a hundred times. The shit with my dad this week has my stress level running at an all-time high, but she wanted me to promise nothing would change between us.

I knew it was nothing but a fucking lie. So, I've kept my head down and focused on everything else going on in my life. Seeing her tonight, I found myself searching her face for any hint.

Did she regret it or did it change anything between us, as it did for me?

I sensed she looked hesitant and unsure when we saw each other. She wanted a night of meaningless sex with someone, without the worry it would ruin our friendship.

Lucky for her, I have experience in one-night stands.

Waving to Dean I'm going to make a quick break, I walk down the hall toward the bathroom.

"You going to tell me what the hell that was about," Graham mumbles behind me.

I want to roll my eyes. Graham is a man of little words, but don't think for a second he isn't picking up on shit going on around him. He reads people. Their facial expressions, their body language, everything.

I promised I would keep my night with Brea between the two of us, but I can tell by his question, he knows something happened.

"What are you talking about?" I ask, deciding to play the oblivious card.

"Don't fucking give me that shit," he grunts. "What's going on between you and Brea?"

Spinning around, I lean against the wall and cross my arms over my chest, deciding this is the best option if I want to avoid him reading into it.

"Nothing's going on. I haven't seen Brea since last week."

His eyes narrow as he runs his hand over his jaw, shaking his head, not buying it.

"Alright. If you don't want to talk about it, fine. Answer me this at least, did you call Callum and tell him about your dad going to rehab?"

I can tell by the annoyed look on his face he knows the answer to his question.

"Why is it my responsibility to tell Callum?" I ask. I want to ask him why he even cares, but I know it's because he's looking out for me. He hates, as much as I do, that all this shit gets put on me.

"The way I see it, if my dad wanted Callum to know, he'd tell him on his own. I'm sick of being stuck in the middle of it. I told my mom the same thing. Callum is stubborn as fuck, particularly where my father is concerned."

I think she's hesitant to tell him in case our father doesn't stick with it. She doesn't want to give him another reason to believe all he's capable of is letting other people down.

"He deserves to know, you know."

"Yeah, well my dad doesn't deserve to hear how he's a piece of shit while he's trying to get better," I spit, uncrossing my arms.

"I didn't expect to see you ever again and what do you know." The sound of the loud shouting has my body tensing. I would know that voice anywhere. The anger in her tone is not one I often hear.

Looking down the hall, I turn my head toward Graham. I can tell he has the same thought I do as we both jog to where her voice is coming from. As soon as I turn the corner, I see Kaleb standing in front of Brea with his hand gripping her forearm.

"So, what, you can forgive Mason for sleeping around, but it's not okay for me to do the same?"

I can feel my ears ringing as the anger rises in my face, heating my skin.

"Stop it, Kaleb, you're hurting me." Brea's pained voice echoes in my head. I vaguely hear Graham's grunt behind me, and I'm relieved to hear he's with us, at least I know he'll have my back if something happens. Clenching my fists, I stalk toward where they're standing.

"No, I want you to answer my question. What is it about your precious *Mase* that has you so willing to overlook his trail of countless women coming from his bedroom?"

As soon as I'm within spitting distance to the fucking prick, I can't help but clench my jaw as I say, "She told you to let her go. I suggest you do as she says unless you want me to help you out."

Kaleb's shoulders tense and I know he wasn't expecting me to come up from behind him. Moving closer so I'm standing near Brea, I see the sinister smile on his face, and it's enough to make me want to deck the fucker right in his mouth.

With a shove, he pushes away from the wall. I move quickly to help her, not wanting her to fall but the move fuels Kaleb's anger further.

"Alright, you need to leave," Graham commands. The venom in his voice is threatening, and I know Kaleb realizes he would be a fucking fool to even think about going toe-to-toe with Graham. He'd lay him out in a fucking instant.

Sliding my arm around Brea's shoulder, I turn her to face me, making sure she's okay. Looking over Brea's shoulder, my eyes find Graham who glances at me, making sure Brea is alright.

"She's fine; I've got her. Get him out of here, will ya?"

With his hand pressed on Kaleb's shoulder, he moves him out of the space and away from Brea. I hear the low murmur in his ear, and I don't have to hear Graham's words to know he's telling him to cool down before making things worse.

"What the hell was that about?" I ask, turning toward Brea.

"He's upset about our fight from the other night is all. I'm fine though; it's not a big deal."

"Not a big deal, Brea? I walked around the corner and see this fucker intimidating you and the scared look on your face. I know you better than this, Brea. This isn't something little to be waved off like it's nothing. Has this happened before?"

I can tell by the flash of anger in her eyes as she grits her teeth, that she didn't like my question.

"No, he has never gotten angry like this," she grunts. "What the hell? Do you think I'd stay with him if he did?"

"I'm fine though, I swear. I'm upset of course, but I'll be okay. Now if you'll excuse me, I need to get ice from the cooler and check on my tables. I'm sure they're wondering where I'm at by now."

"Don't worry about the ice. I'll get it. If that asshole comes around again, I want you to tell me."

Following Brea out, I stop and pull out a bag of ice before lugging it with me to the bar. As soon as I round the corner, I find Graham leaning against the bar as he surveys the crowd.

"How's she doing?" Graham yells over the music as he leans against the wall. I break open the bag of ice and pour it into the cooler. The music is thumping through the speakers, making it hard to hear.

"She's acting like Brea, pretending like it didn't happen or like it's not bothering her," I shout, wiping my hands off on my towel.

"Did you take care of him?"

Graham leans back against the bar and doesn't say anything, only nods his head before searching the crowd for Lissa and Brea, checking on them.

A petite blonde saddles up to the counter and waves her hand at me, getting my attention. Sliding my hand along the bar, I lean closer to her.

"What can I get you?" I shout.

"I'll take a dirty martini." She smiles, running her finger along her lower lip as her eyes roam over my body. Taking a step back, I pick up a clean glass from underneath the bar and pour the ingredients into the cocktail mixer.

Dropping the olive in her drink, I slide the glass toward her and flash her my signature smile. I watch as her eyes light up as her tongue darts out, licking the tip of her finger before bringing the drink to her mouth.

Shaking my head, I don't bother feeding into the attention she's craving. Turning my head toward the server station, I see the annoyance on Lissa's face as she looks back and forth between the petite blonde and me. Behind her, I see Brea turn her head as she saunters toward her tables.

Shit, I hadn't even noticed the two of them approach, and I know it looked worse than it was.

"Are you ever going to grow the hell up, Mason Reid?" Lissa yells, walking behind the counter and starts fixing her own drinks. By the way her arm jerks with the bottle in her hand, she's pissed.

"Excuse me?"

"You heard me," she says, stopping what she's doing as her eyes run over my face. Her eyes narrow as if she's waiting for me to give her the answer she's looking for.

"You want her," she yells, and I can feel my body tense. The sound of Graham's deep laugh behind me has me gritting my teeth. "You want her, Mason. We all know it but the question is, do you?"

"I don't know what the hell you're talking about."

"Riiiiiiight." She laughs, sliding the bottle of vodka on the shelf. "I'm still not buying it. Listen, I'm going to cut to the chase because I don't have time or patience for your cat and mouse bullshit right now."

Her blunt and straight to the point response is earning another laugh from Graham. I can't help but flash him a "fuck off" look. Any other time the guy doesn't say more than two words, much less show emotion, and here he is laughing like this is the funniest god-damn thing he's heard all day.

"I know what happened between the two of you at Dean's house the other night. If I'm honest, I'm surprised it took as long as it did before it happened. Maybe you're still in denial, or maybe you're just stupid, but don't fuck with her heart. You like taking women home with you, but you and I both know, Brea deserves far fucking more than some one-night stand. I would expect something like this from some douche fucker like Kaleb, but I don't from you. So, do us both a favor, figure out what the hell you want and quit fucking with her."

She picks up the drinks and slides them onto her server tray before spinning and facing me. She's close enough to where I can hear her without yelling. I don't say anything, just watch as she leans in closer and says, "You want her, Mason. We all know it," she says, looking over at Graham and raising her eyebrow. I know he heard her as he simply nods his head before looking at me.

Looking at me, I see the smug look on her face. "So, the question is, what are you going to do about it?"

She doesn't wait for me to respond as she turns and walks to the other side of the bar. Graham doesn't stick around either, following along right behind her.

The club is packed, but the area near the tables is less crowded, leaving room for servers to get through to the tables lining the club. My eyes roam, trying to spot Brea, but it's hard beneath the dim lights.

I try to busy myself helping customers but I can't help replaying the words Lissa said as my eyes seek out Brea in the crowd of people. I've known how I feel about Brea for a long time, but have fought against it for months, telling myself it's time to move on after seeing her happy with Kaleb.

When she told me about what he did and then proceeded to tell me she was going to go into the party to find someone to hook up with, I felt like I could hear the blood rushing in my ears and my heart nearly beating out of my chest. It was hard enough to hear and see her with Kaleb. I'll be damned if I was going to watch her march in the house to find someone to take his place.

Over my dead fucking body.

It never dawned on me after all this time, our closest friends may have seen what I am feeling for her, too. I've worked hard to hide my feelings from Brea, respecting her and Kaleb's relationship. Trust is so important to Brea, and I would never want to lose hers.

It's a sure-fire way to drive a wedge between us.

Having someone confront me about her, asking me what my next moves are, takes me by surprise. After Brea and Kaleb had been together for more than six months, I honestly gave up the notion I would ever get a chance with her. She was happy with him, I could see it. Not to mention, they just broke up. It's not like she can get over him and the hurt of what happened overnight, regardless of her wanting to ease the sting.

Turning my head toward where she's serving tables, my eyes immediately lock with hers and I feel it knock the wind out of my chest. She's so goddamn beautiful. Her hair is pulled into a high ponytail. The long strands are curled in waves, hanging down her back. The makeup she's wearing is a little heavier than normal, but she still looks beautiful. I prefer her fresh faced, dressed down in her yoga pants and a t-shirt like she often wears when we are hanging out, but she's breathtaking like this, too.

I watch as her eyes search my face as she approaches the counter, sliding her tray onto the server station. On nights where we're busy, we try to help the servers with their drinks, but sometimes it can be hard to keep up. I don't care now though; I want an excuse to talk to her.

Approaching her, I lean in close to the side of her face and whisper in her ear. "What can I get you?"

I feel her body heat having her close to me, and her body tenses as my mouth rests near her ear. Leaning back, I meet her eyes and watch as they dilate from our proximity.

"Jack and Coke," she whispers loud enough for me to hear. I feel her heated breath against the edge of my lips. She darts her tongue out, wetting her lips before she continues. "And...sex on the beach."

I know she's talking about a drink, but I can't help the grin that takes over my face. Grabbing the bottle of vodka off the shelf, I turn around to face her.

"Coming right up," I shout before flashing her a wink.

chapter nine

BREA

I never thought of myself as the type of person who avoids problems, but it's exactly what I've been doing for the past week.

Mason and I haven't talked about the night we spent together. Aside from a few text messages and small talk at work, we've hardly spoken to each other. Even then, I've done a fairly good job of keeping the conversation short and steering clear of him. I know we promised nothing would change between us, but I can't stop thinking about our conversation in the locker room. I still haven't been able to ask him what it was all about. Maybe I'm just embarrassed he'll say he regrets it.

I don't want to feel like I'm every other girl he's been with. I would hope it would be different between us, but I know I shouldn't expect more than what it is. I wanted a night with meaningless sex and it's what I got, right?

As hard as it is to admit, I'm at the point where now I just miss my friend. I miss the person who was my friend first. Who, when I needed someone, he would come to the rescue. I want it back.

I haven't spoken to Kaleb and, thankfully, he's stayed far away from Velvet. It doesn't mean he hasn't tried to reach out to me. The twenty-seven missed text messages in my phone say something different. I haven't brought myself to read them yet either.

The past few weeks I've done nothing but stress myself. Stress about relationships, school, and finances. I've come to terms it's something I'm going to have to pay on my own, because like everything else going on in my life, I'm avoiding my father, too.

After talking it over with Lissa, I decide to move home and stay with my mom during the summer. I'm going to work a couple of jobs and put money away in savings. Thankfully, Lissa's cousin has decided to come stay with her. It will work out great because she agreed to sublease my room until I come back this fall. I wouldn't go through with it though, if it was going to put her in a bind.

Now I just need to get through the last few weeks of school. Slamming the textbook shut, I sit back against the seat of the couch and let out a huff. I've spent most of the day studying for an Algebra test I have tomorrow and Monday. Math has never been my strong suit, and all these long problems make my head spin. You want me to solve for x? I can't even solve my own ex-problems or best friend problems, so you're asking the wrong girl.

I can't help but laugh at my own joke as Lissa walks into the living room.

"What the hell is so funny?" She stops, turning to look at me.

Tilting my head up, I look at her as my bangs slide in front of my eyes. Blowing the strands out of my face, I flash her a crazy smile, which only adds to her concerned look.

"I think I need a break." I laugh as I muster up the strength to stand and meander toward the door.

"I'm going to go for a walk to The Coffee House," I say, slipping on my shoes. "I'm going to need more caffeine if I'm going to spend the rest of the night cramming."

"Yeah, you may want to get a bottle of wine, too."

"Cause that will help me with studying?" I jest.

"No, but it will certainly help me," she jokes.

Rolling my eyes, I slide my sunglasses over my face. I grab my keys and slide my debit card and wallet into my pocket.

"Hey, I was meaning to ask you, have you and Mason talked about your conversation in the locker room?"

With my keys clutched in my palm, I run the back of my hand along my forehead before looking at her and shake my head.

Grumbling, she replies, "He needs to get his shit together."

She's looking out for me, and I know she's frustrated.

"What more is there to talk about? If it hasn't been said yet, I'm not sure if we're ever going to. I'm ready to just move on."

Tossing a goodbye over my shoulder, I head out the door. While on my walk, I do my best to clear my head and enjoy the fresh air. The time flies by quick. Opening the door to

The Coffee House, the strong aroma of coffee hits me. I was used to it from my days working here as a barista, but walking in the door has me feeling like I'm at home.

Joining the long line forming near the door, I slide off my sunglasses and hang them from the front of my shirt.

"Look who it is, stranger." The sound of Mason's gravelly voice behind me causes me to momentarily tense as I spin on me heel.

"Would you look at that," I say, doing my best to hide my surprise in seeing him here and finding him not alone.

Immediately I regret my decision to just run out the door, wearing only a pair of leggings and a dri-fit t-shirt and my hair rocking a day-old ponytail. I look like I'm getting ready to work-out when all I've been doing is lounging around all day.

Looking next to him, I flash Sierra a smile before turning my attention on Mason.

"What are you two up to?" I ask, forcing a smile on my face. While it's what I say out loud, I'm mentally screaming "what the fuck" over and over.

Smooth, Brea.

"We have a group project due tomorrow. I needed to refuel so we are stopping by here quick before heading to her place to work on it."

I can't ignore the way my stomach bottoms out hearing they'll be going to her place. Especially when I know they have a history of hooking up in the past. More than once even, which even I know doesn't happen often with him.

I hate how insecure it has me feeling.

"Sounds like fun," I say, coming out sounding overly chip-per. Far more enthusiastic than anyone getting ready to go work on a school project. "That's what I'm here doing, too. I'll be heading home, just me. Going to work on studying."

I want to cringe at my choice of words. Of course, it's just you, you idiot. Who else would you be going to hang out with? It's not like you're like Mason, with a new guy draped on your arm every time you turn around.

"Hey, you!" Sara cheers from behind the counter, a bright grin on her face, saving me from this torturous conversation. "It's great to see you! Please tell me you're thinking about coming back for the summer. I miss you here."

The mention of this summer with Mason behind me has me wanting to divert this conversation to safe territory quickly. I haven't yet broken it to him that I'm heading home during the summer. I've been rather busy lately avoiding him and all. I don't want to announce it with him standing right behind me, having him overhear me tell someone else.

"You know, I'm not sure what the summer will bring."

Ordering my frappe and a muffin, I stand off to the side as Mason and Sierra order their drinks. Pulling out my phone, I pretend like I'm engrossed in whatever is on my screen like it's the most interesting thing in the world. I'm terrible at this avoidance thing.

"Thanks, babe," I say as soon as Sara hands me my drink and muffin. "Text me soon so we can get together for lunch."

I grab the bag and turn to head out, already over this attempt to evade studying. I almost wish I would've just stayed home and tried to solve x's problems.

"See ya around." I smile, giving a small wave of my fingers as I slip my sunglasses on.

"Yeah, alright. Bye, Brea," Mason says. I don't have to look behind me to know he is watching me.

As soon as I'm outside and ambling down the sidewalk, I let out a deep breath.

"Jesus fuck," I grumble to myself as I take a drink.

"What was that about?" I hear as my back tenses before coming face to face with Mason once again.

"Good lord, you need to wear a bell. I didn't hear you. You're like a ninja."

I press my hand against my heart. Mason raises his eyebrow, and I know I'm caught.

"What? Nothing! It was nothing."

I'm thankful for my sunglasses providing me with a layer of protection from Mason. I know all too well how he likes to try and read my thoughts like a fucking book. Not working this time. I force another drink to save me from the awkward silence.

"Listen, I wanted to make sure everything was okay. I know we haven't talked much or hung out lately, which is mostly my fault. Everything with my dad and school has been a lot."

As soon as he mentions his dad, I feel like a complete asshole. I've been so focused on what has changed from our night together, and the time we spoke at the club, that I never thought about how things have been going with him and his dad. With everything he's been going through, I know he feels pressured to be there for him.

"It's okay; we both have stuff we've been dealing with and have been busy. I hope everything is going okay with your dad."

He rubs his hand over his forehead, and, for the first time since we ran into each other, I notice the tension in his shoulders and the stress on his face.

"I was hoping maybe we could make plans to hang out soon. The Cavs play the Bulls tomorrow. Maybe, uh, maybe we can watch it together. I just really miss you."

I swallow the guilt I feel rise in my throat. Whenever we would hang out just the two of us, we often would turn on basketball and watch the games together.

"I miss you, too," I sigh, smiling at him. It's the truth. I can't help but want to see him and hang out with him like we used to.

"That sounds perfect. I will probably be studying. Text me and let me know what time you're thinking."

I see Sierra walk out of The Coffee House, looking for Mason. When her eyes land on him, I watch as her face lights up until she sees me staring at her just over his shoulder. I am getting all too familiar with what it feels like to see him the way she does.

"It looks like your friend is waiting for you," I say, pointing over his shoulder. He turns his head and motions to her he'll be just another minute.

Turning to face me, he catches me by surprise when he wraps his arms around me, pulling me close to him. My hands are full with a coffee in one hand and a muffin in the other so I do my best to return the hug without making a mess in the process.

"You're not mad at me, are you?" he asks, whispering into my ear. I feel my heart pound just being close to him again. Taking a deep breath, I inhale his clean scent, leaving me slightly light-headed.

"No," I whisper, pressing my forehead against his neck before I look up at him. Giving him a reassuring smile, I add, "I'll see you tomorrow."

chapter ten

BREA

One thing I inherited from my mom is when I'm nervous, I clean. I don't think there is a space in this apartment left untouched. I could say it's due to the test coming up, but I know it would be a lie.

Mason will be here in a few minutes and it has me on edge, so I flutter around the apartment trying to find something to clean. There's not much left to do considering I've been at it for the past four hours. He texted me twenty minutes ago, telling me he was grabbing us food and was on his way, which means he should be here any minute now.

The sound of his thunderous knocks on the door causes my body to freeze as butterflies in my stomach take flight. I've never felt this nervous at the thought of spending time with Mason. Knowing this is going to be the first time we'll be alone since we were together sends a wave of anxiety rolling through me.

Padding my way across the living room, I unlock the deadbolt as I swing the door open. Standing before me is Mason in a Chicago Bulls t-shirt, a pair of athletic shorts, and tennis shoes. His hair looks wet, like he just showered not long ago. The thought alone has my attention drifting to picturing him standing in the shower as water cascades over his chest and body.

The sound of his throat clearing jolts me from my thoughts, finding an amused look on his face.

"You going to let me in?" Mason chuckles.

"Not in that shirt, I'm not." I laugh.

"Alright," he jokes, moving to hand me the bags of food. Confused, I take them from him as he grabs the hem of his shirt and starts lifting it over his head.

The sight of his abs down to the deep V hidden beneath his pants have my eyes wandering lower as he once again clears his throat.

"You know what, on second thought, you should really leave it on. You're going to do damage to someone's eyes. I don't need this kind of attention from the neighbors," I say, turning on my heel and heading toward the dining room. Mason's deep laugh echoes through the room from behind me as I hear the click of the door shutting. My cheeks heat at my thoughts as I hurry to put some space between us.

"I'll grab us plates," I mutter, setting the bags on the table. I need a minute to myself to get my wits about me.

"Geez, Brea. Just chill out," I whisper to myself. "Take a deep breath and relax."

Walking around the corner with the plates in hand, I plaster a smile on my face and hand Mason his. After we plate our food, we both head into the living room to where I left my textbook and notes for my test on Monday.

I take a seat on one end of the couch and Mason takes the other, although the way he's sprawled out he's really taking up most of the room with the decorative pillow under his arm and his leg hanging over the arm of the couch.

Flipping through the channels, we settle on a show to watch until the game starts. I told myself I was going to use tonight as an opportunity to tell Mason about my plans for the summer. I don't know why, but knowing this conversation is coming is weighing on my mind.

"Got any big plans for the summer?" I ask, not wanting to dive right into it.

"Not really. I'm looking forward to taking a much-needed break. I normally take classes during summer break but this year I decided to focus on working and saving up money. What about you?"

I take another bite of my burrito, buying me time before I speak. Swallowing it down, I decide to rip off the band-aid.

"I'm actually moving home to Cleveland for the summer," I mutter, taking another bite.

"Woah, really?"

I hear the shock and surprise in his tone, and if I'm not mistaken a tinge of sadness, too.

He doesn't take another bite. I can tell he is waiting for me to respond. My eyes are focused straight ahead on the television.

"I'm going to stay with my mom. I am hoping to save a little money before school next fall."

"You're coming back here though, right? What about your apartment? And Lissa?"

"Of course, I'm coming back next fall. I have no desire to stay there any longer than necessary, or ever move there for good. Between running out of my student loan money, needing cash for next fall, and money for tuition, I have a lot to save up for. Lissa's cousin is coming to visit and agreed to take over my lease until school starts."

"Sounds like you got it all figured out."

What he's really saying is, he can tell I have put some thought into this, and he's hurt this is the first time we've talked about it.

"I talked to Craig earlier this week and he agreed to let me take the summer off and will let me have my job when I come back to school this fall."

"Hell, yes, you'll have your job. He knows better."

The way he laughs makes my heart ache a little more thinking about how much I'll miss him, miss this, while I'm gone.

We finish eating and crack open my textbook. I thought studying with Mason would be distracting, but it goes smooth. He explains every problem to me in a way where it starts to make sense. Don't get me wrong, letters and numbers still have no business meshing together. Sprawled on the floor, we are lying next to each other with papers laid out in front of us. When he begins quizzing me, I'm surprised when I start getting them right.

"I think you're as ready as you'll ever be," Mason says, slamming the textbook closed.

"It's a nice way of saying good luck because you're going to need it."

"I'm not saying that and you know it," he says, rolling onto his back, crossing his arms behind his head. I don't even let my eyes focus on the way his muscles bulge behind his head or how his lip curves when he smirks at me.

"The game is about to start. Want me to pop some popcorn?" I ask, leaning back on my haunches and moving to stand.

"Yes, I'm going to need some popcorn when I watch my Bulls crush your precious Cavaliers." His laughter filters through the room, and I can't help rolling my eyes.

"I think I should be saying good luck to you. Your Bulls are gonna need it if you think they'll be able to stop LeBron."

Pulling the popcorn out of the box, I remove the plastic wrapper and stick it in the microwave. I don't hear Mason approach but I feel his body heat against my back. Looking at the microwave, I see his reflection in the glass. He slips his arm around my waist, and I feel my body relax into him. Clutching the edge of the counter, I lean forward and force a deep breath into my lungs.

The microwave beeps but neither of us move. With his nose pressed against my neck, he takes a deep breath before taking a step back and walking into the living room.

I feel like avoiding the subject, and I know we need to talk about what's going on between us in order for us to move forward. Pushing the button to the microwave, I grab the bag of popcorn and quickly pour it into a bowl following behind him.

Folding my legs under me, I set the popcorn on the cushion between us, giving us some space. Or giving me some space rather.

"I'm going to miss this—us hanging out, watching movies, and just chilling. What am I gonna do when you're gone?" Mason says, rolling his head to face me.

"Something tells me you'll have your pick of women who would love to take my place while I'm gone" I force out a laugh as a way of distracting myself from the way my heart aches hearing those words out loud. The thought of him finding someone else, replacing me, even just our friendship hurts.

I can feel his eyes on me once again, burning into the side of my face, as I focus on keeping them straight on the TV. Not even bothering to look at the bowl, I reach my hand in and bring the popcorn to my mouth, hoping he'll let the comment go.

"Is that what you think? That I'm like every other guy who has done you wrong and that I'll be able to replace you?"

Turning my head, I find him staring at me.

"I'm sure Sierra would be more than willing to occupy your free time."

I see it in his eyes, the moment when it hits him. Seeing him with Sierra yesterday and the familiarity in their touch. They may not have the friendship we do, but she has a piece of him I don't.

"Is that what this is all about?" he asks, moving the bowl of popcorn to the coffee table, opening his arms to me. I can't help but raise my eyebrow at him, questioning him.

"What, I've touched you in the most intimate places but you don't want to come cuddle with me now?" he jokes.

The mention of the night we spent together has me hesitating even though I know I want to move closer to him.

"What's the look on your face for?"

"So, you do remember everything from the night of the party?"

"What's that supposed to mean?"

"You remember the night, kissing me, us."

I don't even realize what's happening, he moves so quick. Pushing the coffee table out of the way, he moves his body so he's leaning over me with half his body on the floor, half on top of me.

"How could you think I don't remember?" he asks, but he doesn't give me a second before his mouth is on top of mine. I feel him, all around me, everywhere. Last time I was so overwhelmed, consumed by every touch, I didn't allow myself to feel it.

It's different this time. It's slow, passionate, and all-consuming.

He moves his hands up my thighs, pulling my feet so my legs are open, drawing me closer to him.

"How could you think I could forget this?" he asks, pressing his hand against my cheek. "I will never forget the feel of your lips on mine and your body wrapped around me."

Adjusting a pillow at the end of the couch, he reclines back. Raising his eyebrow suggestively, he looks down at his lap as if asking for me to climb on.

I think about it for a moment but dear God, how can I say no?

Moving my leg so it's between him and the couch, I position myself so I'm on top of him. The friction of our bodies this close to each other causes him to let out a deep groan. My yoga pants against his thin shorts leaves little between us.

I can feel my breathing pick up in pace as I force a struggled breath. I don't miss the glazed look of desire in his depths before a smirk graces his lips.

Running his hand along my side, his fingers skate along the edge of my breast as he twirls a piece of my hair around his finger.

"Come here," he whispers as his eyes meet mine.

I lean forward so our chests are pressed together. The movement causes me to grind against my aching core as he lets out a soft groan.

"Fuck, you feel so good. You keep it up and this will turn into more than just kissing."

Wrapping his hands in my hair, he brings my mouth to his, causing me to let out a groan of my own. I feel his chest rise and fall against mine as he forces his breath through his nose. Loving how our bodies react to each other, I press my pussy into him, enjoying the delicious slide of our bodies connecting. The friction causes a flood of heat as tingles spread through my body.

"I can't stop," I mutter as he slips his hand beneath my shirt. The heat of his skin causes my body to tremble. As soon as his fingers skate along the lace of my bra, I know I want his hands on every inch of my body.

Mason sits forward and pulls my tank top over my head. As soon as my eyes find Mason's, he's lying down. His eyes are blazing, following my every move. Reaching behind me, I unhook the clasp of my bra and slide the lacy material down my arms.

"I want to touch every inch of you," he groans. When his hand covers my right breast, I can't control the moan that slips out of my mouth. The heady feel of desire is causing my eyes to flutter closed.

"She's so beautiful. So perfect." The words come out a harsh whisper, as if voicing his thoughts out loud.

Pulling me so I'm closer to him, he grips my lower back keeping me pressed against his throbbing cock. As soon as his mouth covers my breast, it's like a lightning bolt strikes right through me.

"Mason," I moan, running my fingers through his hair, holding him closer to me. I feel my release surge through me as I teeter on the edge. "I'm going to come."

His eyes turn heavy as he releases my breast with a pop. His mouth is on mine in a heartbeat.

"I want to watch you come," he moans against my mouth.

Wrapping his hands low on my hips, he guides my body beside him with my back pressed against the couch. His hand slips between us and into my underwear. The feel of him through our clothes is nothing compared to his fingertips rubbing circles against my sensitive flesh.

With each flick of my clit, I feel my release simmer below the surface. Mason's hooded eyes stay trained on me. Wanting him with me every step of the way, I slide my hand to the waistband of his shorts and with Mason's help, pull them and his boxer briefs over his hips.

Fisting him in my hand, I swipe the head of his cock with my thumb.

"Holy shit," Mason growls, his movements are jerky as his breath comes out in heavy pants, mirroring the rapid beat of my heart.

All I can picture is how he would react when I finally put my mouth on him. Mason doesn't waste a second, his skillful fingers finding their way beneath the lace of my underwear. Holding my hand up to my mouth, I run my tongue along my palm before sliding it over his hard length, pumping it up and down. The groans that emanate from deep in his chest confirm he's close, which is good because I'm not too far from the edge myself.

"I want you with me," Mason grits out. His free hand moves to his chest, peeling his shirt up, giving me a view of his ripped stomach.

He knows what he's doing as he runs the tips of his fingers down to my opening, plunging two skilled fingers inside me.

My pussy clenches around him as I squeeze my eyes shut.

"Open," Mason commands. The one word forces my eyes wide and immediately they connect with his as he lets out a low hum of appreciation.

"Are you ready?" he asks, as his fingers curl inside me, hitting the right spot. My hand picks up the pace.

My eyelids lower, unable to control my body's reaction and the intensity of the emotions racing through me. His jaw clenches, smothering his moan and before I know it, we're both soaring over the edge, crashing into a sea of bliss. My body jolts through the aftershocks of my release as his cum shoots onto his stomach, dripping over my clenched hand.

Letting out a shaking breath, he peers down at me as he flashes me a devious smirk.

"Damn, Brea. I've got to be the luckiest man alive."

MASON

S tanding in front of the door, I suck a deep breath into my lungs, after jogging up the steps to Brea's apartment. After learning she was moving home for the summer, I told her I wanted to soak up every second of time I can before she goes. That's exactly what we've done. The past couple of weeks with Brea have been amazing. In a lot of ways, we are still the same Mason and Brea we were before the night of the party. Since we are both working on the weekends, we often spend our weeknights together. We've both been focused on school, so I often use the excuse of helping her study just so we can be together.

I am going to miss spending time with her. I'm going to miss the way my eyes search for her when we're working together, how her body feels curled up next to me when we're lying on the couch, and how, although we haven't talked about it, things are changing between us.

I knew we would never be the same after the night we spent together, despite her asking me to promise her they would. The connection between us now is undeniable. Every time we're near each other, it's as if we can't keep our hands off each other. The hunger I have for her is insatiable. I will never have my fill.

My chest aches when I think about her leaving. After how amazing things have been, I don't want to imagine anything other than how things are now. I've been trying to distract myself from the news by working through issues with my dad, school, and my shifts at Velvet.

Tonight, I'm looking forward to spending time with Brea, especially because I know in a few short days, she'll be gone and a piece of me will be gone with her.

My knuckles rap against the hardwood of her apartment door. I hear the muffled sound of Lissa and Brea's voices then Lissa's subsequent laugh as Brea swings the door open. The bright smile she greets me with nearly knocks the wind out of me, and I can't resist the urge to pull her closer. Bending, I wrap my arms around her waist and breathe her in.

"Hey," I whisper in her ear. Her hands skate across my forearms as she presses her body close, relishing the feel of her skin against mine.

"Hi," she murmurs. She peers her head up and, without thinking, I find myself leaning forward and pressing my lips against hers.

"Well, look who it is," Lissa grunts from behind her. I separate myself from Brea but not before I see her roll her eyes at Lissa while smothering a grin.

"Oh, you're at the kissing stage now. That's interesting because I thought for sure I just heard someone say whatever was going on between you two wasn't a big deal," Lissa says, looking at Brea with a raised eyebrow.

"Is that right?" I ask, rubbing my hand along my chin looking at Brea, too. I want to laugh because she clearly doesn't like being called out. "I'd have to say the spark I felt when I just kissed you is a pretty big deal."

Brea's eyes widen as she looks at me before a grin takes over her face.

"I'm going to go get my purse," she mutters as she spins on her heel, heading toward her bedroom. My eyes track her movements until she's no longer in sight.

"Glad to see you are finally getting your shit together, Mase. I'm going to say this but I'm sure you already know," she winks, "but, then again it wouldn't be the first time you missed something spelled out so easily for you. I'm only going to say this once, so listen up. If you break her heart, I'll break your face."

Lissa approaches, her eyes glaring as she pats me twice on my shoulder before walking past, bumping her shoulder into my mine in the process.

Brea rounds the corner, a smothered grin once again on her face. I know she heard Lissa and she's finding it as amusing as I am. Lissa is fiercely loyal to the people who are close to her. She will do anything for them and whatever it takes to protect them.

Holding my arm out for Brea, we turn to leave.

"I won't wait up for you," Lissa jokes, and I can't help but return a grin of my own.

"That's probably a good idea." I wink before sliding my arm across Brea's shoulders.

Walking to the car, I wrap my hand around Brea's and kiss the back of her hand. Her eyes are bright, and I can't help but feel my chest warm knowing I've put that look there.

Opening the door for her, she climbs into the passenger seat of my SUV. The drive across town passes quickly. We make small talk on the way, mostly about school and work.

"So, what's the plan for the night?" she asks.

I feel her eyes as they roam the side of my face. Taking my eyes off the road, I turn and give her a smile.

"What is your favorite part about living in Chicago?" I grin.

"Well, it's definitely not the Bulls," she jokes, slapping her hand on her thigh as she laughs, clearly finding herself funny. I don't even bother looking at her as I shake my head and fight off a laugh, not wanting to encourage her any further.

"Don't give me the side eye. You should've known you walked right into that one."

"Just answer the question," I say, flipping the turn signal as I pull up to a stop light. The traffic is heavy, which is to be expected downtown. Looking over at her, I wait for her answer, hoping I was right in planning our evening.

"I love just walking around and taking in the scenery. The city always boasts something new to explore," she says, pausing. Turning her head, her eyes meet mine and she grins. "Oh, and the pizza!"

Flashing her a broad smile in return, I turn my attention back to driving before someone ends up honking at me. "You got it!"

"Aww, Mase! You shouldn't have." She smiles, leaning her head against my shoulder. "You know me better than anyone, you know that?"

"Damn right, I do!"

We pull into the pizza place. It's a small hole in the wall really, but they are well known for their signature Chicago style deep dish pizza. Brea slides from her seat before I'm able to open the door for her. Meeting her on her side, I grab her hand and pull her in closer, ushering her inside. She bounces on her feet, excitedly, before looking up to land a small kiss on my cheek.

The restaurant isn't busy, thankfully. We step up to the counter and order our pizza while we wait for a table. A few minutes later, a young kid, who looks like he's probably no older than sixteen, lets us know our table is ready.

He seats us near the corner of the restaurant. Sliding into the booth, the server takes our drink order and leaves us alone.

Sitting in front of Brea, I find myself taking in every feature on her face. It's as if I'm memorizing what she looks like, cataloging her smile and the way her green eyes light up. The soft lines of her dimples to the hoop in her nose and how her long eyelashes look like feathers every time she blinks. She is so beautiful.

"What?" Her brows furrow in concern, shaking me from my thoughts as she runs her hand through her long chocolate brown hair.

"How are you feeling about the move?" I ask, changing the subject. By the look on her face, she picks up on my less than subtle attempt to move the conversation away from what is really on my mind.

Letting out a sigh, her eyes look around the dining room before falling on mine. I immediately regret the direction this has taken. I watch as she runs the tip of her finger along her bottom lip, as if she's now the one lost in thought.

"I'm not excited about it, if that's what you want to know. It's for the best though." She does her best to reassure me. "My mom called me earlier this week and told me she has been thinking about putting the house on the market. Which is weird. I know it's what she needs though, ya know? I think it's her way of coming to terms with the fact it's time for her to move on."

"Maybe it's the step she needs to take to fully close that chapter of her life."

She nods her head. "She seems good, better actually. I'm not sure what the change is, but she almost sounds happy."

A puff of air leaves her mouth as her eyes turn toward the window. I feel her tension ease a little as she admits it out loud, as if hearing the words help her come to terms with things.

"That's good. I'm sure she is glad to have you coming home to stay with her. I'm kind of jealous, actually."

A warm smile spreads across her face. "You know we'll still keep in touch while I'm gone. We can FaceTime and you'll keep me updated on how things are going at Velvet."

I watch as she runs her hand through her hair once again. The long strands look like silk resting against her chest.

I want to reach out my hand and run my fingers through them.

"Have you talked to your dad? Does he know you're returning home for the summer?"

A look of guilt passes over her face as her eyes focus on something behind me before finding mine once again. I know she is still angry with him for how he treated her mother and the secrets he kept from them both. It doesn't change the fact I know she wishes she could still talk to him. Trust is big with Brea though, and it will take time before he earns it again.

"No, I haven't talked to him since spring break actually. What's there to say, you know?"

"Well, there is the matter of tuition. He did commit to paying for it when your parents divorced. So, what, he's just going to stiff you on it because you decided not to show up for Christmas last year?"

I hear my frustration seep into my tone. Just knowing, if he wasn't such an ass, she wouldn't be leaving me for the summer. I watch as her fingers massage the skin of her forehead. Now I feel terrible for the direction our conversation has gone. This is not how I want our last night together, just the two of us before she moves, to end up like.

"I'm sorry, let's not talk about it tonight. Okay?" I ask, sliding my hand across the table and wrapping it around hers. She flashes me a sad smile before muttering a quiet "thank you."

The waiter approaches our table with our food. I move as he sets the deep-dish pepperoni pizza between us. Brea's eyes sparkle as if she just saw a newborn puppy.

After serving our first slice and asking if we need anything else, he hurries away leaving Brea and I alone again.

Raising up her pizza to me, she holds it between the two of us. I can't help but grin at her, as I tilt my pizza to her in "cheers."

"In pizza we crust." She laughs before taking a big bite. The cheese is so thick it makes it hard for her to bite through as strands of cheese hang from her mouth. Using her hand, she covers her mouth as she slowly chews, bringing in the wayward cheese as she eats.

I watch as her eyelids flutter closed as she lets out a deep hum, thoroughly enjoying the bite, and I'm struck frozen in place watching her. I move to adjust myself in my jeans to avoid pulling her out of her seat and dragging her back to the car.

Who would've thought watching her eat pizza could be so arousing? Never mind, who am I fucking kidding? Watching Brea do anything is enough to get my blood flowing, and I know if I don't look away, I'm running the risk of sporting a fucking boner right here in this restaurant.

As soon as her eyes open and meet mine, I don't even work to cover up the look of desire on my face. By the rosy color that fills her cheeks and the rise and fall of her chest, it's obvious she's just ask affected by my reaction to her as I am. Her tongue darts out, licking the trace of pizza sauce from her lip, and I don't bother to hide my grunt as I think about her tongue licking other areas.

I rapidly divert my gaze away from hers, letting out a cough to clear my throat. I hope no one else witnessed the little show she just gave me. Brea's a fucking knockout, and she always men turning their heads. If they were to see the look on her face and the sounds coming from her mouth, I wouldn't hesitate in telling them to take a fucking hike.

"How are things going with your dad?" she asks. I'm grateful for the change in conversation.

"He's doing good. Really good. He called me yesterday. I guess they'll be releasing him from rehab tomorrow sometime."

"Mason, that's great! Has he decided what he's going to do?"

"Yeah, he's actually considering moving home. Well, closer to home anyway. When I was younger, he relocated to Florida to work for the law firm there. In one of the letters he sent, he mentioned how he was thinking about moving to Des Moines. It's about an hour or so away from where we lived in Arbor Creek."

It was hard only having limited communication with my father, but he regularly sent letters about his time in rehab. Although I couldn't hear his voice until recently, I could see the change in the limited interactions we had.

I'm relieved he is considering making the move. I know being closer to home and our family will be good for him. Although he and my brother, Callum, haven't talked going on two years now, I know being closer to my grandmother will help.

I still feel somewhat to blame for what happened on New Year's. He won't admit it because I know he doesn't want me to put that on myself, but after spending the holidays alone he went on a long drinking binge. He told me in one of his letters how much he regrets the decisions he made that led him to living on his own in Florida. It's one of the reasons why I've always found it in me to stand by his side, despite his issues with Callum.

"I know he'll be happier just being closer to you," she says, reaching her hand out and rubbing it along my forearm.

"I am, too," I confess, looking at my pizza as I take another bite.

After we finish eating, we sit here for a little bit longer. I'm grateful it's quiet here, allowing the waiter to give us some space.

We talk about the job Brea has lined up for the summer and her plans to spend time with some of her high school friends. As much as it kills me to know I'll be away from her for three months, it makes me happy as she talks about the people she'll be spending her time with.

"Where are we going now?" She smiles as she stands up from the booth. I ease my arm around her lower back, bringing her closer to me.

"You'll have to wait and find out," I say as we walk through the restaurant and out the door.

I hold the door open to let another couple in, as Brea stands off to the side next to me. As we turn and head toward the parking lot, I spot a familiar face approaching me. I know Veronica from my psychology class, but we also have hung out a few times at a couple of parties we've been to. She's a pretty girl. Her blonde hair and big gray eyes were the first thing I noticed when we first met.

I force a smile on my face, hoping she'll take a hint when she sees my arm around Brea.

"Mason, hey!" With a radiant smile on her face, she approaches me and I feel the frustrated growl vibrate deep in my chest as her arms envelop my waist. My body tenses, immediately turning cold as Brea releases my hand and takes a step away from us.

My head swings her way, hoping to convey a look that says I'm sorry. Her eyes are looking everywhere but at me, and immediately I feel like an asshole.

Damn it.

chapter twelve

BREA

Letting go of Mason's hand, I take a step away and wrap my arms around my waist. As soon as I do, it's like my body instantly feels cold, and I do my best to look anywhere but at the beautiful blonde pressed against him.

I hear him mutter out a small 'hey' as he takes a step away moving closer to me. I can feel his eyes boring into the side of my face, but I can't bring myself to look at them. The familiar way she approached him leaves me with a sense of uneasiness, and I know without a doubt they have a history together.

A history involving him, her, and no clothes.

The thought of sharing Mason with someone else now, after I know what it's like to have his hands on my body, has my heart beating wildly in my chest. I can feel the emotions racing through me, bubbling up along the surface.

I blink past the tears that are forming as Mason slides his arm around me. In the mix of my racing thoughts, I've closed out their conversation. My body fights off the tension as he presses me against his side, and his touch alone has all my fears melting away.

"I'm actually on a date with my girl here," Mason says, running his arm along my forearm up to my shoulder, pulling me closer to him. I must've missed the question, but if I had to guess she was probably asking what he's doing tonight. More like, she wants to know if there's a chance it will be her.

I let my eyes rake over her as red-hot jealousy courses through me. Her eyes meet mine, and it's as if for the first time she's noticing I'm even standing next to her.

She forces a fake smile as she holds out her hand to me in greeting. "Hey there, I'm Veronica. I'm a friend of Mason's."

The way she says "friend" has me smothering a laugh. As petty and childish as it may be, I want to correct her. She may know Mason, as in familiar with what he looks like beneath his clothes, but that doesn't mean they're friends.

I want to tell her while she may think they are friends, I know who he really is on the inside. That's the part of him that truly matters. I remind myself it's me he cares about and, as hard as it may be to admit it right now because I'm upset, I know he would never want me to be hurt by their interaction tonight.

That thought has me tamping down my anger and wrapping my arm around him. His eyes seek mine, as if trying to gauge my reaction, although feeling the tension still rising in my shoulders. I flash him a small smile, just needing him to know that above all else, I trust him.

"I've got big plans for this one tonight, so we'll see you later," Mason voices, raising his hand and waving as he moves us to turn. As soon as we're a few steps away, he turns his head, bringing his mouth to the side of my face.

He takes a deep breath with his lips pressed against my ear and whispers, "I'm sorry."

Hearing the worry and concern in his voice, I don't even second guess it as I mutter out a quiet, "I know."

Once we approach his car, he grabs my hand to stop me before opening the door, turning me until I'm facing him. Pulling me closer, he leaves no space between us.

The worry and concern I heard a moment ago is written all over his face.

"Do you know?" he asks, searching my eyes for any clues for how I'm truly feeling.

"I know you understand how important trust is to me and would never do anything to hurt me."

He leans in closer, pushing me against the side of the SUV. With his palm pressed against the side of my face, he brushes away my hair as he tilts his head in closer to my mouth.

"Tell me you know how much you mean to me," he breathes. His words feather along my lips. "I need to hear you say you feel this between us."

"I know," I choke out. "I know because I feel it, too."

As soon as the words are spoken, his mouth crashes down on mine. He presses his body into me, and I feel his heartbeat through the palm of my hand. The steady rhythm is matching the heavy beat of my mine, so in tune with one another.

He traces his tongue along the edge of my mouth and I open for him. As soon as our tongues connect, I feel the strangled groan vibrate through his chest. All I can do is fold my arms around his neck, pulling him in closer and hanging on for the ride. When our lips separate, I squeeze my eyes shut as he kisses a line along my jaw, toward my ear, as I struggle to inhale a breath and calm my racing heart.

"When you're gone, I want you to think about this moment. I want you to remember how it feels to have your lips on mine," he mutters, pressing himself closer to me. His hard length is pressed against my stomach, causing my body to quiver. "I want you to remember how just having the taste of your lips on mine makes my body ache to be inside you again," he says, leaning in, pressing a soft kiss to my lips, and I can hear myself sigh as he does.

"God-damn, all the little sounds you make as you come alive for me. They are forever burned in my memory. When you're gone and I'm alone at night, longing to have you near me, those will be the noises I think about when I'm missing you."

Before I have a chance to say anything, he takes a step away, pulling me with him. He turns me so I'm facing the car.

With his body pressed close to mine, I can feel his cock against my ass. I can't stop myself from leaning against him as his hands grab my hips, helping guide my movements.

"Fuck, I'm going to miss this when you're gone," he groans in my ear as his tongue darts out and flicks my earlobe.

Tilting my head back against his shoulder, his hand skates up the front of my shirt, cupping my breast in his palm.

"Mason," I whimper as I turn my head seeking his lips.

Trailing kisses along my cheek toward my ear, he whispers, "Get in," before grabbing the handle of the door. It takes a second before I realize he's opening the back passenger door. I do as he says, climbing inside.

"If this is my last night with you, I need to get my fill of you before you go. We'll start here because I can't wait, but this won't be the last time."

His mouth curves up on one side. The smirk on his face makes my stomach do a flip.

He climbs in with me, sliding his hand along the back of the seat. His hand runs along the side of my face, kissing me deeply.

"I always knew it would be like this between us," he says, running my hand along his chest, letting me feel the rapid beat of his heart. "You make me feel things I've never felt before. Crazy things, Brea." He searches my eyes before grabbing my face, pressing a soul-shattering kiss against my lips.

When we break apart, I see the change in his eyes. The sweet, romantic side of Mason is gone and has been replaced with a look of fiery, passionate side.

Sitting back, he runs his tongue along his lower lip.

"Unzip your pants and come here. I need to feel you."

Pulling out of the restaurant parking lot, I run my fingers along my mouth. They tingle from Mason's rough kisses. The heady mix is leaving me light headed.

Peering over at him, I watch as he adjusts himself in the seat. I bite my lip watching him, knowing what we did merely took the edge off but wasn't enough to sate the need growing between us.

He doesn't tell me where we are going, and I don't even bother asking as he grasps ahold of my hand, driving us across town. As soon as we get closer, I know where we are. The sun has begun to set, painting the sky a beautiful hue of orange, purple, and blue.

One of my favorite parts about living in Chicago is taking a walk along the Navy Pier. I love how beautiful and peaceful it is right before sunset.

It takes a few minutes for us to find a spot to park. After we pay for the meter, he grabs my hand and we walk along the water. Neither of us says anything nor do we move to let go of each other's hand.

"There are times when I miss being home in Arbor Creek," he says after a while, breaking the silence. "It's very different from living in Chicago and the fast-pace life. Arbor Creek is small, hell, it would probably take you ten minutes to walk the span of downtown. It's quiet and peaceful. I'd love to take you there some day, show you what it's like."

Turning my head, I look up at him and I feel warmth in my chest as I think about visiting where Mason grew up and meeting the people who made him who he is today.

"I would love that." I smile.

He raises our joined hands up to his mouth, pressing a small kiss along the back of mine. He traces his lips along the skin, and I feel myself let out a deep breath at how my body reacts to his touch.

We approach a spot along the water. It's truly beautiful with the sunset as the backdrop. I stop to look at the view, leaning in close to the railing.

"It's so beautiful," I whisper as Mason leans in close behind me.

With his arms surrounding me, we stand here in the quiet stillness watching as the sun sets and the water laps against the rocks. The downtown lights cast a soft glow on the distant edge of the water.

"Yes, you are," he sighs, leaning his head close to my shoulder.

Running my hands along his arms, I wrap our fingers together. Up until this point, I haven't allowed myself to think about how much I'm going to miss Mason when I'm gone.

So much has changed between us in the past two months. We haven't discussed what is happening between the two of us. Tonight, when he called me his girl, something in me changed. I can't help but wonder if he only said that because his past was standing in front of us.

Either way, it made me realize regardless of what is going on between us, I don't want him to feel obligated to continue with this while I'm gone. He's never been one to commit to anything serious, and I can't expect him to wait for me until I get back. More importantly, I don't want to risk losing who he is to me. Distance can weigh heavily on a relationship. It isn't fair to put that kind of strain on us before we really have a chance to see what this could be.

I make myself a promise to tell Mason before I go that I don't expect him to wait for me. I want him to be happy, and if someone comes along while I'm away that does, I want him to know it will never change who he is to me.

As much as it would hurt to never again feel the way I do when we're together, or have his lips on mine, I would much rather have him in my life as a friend than not at all. The truth is, I don't know what I would do if I lost him. So, I'll hold onto whatever I can have, even if it means loving him all alone.

chapter thirteen

MASON

Pushing open the door to the gym, I jog down the front steps. Keeping my head bowed against the rain, I adjust my gym bag on my shoulder as I pick up the pace. Clicking the lock on the remote, I slide into the driver's seat of my Range Rover.

My phone vibrates with an incoming text message.

Callum: The bus arrives a little after 6:30. See you then!

I woke up this morning to messages from both my dad and Callum. My dad was informing me he was still planning to be released from rehab today, and I'm sure any time now he'll be calling. Callum, on the other hand, let me know he was thinking of taking an impromptu trip to Chicago for a visit. Wrapping up my last class this morning, it was nice to think of spending the weekend with my brother, especially since Brea is heading out of town tomorrow morning.

Callum still lives in my hometown of Arbor Creek. While we always had a close relationship growing up, we have had our difference of opinion when it comes to our father. Callum is the oldest of the two of us by two years. When our parents divorced, our dad moved to Florida. Although they rarely saw each other, much less spoke, Callum had chosen to side with our mother, and after he graduated from college, he cut off ties completely.

I've never understood how he could act as though our father was not a part of his life, regardless of the mistakes he's made. He believes his faults are worth cutting all ties and never looking back.

Since I was younger when our parents divorced, I don't remember the details of what happened to cause our parents to split, unlike Callum. If anything, I know he did his best to shield me from their fights. I know now he was only trying to prevent me from going through the same resentment and turmoil he has gone through.

Checking the clock on the front dash, it's a little after six. Putting the car in reverse, I ease out of the parking spot and head downtown to the bus station. Callum normally doesn't mind driving, but insisted he didn't want to bother with finding his way around the city on his own and asked if I'd pick him up when he arrived.

Twenty minutes later, I pull up in front of the bus station to find my brother leaning against the side of the brick building. His head is tilted down, focusing intently on whatever is on his phone. Honking the horn, I see him jolt his attention, lifting his head up to meet mine.

Holding his middle finger up at me, he chuckles as he drags his suitcase along behind him. Rolling down the window, I can't help but crack a grin when I see the annoyed look on his face.

"Quit fucking around already and get in the car." I laugh.

"You weren't sitting here that long and you know it. Shut up!" He smothers a grin of his own.

Depositing his suitcase in the backseat, he opens the passenger side door. Clapping his hand in mine, I lean over and give him a half hug.

"Good to see you, bro."

"It's good to see you, too," I say, adjusting my sunglasses on my face.

"I was thinking we could head to my place for a little bit. Graham will be there so you can catch up with him. If you're up for it, we can head to Velvet later. I have a friend who is heading home for the summer, so I want to say goodbye to her before she leaves tomorrow."

The mention of Brea and her trip home leaves a weighted ball in the pits of my stomach. I have been trying to avoid thinking about it. I hate being reminded she'll be gone for three months. I'm going to miss her, but I understand why she's doing this. If I thought I stood a chance at convincing her, I'd beg her to move in with me for the summer.

"Sounds good, man. How is Graham doing anyway?"

I hear the concern in my brother's tone. It's the one thing that Graham hates to hear when people ask him how he's doing. The events of the past weighs heavy on Graham, and he works every day to fight off the demons who lurk around every shadowed corner.

"He's doing alright. Next month will be four years since the accident. I think the date is looming over his head."

Callum runs his palm across his chin, letting out a deep sigh.

"I can't believe it's been that long already. He still hasn't been back to Arbor Creek, has he?"

"Nope, but I know he'll be glad to see you."

We spend the rest of the drive catching up on how things are going. Callum talks about his job working with our stepfather, Randy, and how our mom is doing. As much as I love living in the city, it's nice having this time with my brother. There will be a day when I will move home to Arbor Creek, but for now I'm enjoying my life here.

Turning into the lot of my apartment, I pull my car into a parking spot. Callum leaves his suitcase in the car, after asking if I'll swing by his hotel room before we go out tonight. Unlocking the apartment door, I swing it open and am struck dumbfounded, standing still when I see Graham leaning over the counter in our kitchen as my father stands in the dining room.

"Dad," I say, surprised to see him standing there. The first thing I notice is the clear look in his eyes replacing the glossy bloodshot look he often wore.

Walking around the table, I wrap him in my arms, patting him on the back. It's good to finally see him, and for a moment, I find myself forgetting I left my brother standing behind me.

"What the hell is this?"

The pissed off tone changes the mood in the air instantly. The tension in my father's shoulders as his body tenses, not expecting to see Callum here either.

"Son," my father says as I move to step away. Looking between Callum and my dad, I know I should stop it. It's like trying to stop on an icy road when you're going too fast. You can see what's coming in front of you and try with all your might, you want to stop it but you can't.

"Please don't tell me you let me come all the way here for some fucking reunion. I meant what I said two years ago, I don't care if I ever speak to you again. Yet, look, here you are!"

"Callum, shut the fuck up!" I yell, pissed at the blatant disrespect he has for our father.

"It's okay, Mason," my father says, holding his hands up at me. Turning his attention to Callum, "I didn't realize you would be here."

Callum lets out a frustrated breath as his nostrils flare.

Guilt passes over Graham's face as he looks between me and Callum. He couldn't have known this would've gone down this way. Callum's trip was planned at the last minute, and I thought my Dad was still in Florida. There are so many questions, but I know as soon as I ask them, it will only start another argument. Regardless of the fact my father has put himself through rehab to try and get healthy again, Callum is bound to focus only on what he did wrong to end up there.

"I've got a hotel room at the Westin downtown," my Dad says, turning to face me. "How about you give me a call tomorrow when you have some time?"

Nodding my head, I grip my dad's shoulder. Keeping my voice low so only he can hear me, I whisper, "It's good to see you. You look good."

He flashes me a sad smile, heading toward the door. I watch as Callum moves out of the way, crossing his arms in front of him, focusing his attention on the floor. As soon as the door shuts behind him, Callum's eyes find mine. The tick in his jaw confirms he's riding the edge of frustration.

"What in the fuck?"

"Listen, I had no idea you were going to be here," Graham interjects, facing Callum. "You have to know I would've given you a heads up. He just got here a few minutes before you did."

Callum runs his hand over his face. The frustration on his face a match for what I'm feeling course through me. This is not how I expected our night to go.

"I need a fucking drink," Callum grunts.

Opening the door to Velvet, I let the feel and the beat of the music flow through my body. The lights are dim and it takes a second before my eyes adjust to the change in lighting. Brea texted me earlier today reminding me tonight is her last shift before she packs up and heads home. She has a meeting with her boss of her new job so she wants to head off early in the morning, which means I have less than twelve hours left with her.

Moving through the hordes of people toward the bar, I don't even bother to see if Callum is behind me. His sour disposition has changed the mood for the night, and I don't want his attitude to put a damper on my last night with Brea.

I don't even bother waiting at the bar to order. Leaving Callum standing there, I walk behind the bar and grab him a beer, ringing him up on the register. Pulling the cap off the top of his Busch Light, I slide the bottle along the counter toward him.

Lissa saunters toward the bar, loading her drinks onto her tray. Leaning in close to her, I yell in her ear over the loud music.

"Where is she?" Knowing she knows exactly who I'm looking for.

"Uh, I think I saw her head into the back. That was a few minutes ago though."

Nodding my head, I hold my finger up to Callum, letting him know I'll be back, as I turn in search of Brea.

After checking the cooler and the employee locker room, I come up empty and resign myself to waiting at the bar in hopes of finding her there.

Rounding the corner, I stop myself short when I see a long-haired brunette with her arms wrapped around none other than my brother.

Bounding my way over to where they are standing, I struggle to contain my anger.

"Care to explain to me what you're doing?" I shout over the music.

Callum doesn't say anything, instead raises the beer bottle to his mouth, wearing nothing but a smirk. He's lucky I don't knock the smug look right off his face.

As soon as Brea steps away from him, I see the confusion on her face as she turns to see me standing behind her, bouncing her head between me and Callum.

"Sorry, Mase," Callum grunts out a laugh. "I think your friend here thought I was you."

I grunt at the way Callum emphasizes the nickname Brea uses for me.

Looking down at her, I claim her waist and pull her closer to me. She comes easily, returning my hug. I hear Callum chuckle behind us, but I tune him out as I lean forward pressing my nose against where her shoulder and neck meet.

"I'm going to miss you," I whisper in her ear. She doesn't say anything in return, only nods her head.

"Did you get your final grade?" I ask. She has been stressed about keeping her grade up in her Algebra class so she doesn't lose the scholarship she is receiving for part of her tuition. She's been stressing about it since taking the test that accounted for half her grade.

"I passed."

Despite the dim lights, I see the grin on her face as her eyes light up.

"I knew you would, baby." I smile back, squeezing her tighter, pressing her closer to me which makes her grin grow even wider.

"Can you try to get away for a little bit and take a break?"

"Yeah, let me see if Lissa can cover my tables and we can head outside for a bit."

I know Craig wouldn't be happy about me stealing her away after she got here, but it's still early. It's not quite as packed as it will be soon. If I don't talk with her now, I may not get the chance until closing, and I'm not sure Callum is planning to stick around that long.

Brea sneaks away to check on her tables and find Lissa.

Waving Farin over, I order a beer and head to the high-top table Callum is sitting at. Sliding onto the barstool, I watch the crowd of people on the dance floor.

This isn't how I expected my night with my brother to go. The last time we were together, we hit up the bar in downtown Arbor Creek. Brodie's is more of a small-town bar, nothing like the size of Velvet.

"So, who was that?" Callum shouts.

"Just a friend of mine," I grunt in response, not wanting to get into it with him right now.

"Is that right?" he asks, calling me out. Callum knows I don't get close to women, at least not like that in public.

"That's right," I say, rolling my eyes at him.

Turning my head, I expect to see Brea but come face to face with Sierra. Although she and I have been friends for some time, we haven't hooked up since the night my dad was arrested. I know she is still interested, hell, otherwise she wouldn't even be trying to talk to me.

I don't need Brea to see me talking to her either.

"Alright, tell me who this is! You're clearly related because you look like you could pass for twins."

Callum snorts, finding it funny that for the second time tonight, we've been mistaken for looking alike.

Grabbing her hand draped across my shoulder, I move to her so she's standing at my side and flash her a wink, not wanting to be rude.

"This is my older and less handsome brother, Callum."

Callum chokes out a laugh.

"Now I know what I've been missing being away from school," Callum says, winking at Sierra.

Brea picks that moment to approach our table. I see the forced smile on her face when she sees Sierra standing with us.

Pulling Brea closer, I press my mouth against her ear. "You ready now, baby?"

She leans back and looks me straight in the eye, as if trying to say something without using words.

"Alright, let's go." I smile, grabbing her by the hand.

After signaling to Callum I'm heading out for a bit, I follow behind Brea as we walk toward the back of the club and out to the patio. It's quiet though, and it will give us a little bit of privacy we won't get inside.

Opening the door, a wall of humidity hits my face as I take a deep breath, inhaling the warm air. Brea leads me to the corner, away from the groups of people standing outside talking. I don't go any further without having her in my arms, as I pull her closer, wrapping around her waist tightly. She lets out a small yelp, taking her by surprise.

With her arms at my neck and mine draped around her waist, we stand like that, just taking each other in. I'm going to miss the feel of her small body pressed against mine, the fruity smell of her shampoo, and her soft skin.

Running my fingers along her lower back, I run my hand underneath the cotton of her t-shirt. I feel her body tremble beneath my touch. Knowing her body reacts this way to my touch spurs something inside of me.

I press my mouth against her forehead and inhale the smell of her.

"Promise me nothing will change between us while you're gone," I whisper. "Promise me, even though we're going to spend the next three months apart, we'll pick this up when you're back."

"Mason, I don't expect you to stay single while I'm gone. A lot can happen in three months," she says. I hear the edge of concern in her voice. What she's really saying is a lot can change.

She doesn't look me in the eye, focusing her attention over my shoulder. Knowing this will be what she remembers when she's gone, I want to leave her with something memorable. A moment between the two of us to hold onto.

"Brea, I know this is all so new between us. I need you to know I will always be here as your friend, but hear me when I say there is nothing that will make me change my mind about what I want. There is no one else, no amount of time, or anything you can say, that will make me change how I feel. I've known this for a long time and kept it to myself because I wanted to respect what you had with Kaleb. Now that I can show you, I'm not going to fuck it up."

"Everything you know about relationships end in heartbreak. I'm not looking or going anywhere, Brea. I promise I'm going to be here when you come back and, baby, when you do, I'm going to continue to show you I will never hurt you."

I press my mouth against her lips. The moment they connect, it's like a spark lights between us. Hearing the small whimper pass her lips, I struggle to fight off a groan of my own.

God, I'm going to miss this girl.

chapter fourteen

BREA
july

Pulling my car into the driveway, I turn the key in the ignition. I lean my head against the headrest and let out a deflated sigh. This wasn't how I planned to spend my twenty-second birthday on a Friday night. I just got home from work. My boss let me out an hour early, only to come home, take a long bath, and binge watch Netflix all night.

To be fair, I'm looking forward to eating a bowl of ice cream and watching One Tree Hill again for the millionth time. Although, if I had it my way, I would be hitting the highway straight to Chicago to see Mason.

Checking my surroundings, a big red pick-up parked next to my mom's car immediately catches my eye. I'm surprised. For one, that my mom is even home already. Usually, I beat her here. And two, wondering who could possibly be here with her? She never mentioned anyone having to stop by to fix anything. I notice the license plate reads Stark County as I jog my memory wondering who it could be, but I come up empty.

I grab my purse and lunch pail from the passenger seat before opening the door. It's been a little over two months since I moved home with my mom, and so far, things have been going better than I expected. When I arrived, I thought I'd find the same woman I saw when I visited during spring break. A woman who was still mourning the loss of the life she once had. Instead, what I came home to was someone else entirely.

Growing up an only child, I was close with both of my parents but always had a closer relationship with my mom. Their divorce rocked the both of us. Recalling how apprehensive I was about my temporary move, I felt guilty over how much I had dreaded coming home. Looking back on it now, I'm so grateful I went through with it because, in a way, it allowed me to reconnect with the mom I had before our world was turned upside down.

On the nights I've been lonely and missing Mason, she's been there trying to pull me out of it. She knows all about Mason, having met him when she came to visit in Chicago, but what I haven't told her is how our relationship has changed. Or at least, how the emotions have grown for me. We have our girls' nights where we'll hang out, watch recorded episodes of Dateline while drinking a glass of wine, but whenever Mason calls, she will always flash me her warm smile and waves her hand at me to go talk to him. I'm sure she senses something has changed, but she hasn't pressured me to open up about it.

Climbing the steps of the front porch, I turn the door handle, unsure if it's locked. Finding it unlocked, I push the door open and take a tentative step into the foyer. Slipping my shoes off, I bend over and put them in the mudroom located off to the side.

I listen for any indication someone could be home but the house is quiet, except for the soft hum of the dryer. Climbing the stairs, I head into the kitchen to unload the contents of my lunch before heading for a hot bath. It's been a long day and the thought of a bath bomb sounds heavenly.

As soon as I step into the kitchen, I'm met with a grunting sound followed by a moan behind me causing me to freeze as my mom's laughter filters through the air. Turning my head, I feel my eyes widen when I find my mom pressed against the counter and a tall man standing in front of her. I am not able to see his face as it's pressed against the base of her neck. He's dressed nice in a pair of khaki shorts and a polo shirt. Her head is tilted back, her eyes closed, resting against the kitchen cabinet.

Another groan filters through the air, and it jolts me into action as I set my lunch bag on the counter, not bothering to make my presence known. I'm too shocked and surprised at what I just witnessed to even consider talking about it at this point.

I quietly tiptoe my way down the hall, which isn't easily done with the old wooden floor creaking below each footstep I make. The sound of my mother's laughter follows me, and the moment I step into my room, I let out a sigh in relief.

"What in the hell?" I whisper-shout to myself. As shocked as I am and kind of grossed out for seeing my mom with some guy I've never met, I also can't help but wonder if he is the reason she's been so happy lately.

I tell myself that if that's the case, I know she'll tell me in her own time.

Tossing my purse onto my bed, I pad along the soft carpet of my bedroom and into the bathroom. Turning on the faucet, I reach my hand under the water to check the temperature. Standing in front of the vanity, I slide open the drawer to grab a bath bomb and quickly unwrap the plastic before dropping it into the tub. I watch the colors turn the water a beautiful array of blues, purples and pinks. Unzipping the front of my pants, I slide them off and toss them into the hamper. Grabbing the hem of my t-shirt, I slip it over my head, adding it to the pile.

I reach my hands up to tie my hair into a high bun and turn my music app on. Stepping into the bathtub, I ease my body into the warm water.

This is one amenity that you won't find living in a small apartment in downtown Chicago without paying a hefty price. This bathtub is one of my favorite things I've always loved about living in this house. I remember growing up how it felt like swimming in a pool. It's big enough for two, maybe three people, to sit in here comfortably.

Leaning my head against the edge of the tub, I close my eyes feeling the stress of the week and the tension in my body ease away. I don't know how long I'm sitting here when the ringing of my phone jolts me awake.

Raising my hand out of the water, I pat my palm on the towel next to me before picking up the phone, swiping at the screen to connect the FaceTime call with Mason. I ease under the water, holding the phone in front of me when his face appears on my screen.

"Happy Birthday, beautiful." He smiles.

"Thank you," I hum, smiling at him.

I can tell Mason's trying to see where I am, thinking I'm just getting off work. Adjusting the phone in my hand, I can tell the moment he realizes where I am when a huge grin takes over his face. He lets out a deep grunt, muttering to whoever is next to him he'll be right back and after that he's on the move.

"Hold on for a second, Brea," he says.

"Are you," he stops to clear his throat. "are you in the bath?"

His voice is low as it echoes around the room he's in. I hear the edge of exasperation in his tone.

"Yeah, I got off work early. It's been a long week so I decided to come home and take a bath."

The lighting on the screen goes dim, followed by the sound of a door clicking shut.

"I wasn't expecting to see you...like that," he chokes out. "God, I fucking miss you. I need you to know it's killing me to be away from you, especially today. I wish I could be spending your birthday with you."

My heart warms hearing him call me "baby." Mason has always hated nicknames. He used to grunt and groan when I would call him Mase in front of his friends. While we've kept in touch while I've been gone, there is a pang of loneliness I feel after not seeing him this long. As much as it helps to be able to see his face when he video calls, nothing would beat the feel of having him next to me.

"I know you do and I miss you, too. In just a couple of weeks, I'll be back in Chicago and you will get sick of me soon enough," I joke.

I watch as he runs his hand through his hair, holding the camera away from him. My eyebrows furrow as concern sets in. Something seems off, and I don't know what it is.

Sitting up in the tub, the water splashes around me but I'm careful not to drop my phone.

"Mason, talk to me."

He doesn't say anything for a moment before turning the camera back to face him. I see the hurt in his eyes, causing my heart to drop, fearing what he will say next.

"What's wrong?"

"I just hate you're there and I'm here. Being away from you," he chokes, "it just fucking sucks, Brea. I want to hold you, kiss you, and to properly wish you happy birthday."

Leaning forward, I pull my knees up to my chest, holding the phone out in front of me. A piece of hair falls out of my messy bun, draping over the edge of my face.

"I'll let you make it up to me when I get home, I promise." I smile, hoping to ease some of his worry.

His face lights up, and the grin that I love so much is once again back on his face.

"Got any big plans to ring in your birthday? The big two-two!" he asks, changing the subject.

"Oh, yeah, big plans that involve me and this bathtub, then becoming one with the couch while I binge watch Netflix."

"Is that right?" he jokes, his lip curving up in a smirk. "You're a little party animal, babe. I wish I was there to Netflix and chill with you." He laughs, flashing me his devilish grin.

There's the Mason I love. He doesn't show this side of himself to everyone, the light and carefree side. The side of him that jokes just to put a smile on my face. No, this is the side he reserves for me.

"Netflix and chill, huh? Is that all I am to you?" I chide.

"You mean more to me than anything in this world, Brea. Don't you know that already?" His tone is serious but the smile on his face shows me he means it.

"While I'm confessing my heart to you, I think I should also say it's killing me to know you're sitting there relaxing in the bathtub," he grunts, "naked...all by yourself."

"You know, you could always come up here and visit me if you want."

The sound of his pained grunt echoes through the room.

"I hope you know I would, if I could. Craig is three weeks away from opening Hard Stop. I've been spending ten to twelve hours a day here helping get things ready, plus working my shifts at Velvet on the weekend."

Craig, the owner of Velvet, has been working to open a new restaurant. The club has been so successful, he felt it was time to venture out into other businesses. Since Mason has been on summer break and needed the extra money, Craig hired him to help between the two businesses. I know Mason mentioned Graham has been helping him more as well, taking on more responsibilities at Velvet. The last time Mason and I talked, he mentioned how Graham was offered a position in management, helping run the security overseeing both businesses.

"Yeah, I know," I say, nodding my head. I lean forward to pull the plug on the drain, letting the water out.

"I should probably get to work. I'm sure Craig is wondering where the hell I'm at," he says. "I'll call you when I get home tonight."

We both say our goodbyes with the promise of chatting later. I know Mason wishes he could be here. After we disconnect the call, I set the phone on the edge of the tub. Moving to stand, I dry myself off before wrapping myself in a towel. I spend some extra time putting my lotion on before I head into my bedroom in search of something comfy to wear.

As soon as I enter my bedroom, the scent of flowers that I hadn't noticed before, fills the air as my eyes fall on the huge bouquet of red roses sitting on my dresser. There are easily two dozen roses and immediately I smile, thinking of Mason. He had already sent me a present earlier this week—a massage at the local beauty salon. I should've known he would find another way to make me smile and this is one of them.

Leaning in close, I inhale, deeply appreciating the smell that permeates the air before picking the card off the plastic holder. Flipping open the envelope, I ease the card out.

Happy Birthday, sweetheart. I miss you! ~Kaleb

After the argument at Velvet, I haven't spoken to Kaleb despite the fact he continues to text message me occasionally. Even then, I hadn't even bothered to read his messages until one night when I got curious and read through them.

I would have thought by now he would take the hint and realize I'm not interested, but he was always persistent.

I don't want to hurt him and I understand him wanting to try and make things right between us, but I will never be able to get over what he did to me. There is no moving on from that, regardless of what misplaced feelings he had toward my relationship with Mason. I would've thought he knew me well enough to know it, too.

Sliding the card back into the envelope, I pull out a pair of yoga pants and a t-shirt from my dresser before making myself comfortable on my bed.

Even with the TV turned on and One Tree Hill playing, I can't stop thinking about how to explain to Kaleb it must stop or how I will break it to Mason. I know after the last time I saw Kaleb, he wouldn't be happy with me for not mentioning he has been continuing to contact me. With the way things ended with Kaleb, the guilt I felt early on seeps in. Did I really give him reason to question my friendship with Mason when we were together? Whenever we would run into Mason when we were out with friends, I always tried to make Kaleb feel like there was nothing to worry about. Didn't I?

Opening the passenger door to Kaleb's BMW, he jogged around the front to grab the door, holding his hand out to me. His strawberry blond hair was longer on the top. It looked a little wild, swept to the side in a boyish sort of way.

Placing my hand in his, I grinned up at him as I stepped out of the car. "You look gorgeous tonight, sweetheart," he said, grinning down at me.

Taking hold of his forearm, we walked toward the Sports Bar. Kaleb was a big fan of the Chicago Blackhawks. They had made it to the playoffs, so there we were, ready to cheer them on.

Inside we were greeted by a swarm of black and red as fans prepared to cheer on the Hawks. Kaleb kept a hold of my hand as we made our way through the crowd of people toward the table his friends often commandeered. Kaleb turned to me, nodding, indicating he was going to get a drink from the bar. I responded with a nod before he flashed me a smile, leaving me to grab our drinks. I continued to weave my way through the packed tables. People were standing around talking, so I was careful not to bump into anyone with a drink in their hand.

A strong arm snagged my waist, pulling me in. Any tension I felt in my body when I was taken by surprise was gone when I heard the soothing sound of Mason's voice in my ear.

"Where do you think you're going?" Mason laughed, as he spun me in his arms.

Smacking him on the chest playfully, I shouted, "What do you think you're doing?" Raising my eyebrow at him in question, I perched my hand on my waist, heavy on the sass.

He shook his head at me, "What does it look like?" I saw the sparkle in his eye.

How could I be mean to him now? "Oh, alright, I guess," I say, as he let out a loud laugh, embracing me in a hug.

Peering up at him, I said, "You really did have me freaked out for a second before I realized it was you, creep," I joked, pushing against his chest once again. I took a step back, only to bump into someone behind me.

Spinning around to apologize, I peered up to find Kaleb. The look on his face was stone cold and his expression was unreadable.

"Hey, sorry," I muttered loud enough for him to hear as I leaned in, cuddling closer to him. "I was just saying hi to Mason."

"Of course, you were," Kaleb said flatly. "Where Mason goes, you always follow."

Turning to face Mason, I hoped to convey how sorry I was for Kaleb's comment only to find a small grin lining his mouth.

"Mason's one of my best friends, Kaleb. You know that," I said, taking my drink from his hand. "Right, Mason?" I asked, turning my head toward him once again.

"Yep," he said with a pop. "Best friends."

As much as I wish I could take back the night I walked in on Kaleb, I'm certain if that night would never have happened, Mason and I wouldn't be where we are today. I believe everything happens for a reason. Today, I'm not going to let the guilt I feel over the past affect me because regardless of how we got here, I know I am looking forward to what my future has in store with Mason.

chapter fifteen

MASON
august

Rubbing my fingers over my eyes, I lean back in the office chair and quickly check the time on the clock. I've been counting down the minutes all day until it's time to head out of here.

I've spent most of the summer busy working, doing everything I can to keep my mind off Brea and how fucking much I miss her. Knowing in just a few hours she'll be back has me distracted and unable to focus.

It's a little after four o'clock when I shove my chair away and bound out of the office. I've been spending a lot of my time during the week at Hard Stop, the restaurant Craig recently opened, located close to downtown. After spending the weekdays here, I've been keeping myself busy working my shifts at Velvet on the weekends. Craig gave me the weekend off knowing Brea was coming to town but I ended up going into the restaurant today to stay busy. I've been going out of my mind at the thought of seeing her.

"I'm going to head out. Brea should be here in a couple of hours and I want to get a shower before I do," I say, tilting my hip against the doorway leading into the stockroom. Craig is leaning over a stack of boxes, flipping through what appears to be the invoices.

Peering his head up to mine, he nods his head, "Alright, you tell her to come see me once she gets settled in. I promised her she'd have a job when she came back to Chicago and I mean it. Although now, I think I'll give her the option of picking where she wants to be."

I know Craig has been looking to hire some waitresses, and it would be a great opportunity for her to pick up hours during the week, but this is our last year of college. I don't want her to stress herself out.

"Yeah, I'll talk to her and let her know."

After we say our goodbyes, I head out the side entrance toward where my Rover is parked. As soon as I approach the SUV, I feel my phone vibrate from my pocket, and the hope that it's Brea has me reaching my hand inside to check to see who it is. Instead, I find a missed call from my mom.

Ever since Callum left Chicago, we haven't spoken to each other, although it's not without a lack of me trying. I've made several attempts to reach out to him, but he's a stubborn and prideful person, and my efforts have been futile. The last time I spoke to my mom, she told me Callum has shut down and refuses to talk about it with her or my stepdad, Randy. My phone vibrates in my hand again as a notification appears indicating she left a voicemail.

Clicking the message icon, I press play as I raise my phone against my ear.

Hey, sweetie, I was just calling to see how your week is going and to see what time Brea is supposed to be back in town. It worries me knowing that girl is driving all that way by herself. I was just wondering if you talked to your brother at all? I know he's as stubborn as a mule but I think he'd like to hear from you. Anyway, I'm sure you're busy so don't worry about calling me tonight. If you can though, will you try to give Callum a call? Alright, I'll talk to ya later. Love you, sweetie.

I can't help but smile at my mom. That woman couldn't stop herself from meddling in what's going on with people's lives and relationships even if I begged her. She has good intentions though and a heart of gold.

Tossing my phone on the center console, I decide I'll head home and take a quick shower and, if I have any time before Graham and I head over to Brea's, I'll try giving Callum a call.

It doesn't end up taking me long at all to get home and get myself ready. I think the anticipation of seeing Brea has me racing to get in and out as quickly as possible. With forty minutes to spare, I pick up my phone and decide to give Callum one last try. If he doesn't answer after this, I'm throwing in the towel. The ball will be in his court, and whenever he decides to pull his head out of his ass, the door will always be open.

Scrolling through my phone, I click Callum's name and press the phone to my ear as it rings.

"Reid." Callum's voice grunts into the receiver.

"It's about time you learned to answer your phone," I grumble. He doesn't respond right away and, for a second, I think he disconnects the call.

"I don't have time for this right now, Mason. What the hell do you want?" I hear the edge of frustration in his tone, and it only adds to my annoyance. Why the hell is he pissed off at me?

"You going to keep avoiding me forever? Doesn't it get old after a while, running away from all your problems?" The last comment was a low blow but still. He's acting like a jackass and he deserves to hear it.

"Just cut to the chase, what the hell do you want?"

"You know it's been two years since you've talked to Dad? I've tried to stay out of your problems, but the way you spoke to him when you were here was bullshit, man. It's fucking disrespectful."

"I'm not the one with problems. He is! He has a fucking problem with drinking too much and putting his hands on women, specifically our mother. Now THAT is disrespectful, Mason! The only thing I want to know is why you don't see his behavior as being an issue?"

"Dude, he has paid the price for that. How long are you going to rake him over the coals and crucify him for it? Maybe if you had stopped acting like an asshole and listened to what he had to say when he tried talking, you'd feel differently."

It's the fucking truth! He didn't even give our dad a chance to explain why he was in Chicago, instead treated him like shit to the point where he left and went to his hotel. If he pulled his head out of his ass and talked to him, maybe he'd get the full story. I get he made mistakes in the past and it pisses me off to hear how he treated our mom, but he also deserves to hear him out and that's something Callum has never given him.

"That's what you're not understanding, Mason. I don't give a fuck what has he has to say anymore, the same goes for you. I'm done with this conversation."

Tossing the phone on the coffee table, I rub my hand over my face.

"God, he's such an asshole," I spit, running my fingers into my damp hair. The sound of a can top popping has me peeking my eye open, expecting to find Graham standing in front of me.

Tilting my head up, I wait for his inevitable question to come but instead he just holds out the can of beer to me. I don't even hesitate to take it from him, pop the top, and take a long swig.

"Thanks, man," I say, wiping the back of my hand along my mouth.

Graham doesn't say anything, instead, takes a seat on the other end of the couch, leaning over to pick up the remote. I don't try to talk about it, too pissed off after the bullshit Callum just said to even bother going into it. Instead, I focus on the television and watch as Graham flips through the channels, settling on an episode of That 70's Show.

Taking a long pull from my beer as I check the time on my watch, we still have thirty minutes before it's time to leave for Brea's.

When we talked on the phone earlier this week, she made me promise tonight she could get her friends together for pizza and to hang out. As much as she wants to settle in, I know she misses her friends more than anything. Graham and I decided we would help her get the stuff she moved out of her room in Cleveland and into her apartment.

Just the thought of Brea being in Chicago has me letting out a sigh of relief.

"You want to talk about it?" Graham asks, turning down the TV. I feel his eyes burning holes into the side of my face.

"He's just an asshole. What more is there to say?"

"He is your brother."

To anyone else, you'd probably miss it but I hear the edge of sadness in Graham's voice. He hates seeing Callum and I fight like we are, and I feel the guilt rise in my throat. Ever since the day Graham lost his cousin, Gage, who was more like a brother to him, in a car accident, he hasn't been same. The regret and blame he has placed on himself from that night haunts him.

"I know, but he's bull-headed and won't give it up. I'm sick of being stuck in the middle of him and my dad."

"Then don't put yourself in the middle of it, Mason. It's that simple. It's not your battle to fight. You can be there for your dad without choosing sides."

"I just don't want to talk about it tonight. Brea will be home soon, and everything will be better."

Graham is the only person who knows how much I've truly struggled having her away. If it wasn't for Craig needing my help, I'm certain this break would've caused me to go out of my mind.

Before Brea left, she was worried I was going to turn my attention to someone else. The truth is I've put so much focus into working and going to the gym, I haven't given myself time to focus on anything else but her. The only parties I've been to include Graham and I, this couch, and a six pack of beer between the two of us.

Don't even get me going on the fact that this is the longest I've gone without getting laid in a long fucking time. It's resulted in a lot of cold showers and a few memorable FaceTime conversations with Brea.

In all honesty, it's really time for me to get my shit together and start thinking about what the future has in store. I'm getting ready to go into my senior year of college, and I have a lot of work to put in before I can start law school the following year. It's time I look at the path my dad has been on and use his mistakes as a lesson.

"It's days like today I'm grateful we live here," I joke, changing the subject as I turn my head toward Graham.

I can tell he's lost in thought, his eyes lacking focus, as he nods his head. If I had to guess, his mind has drifted back to Gage.

"Do you ever think about going home to Arbor Creek? I'm sure your mom would like to see you."

"I can't." The emotion seeps into his words, coming out gruff.

"You can't or you won't?"

"Nothing good would come out of going back there. Not now."

I don't want to tell him he's wrong because I know it's no use. Graham left behind a lot when he left Arbor Creek three years ago. I know he doesn't think he deserves it but there are people who love him, who want to see him.

I guess we're both just too stubborn for our own good.

"What time did Brea say she'd be home?" Graham asks, picking up the remote again, flipping through the channels.

"She said she would be here around six or so." I hit the lock button on my phone, checking the time. "We have about twenty minutes if you want to start heading that way."

With a nod of his head, Graham stands up and heads down the hall, leaving only the sound of his heavy feet padding on the hardwood floors.

Sometimes the past is too hard for some of us to get over.

chapter sixteen

BREA

Two knocks sound on the edge of the door as I shut my suitcase, zipping it shut.

"Come in," I say, as my mom peeks her head into my room.

Her long brown hair is pulled up high in a ponytail. We spent most of the past month getting everything cleared out of the house to prepare for her to sell the house. This last weekend I finally went through all my stuff I kept here when I went away to college and decided what was worth keeping and taking with me to Chicago. Aside from some of the keepsakes my mom offered to hold onto for me, the rest is getting packed up in boxes as I get ready for the trip back to Chicago later today.

"How is packing coming along?" she asks. She's dressed in a pair of track shorts and a tank top. She's been spending most of the morning repainting the living room to prepare for Monday when the realtor stops by to take pictures of the house. This is likely the last time I'll be in this house and the thought has me a little nostalgic.

Careful of where she steps, she maneuvers through the room toward where I'm sitting and takes a seat next to me on the edge of my unmade bed.

"Good, I think I'm almost done."

I pat the beads of sweat on my forehead on the sleeve of my t-shirt, heaving my suitcase off the bed and onto the floor.

"This is the last of it I think," I say, looking around the bare room.

I understand why she's selling it. The house was already too much space when it was just her, my dad and I living here. Now that she's here by herself, it's more space than she could ever need. Although she would never admit it, I got the feeling the walls felt like an echo of the past she was ready to leave behind. In a way it felt like we were closing the chapter on that part of our lives.

It was about a week after I walked in on her and David, who I now know as her boyfriend, before she finally revealed the truth behind her motivation to move. She was finally ready to move on with someone who made her happy and hearing that made me happy for her. It was time for us both to close this chapter together.

"Have you spoken to your father and told him you're leaving?" she asks. As hard as their separation was, it was my mom who has encouraged me to reach out to him and try to heal our relationship.

"He called a little bit ago, but I didn't answer."

"Brea, honey, you really should see him before you leave, or at least call him. I think it would be good if the two of you talked." I let out a sigh, not wanting to do this with him while knowing she's right. "He deserves to hear the truth behind how you feel."

"I've tried talking to him about it. It's like he doesn't even hear what I'm saying. I don't want to go over to his house, nor do I want to meet his happy little family. To be honest, I don't think I'll ever be ready."

"They're your family, too, Brea. Regardless of your father's poor decisions, it's not Kyla and Kaden's fault," she says, referring to my twin brother and sister. I've heard about them and even seen pictures of them the last time I was out to lunch with my dad. I know it's not their fault, but something about meeting them feels like I'm betraying my mom.

As if she can read my mind, she says, "Healing this part of you, Brea, does not mean you are disloyal to me."

I feel the tears well up in my eyes as I hear her voice the one fear that has been holding me back from moving forward.

"I just can't forgive him for what he's done to you, to our family. The hurt he has created and left in his wake," I say, running my finger underneath the brim of my eye wiping away an errant tear.

"I think you've carried far too much with you that wasn't your burden to carry, sweetie. You were older and it's hard to keep things from you, but I'm sorry you had to go through this with me. One thing I've learned through all of this as even the people you don't think have earned it, deserve forgiveness. Not for them, not because they deserve to have their mistakes overlooked, but because sometimes the only way for you to heal is to let go of the anger and hurt you're carrying. Forgiveness isn't about them, it's for you."

She doesn't continue to push me or say anything more as she stands up and wraps her arms around my shoulders, pulling me in for a hug. I fight off the tears that threaten to spill down my face, but it's no use.

The woman standing before me has been through so much the past four years. Hearing her say she has forgiven my dad and is moving on goes to show her true strength.

"I'm going to miss you, sweetheart," she whispers in my ear. "It's been so nice having you home but I want you to remember no matter where I live, you'll always have a place to stay." With that, she leans back and gives me a big smile before turning and walking out of the room.

Taking a deep breath, I pick up my phone and scroll through my missed calls, finding my dad's name. Before I change my mind, I click on my father's name and raise the phone to my ear. It rings twice before he answers.

"Brea, what a wonderful surprise. How are you?" he asks. His rough voice is reminding me all too much of the man I knew growing up.

"I'm okay," I say, letting out a sigh. The emotions rolling through me make my voice sound like I'm croaking. "Do you have time today to meet for lunch?"

"You're in town?" he asks, sounding surprised.

"Uh, yeah," I say, not wanting to tell him the reason why I was home for the summer. "I'm getting ready to head to Chicago though later today. If you're free, I was thinking we could meet before I head back."

"Yeah, sure. Of course."

We make plans to meet for lunch in two hours, which gives me plenty of time to finish loading up the rest of the boxes, shower, and get ready. All this packing and moving stuff has left me sticky with sweat. I promised Mason I would be home in time for our pizza date with Lissa and Graham.

As if on cue, a text from Mason comes through my phone.

Mason: I'm counting down the minutes until you're here. I can't wait to see you.

We've spent most of the summer texting and FaceTiming each other. Thank goodness, I am on an unlimited plan because between my nightly calls with Mason and my two hour long catch-up sessions with Lissa, I've been putting some miles on this bad boy.

An hour and a half later, I'm wrapping my arms around my mom's waist as we say our goodbyes. She makes me promise I'll come visit her for Thanksgiving or Christmas, and I reassure her that I will, as well as calling her when I get back to town.

I pull up to the small Italian restaurant, Portobello, a little bit later. Portobello has the most delicious food, and anytime I make it to this side of town, I like to try and stop for lunch. The rain has started to pick up over the last hour, leaving the sky a murky gray. Keeping my head tilted down, I quickly swing my door open and make the run toward the front door of the restaurant.

The aroma hits me as soon as I open the door, causing my stomach to growl. It dawns on me that with a long list of things to get done before I hit the road, I didn't even take time to eat breakfast this morning. My eyes scan the tables looking for my father. When his head tilts up and he sees me, his eyes light up as he waves at me.

I flash him a weak smile, as I make my way over to where he's seated facing the door.

"Hey, Brea." His warm smile greets me. I can't help but feel the twinge of sadness at how familiar and different this seems.

"Hello," I mutter, sliding into the seat across from him.

"This is such a pleasant surprise. I didn't even know you were in town. When did you get here?"

I should've thought about this question before I got here, how I would answer it. Then I remember what my mom said earlier, how he deserves to hear how I'm feeling.

"A few months ago," I say, clearing my throat. "Um, the end of May actually."

I see his eyes widen in shock as his Adam's apple bobs as he swallows. "Oh, I had no idea."

"It's okay, how could you? It's not like we've talked or anything."

"Yeah," he says, letting my response hang in the air.

The waitress walks over to our table and asks if any other guests will be joining us before taking our order. I almost wish she'd stay because the moment she walks away, I feel the awkwardness of this lunch settle in.

"So, what's new? How are things going?"

"Not much, just getting ready to move back to Chicago for the school year. I'm starting my senior year so after this year I'll have my Bachelor's Degree in Elementary School Education."

"Wow, that's really great, sweetheart. I'm so proud of you. I always knew you'd work with kids. You're so great with them."

"Thanks."

I can tell already this conversation is going to be hard. I feel my palms sweat as I run through all the things I want to say, but am not sure how to put it out there. Running my hands along my thighs, I try to wipe away the moisture as I peer out the window. The rain has started to fall heavily, beating down on the roof of the restaurant.

"How are you and the family?" I ask. The question was intended to be genuine but even the words come out snarky to my own ears.

"I'm doing good, we're..." he pauses, and I sense his hesitation to continue. "We are all doing good."

Nodding my head, I force a smile on my face. "That's good," I retort. Immediately I wish I would've never called him and asked to do this. I understand what my mom said when she told me he deserves to hear how I feel, but honestly sometimes I feel like he doesn't deserve to hear from me at all. I can forgive him, release myself from that burden, without having to sit at this table and look him in the face.

"Is everything okay?" he asks, the hesitation still clear, and I almost want to laugh. The man who I grew up looking up to, who I was certain didn't fear anything, is sitting here holding a conversation with me like one wrong move could send the whole world crashing down around him.

Isn't that funny though? Isn't that what he did to us when he decided to serve my mom with divorce papers without any indication they were coming? Come to think of it, I don't think he's ever stood up to impact his actions like the rest of us have had to. Instead, he hid behind lawyers and text messages.

"It will be," I say. The words are spoken with absolute conviction. "Why did you do it?"

His eyes narrow, as if he's waiting for me to say more, as if hoping there's more to the question or maybe he's wishing he didn't hear me at all.

"I'm sorry, sweetheart. Do what exactly?"

"Oh, spare me! You know *exactly* what I'm talking about so don't play coy. I can't sit here in this restaurant and do this lunch with you without putting this out there. Why did you have an affair? Why did you not only start a family with someone else, but hide it from the family you already had? Why let us all go the past seventeen years living a fucking lie?"

"Watch your mouth," he spits, looking around the restaurant. His face turns red in embarrassment. "If you want to do this here, right now, you'll speak to me with respect. Do you understand?"

I can't help but throw my head back and laugh. "We're going to talk about respect? Really?" I laugh again. Very rarely do I ever get pushed to the point where I react like I want to this second. The last time was when I walked in on Kaleb with that girl and even then, I was struck frozen, unable to form words.

I'm done being a pushover, letting people walk over me and my emotions. More importantly, I'm done letting my fear that I'll end up heartbroken if I ever let someone close to me again keep me away from moving forward in my life with Mason.

"Answer the question," I say flatly.

"It wasn't supposed to turn out this way, okay? This wasn't how it was supposed to be."

I can't help but roll my eyes at the sudden emotion on his face.

"Fine, you want to know the truth? I'll give you the truth, Brea. I was in love with Patricia from the moment I first met her." I feel my body turn to ice as I look at him. My eyes narrow once again as I watch him fold the wrapper of his straw between his fingers. "Like I said, it wasn't supposed to happen like this. We met when I was just a junior in high school; she was a sophomore. She was a new student that school year and I remember when I first saw her it was like she was the only person who existed."

"Get to the fucking point already."

"Brea," he commands, not liking my attitude.

"I don't give a shit how the two of you met. I really don't."

"You asked so I'm telling you. Now if you want to hear it, you'll shut your mouth and listen to me."

Sitting against the seat of the booth, I cross my arms in front of my chest and wait for him to continue. It's that moment when the waitress approaches the table bringing both our entrees and drinks. I can tell she was waiting for the best time to interrupt us, and I feel bad for making this uncomfortable for her. I flash her a small smile as a thank her as she nods her head and walks away.

I take a bite of my food but with my stomach tied up in knots, now I can't even eat. I set my fork down on my plate as I take a drink of my water, waiting for him to continue.

"Patricia was younger than me so when it came time for me to head off to college, it put a lot of strain on our relationship. I was in my first year of pre-med and the class workload was more than I could carry. She was enjoying her senior year of high school, getting ready to graduate, going to prom, that sort of thing. She wanted me to be there for all these things, but I kept failing. Everything was falling through. She told me she wanted someone who was going to be there for her through the hard times and she left."

"I hadn't spoken to her in over two years when I met your mother. She looked a lot like you do today with long brown hair down to the middle of her back. Her big green eyes were so full of life, I couldn't help but fall in love with her. It was like I forgot everything around me when she was near me. We dated all throughout our senior year of college. We were only a few months away from graduating when we found out she was pregnant with you. All that kept playing through my head was what Patricia said to me that day when we broke up, that she wanted someone who was going to be there for her through the hard times. I didn't want to lose your mom so I proposed and it was a month after graduation when we got married.

I knew my parents weren't expecting to get pregnant when they found out about me. Although I was a surprise, they always told me I was a blessing to them.

"Although I knew I still loved Patricia, I knew that a life with your mother would make me happy. I didn't speak to Patricia until you were about six years old. Your grandfather was not doing well; they thought he had a heart attack. He was too young to be having any health problems so I flew home to be with him. I felt if I was there, I would be able to talk to the doctors and really understand what was going on. I wasn't expecting to see her that night, and it was never supposed to happen how it did."

Looking up at me, he says, "I loved you and your mother, but I... I loved Patricia, too. So, imagine my surprise when she walked into the hospital room. She was the nurse at the hospital. We had gotten some bad news about your grandfather that day, and when I was standing in the hallway, she comforted me. She offered to take me across the street to a small pub in town for a drink."

I sense where this conversation is going and I want to stop him. Holding my hand up, I interject, "You can spare me all the unnecessary details. I know what happens from here. You cheated on my mother and she got pregnant."

"Brea, you have to know it wasn't supposed to happen like this. I swear to you."

"Yeah, that's what you keep saying but it sounds like a load of shit to me. You had the choice of going with her to that bar, and you had a choice to fall into bed with her. Those were choices you made and because of your LIES, you've torn our family apart. Was it worth it?"

"I hate how it happened, Brea. I really do, but I've always loved Patricia and in the back of my mind, there was always the hope we would one day be together again. I know I'm going to hurt you, but you are asking for the truth and I want to give that to you. I don't want to bring you or your mother any more pain than I already have."

"When Kyla and Kaden were born, I knew I couldn't walk away from them. I just had gotten so caught up in everything, it broke my heart to think about hurting your mother or leaving you. Patricia and the kids ended up moving closer to Columbus, which is where Patricia works now.

We talked about me separating from your mom but I just couldn't bring myself to do it. There were times where we split up, she hated knowing what we were doing and, again, wanted someone who was going to be there through the hard times. For about six years, we had split up and communicated only about the children. I would take trips to spend time with them, but it was hard. It was hard being near her and knowing that after all this time, there were unresolved feelings there between us."

Hearing him mention Columbus brings back all the memories of when he would go away on work trips. It's about two and a half hours away from where we lived, but he always said it was just easier with the long days at the hospital to stay there and travel home on the weekends.

"I didn't want to put you through a divorce while you were still in high school. I know when everything came out, it would be hard on both you and your mom. I fully planned to wait until you were eighteen, but then your mom found out, although there were times I thought she knew all along. I just got sick of all the lies and secrets. By some miracle, Patricia still wanted to be with me. The twins had just turned eleven and were starting to ask questions. So, I took the only way out that I knew and filed for divorce."

Folding my arm around my waist, I rub the pad of my finger along my lower lip. I struggle with the urge to tell my father what I think of him as I bite down on the edge of my fingernail.

"This doesn't change the way I feel about you or what you did. If anything, this only makes me angrier," I breathe out, looking out the window at the rain falling steadily on the ground. "I don't think I'll ever want to meet her or your kids.

I know it's not their fault, but you can't expect me to want to play family with them. They are not family. I appreciate you finally telling the truth; it's about time I heard it. At this point, I don't know if or when I'll be ready to talk to you again. I just need some time and space. I understand you loved her and you wanted to be with her, but you didn't have to go through all of this and hurt these people in the process."

I reach over and take a long drink of my water before setting the glass on the table. "I'm going to go. I am not feeling very hungry now. I'll probably just get a sandwich when I'm on the road."

Sliding out of the booth, I stand and turn around to face my father. I see the heart break and regret on his face. I remember the one thing my mom said to me this morning.

"I need you to know I forgive you, and it's not because you deserve it. I need to forgive you for me because, at this point, it's my only hope I have of moving on. I hope you also find a way to forgive yourself, too."

Walking out of the restaurant, I take a deep breath. Despite the information shared with me today, I can't help but breathe a little easier as the weight is lifted off my chest.

Sometimes to heal, you need to let go of the anger and hurt that you're carrying.

chapter seventeen

BREA

Adjusting the bag in my hand, I slide the key into the lock and swing the door open.

"Lissa," I call out, hoping she's home. I saw her car parked outside, but for all I know she could still be at Adam's.

"Brea!" she shouts, as she comes barreling down the hall. As soon as she rounds the corner, her arms fly out ready to hug me. "I'm so glad you're here. You're home!"

I stand here with two bags slung over my shoulder and a duffel bag in my hand, not feeling nearly as enthused as she is. This whole day has been emotionally draining.

"Sorry, here! Let me help you," she says, racing over to take the duffel from my hand. It's been awhile since I've made the trek up the two flights of stairs to our third-floor apartment. I feel myself a little out of shape already as my chest heaves with every winded breath.

"How was the drive?"

"Not as quick as I would've hoped," I mumble, slipping my shoes off near the door. Standing in front of our rocker recliner, I fall back on the seat with a huff. The air conditioner is on full blast, all thanks to my amazing roommate who appreciates the feel of bought air.

"Why's that?" Lissa asks, rounding the couch, sitting on the end with her chin perched on her fist.

"I met with my dad for lunch before I left," I say, leaving that little fact in the air. Lissa and I talked several times while I was away so she's aware I hadn't spoken to my dad while I was gone.

"How'd it go?"

"I'm just glad it's over. I'm surprised Adam's not here with you," I mention, changing the subject. When I talked to her earlier, she mentioned he might join us, but now looking I realize he isn't here.

She doesn't say anything, looking down at the throw pillow on the couch. She rubs her finger along the silk edge, and I can tell something is bothering her.

"Everything okay, Lis?"

"Yeah, everything's great." She looks up at me with a sad smile. "We are just starting different parts of our life, and I feel like we are moving in two different directions now. Adam graduated and he got a new job where he's already been promoted. Here I am getting ready to start my senior year. Things just feel...different."

"It's just a lot of new things happening at once. I'm sure you will both get settled into your new normal again soon."

I watch as Lissa nods her head agreeing, but I can tell she still isn't too sure.

"Have you talked to Mason today?" she asks.

"I texted him to let him know I was almost here but that was about an hour ago. He should be here with Graham in a few minutes. They are going to help me unload the stuff I brought from home."

As if on cue, two knocks on the door sound as Mason and Graham come walking through the door.

"Yes, sure! Just come right on in," Lissa grumbles, clearly annoyed how Mason just waltzed in unannounced. Graham flashes a look of apology to Lissa as he turns to close the door.

Mason, however, completely ignores her as he come straight to me. I can tell by the look on his face something is bothering him but he doesn't waste any time as he pulls me up from the chair and into his arms.

His hands are pressed against the side of my face, brushing the strands of hair away as his lips crash down to mine. I should've known it was coming; he's promised me for weeks what this moment would be like. My hands clasp around his strong arms, feeling the smooth skin of his muscles as I hold on for the ride.

I feel his tongue run across my lip, eagerly seeking entrance into my mouth. He knows all the right ways of tangling his tongue with mine, showing promises of what's to come later.

His hands are molded against my lower back. Mason breaks our kiss as his lips skate across my cheek up toward my ear. The feel of his hot breath against my skin leaves goose bumps in his wake.

"I'm so glad you're home," he whispers low enough for only me to hear. "Promise me I can have you alone sometime tonight."

He leans back, meeting my stare before his eyes travel down to my mouth as I bite my lip, smothering my wayward smile. Mason's mouth curves up before he presses his lips against my forehead before taking a step back.

"Hey, Graham," I say, raising my hand, feeling somewhat embarrassed. He surprises me with a wide grin that takes over his face.

"Glad to have you home, B!"

"Is your car unlocked?" Mason asks. By the tone of his voice, I am picking up something is clearly bothering him.

"No. Here, let me get my keys."

Walking into the dining room, I grab my keys from where I tossed them when I walked in the door. I turn to hand them to Mason and without another word, he shoulders past me and heads out the door.

"It's wonderful to see you, Mason. Always a pleasure," Lissa says after the door shuts behind him, looking at me as she rolls her eyes. "I'll be in my room."

Giving a small wave to Graham, she makes her way down the hall to her bedroom.

"Everything okay with him?"

"He got into it with Callum earlier. They haven't been getting along, and today it all blew up."

I'm aware Mason hasn't spoken to his brother since Callum visited this past May. He's mentioned to me a few times how he's tried to reach out to his brother, with no response. There were nights we would stay up late talking, in hopes getting it off his chest would make him feel better.

"Is he okay?"

"He'll be fine. Believe it or not, he's happy you are home. I don't know how honest he was with you, but he missed you. More than I think he'd like to admit."

"I missed him, too," I mumble, looking to my hands while running my thumb along my fingernail.

"I'm going to head down and help him unload your stuff. Like I said, it's great to have you back, B." He reaches out and touches my shoulder reassuringly. Without another word, he turns and heads toward the door.

Picking up my bags I left by the door, I lug them over my shoulder and bring them to my bedroom. I'm thankful when I find my room nearly the same as I left it. I turn on some music as I start unloading clothes, hanging them up in my closet.

I'm so lost in the sound of the music that I don't even hear Mason as he enters the room. Bending down, I line up my sandals on the floor of my closet. When two hands grip around my hips, catching me off guard, I nearly do a somersault forward.

"Good God, you scared the hell out of me."

"Who else would have their hands on you like this?" Mason asks, as I stand turning myself to him. His arms wrap around my waist, pulling me close to him again. All signs of whatever was bothering him before are gone.

"No one." I defend. "I just didn't expect you to come up on me unannounced. I didn't even hear you."

"How could you? Not with this playing." He laughs, pointing to where my phone is docked on my iHome as Ariana Grande plays through the speakers.

"What? You don't like this?" I ask, letting my hips move to the beat of the music. He takes a step away from me, biting his bottom lip as he lets his eyes roam over my body. Laughing, I smack him on the shoulder.

"If you're going to be in here, you need to help put stuff away. Otherwise, you'll just be a distraction."

"It's been almost three months since I've last seen you. I'm going to distract you all I want."

"Alright, well if that's the case, sit," I say, pointing at my bed. I can see the hopeful look on his face, paired with his devilish grin, as if thinking we're taking this somewhere else. "Where is Graham?"

"He and Lis are in the kitchen ordering the pizza. Graham is just going to go pick it up quick since it's not too far away."

My phone chimes play through the speakers of my iHome. Turning down the volume, I pick up my phone from the dock.

I bite on my lip as my brows furrow when I see who it is.

Kaleb: Welcome back to Chicago. Can we meet up at some point to talk? I've missed you, B.

"Everything okay?" Masons asks, shaking me from my thoughts.

Closing out of the text message, I set the music on low.

"Yeah, sorry. It's nothing important," I mutter, pushing the text out of my mind.

I feel terrible for lying to him but I'm not prepared to talk to him about Kaleb, especially after I practically just walked in the door. I'm not planning on seeing Kaleb so the way I see it, what's the point in bringing it up.

"Alright, it's time to spill it," I command, changing the subject.

Bending forward, I pull more shirts from my duffel bag. Grabbing hangers from my closet, I walk to where he's lounging on my bed and start sliding shirts on each one.

"Spill what?"

He's trying to avoid this conversation, so I'm going to have to drop it or force it out of him. I decide to go with the latter.

"Graham told me something went down with you and Callum. He didn't tell me what, but it was enough to tell me I need to ask you about it. So, spill it."

Flashing me an unamused look, he rubs his hand along his jaw as he falls back on the bed.

"I'm just fed up with him and his arrogant ass attitude all the time. After his trip to Chicago, he has blown off both mine and my dad's calls and texts. I know how he feels about my dad. Hell, I understand it, but he won't even let me get a fucking word in edgewise to talk to him. He had no idea when he got here, Dad had just put himself through rehab and was released. I mean, damn, the least he could do is hear him out."

While I understand how Mason feels, like the news of his dad's release from rehab could change things, he also needs to understand some mistakes are not always easy to overlook.

"He still doesn't know about his arrest or stint in rehab?"

I'm almost shocked. Mason is from a small town in Iowa named Arbor Creek. While the city I'm from isn't small, I know all too well how word can travel like wildfire.

"Nope. My mom and Randy know, and I told my friend, Brannon. While my Mom doesn't like the idea of us fighting, she thinks Callum's feelings about our dad need to be worked out on his own. Even though the woman likes to meddle in people's business, she doesn't want to get in the middle."

"Well, she's not wrong you know. You can't force him to feel something that he doesn't feel. Hell, before I left, my mom told me I should find it in me to forgive my dad for his actions leading to the divorce. It just doesn't happen like that for everyone. Sometimes you have to let people heal on their own terms."

"When you put it that way," he mutters, as if piecing together that although our situations are very different, Callum and I are both justified to feel how we do about our fathers.

"It's good to have you home," he confesses, grabbing the pillow from my bed, tucking it beneath his head, making himself at home. "I know we talked on the phone and all, but having you here like this is different. Sometimes I just need you next to me, knocking sense into me." Leaning over, he grabs my hand, pulling me to sit beside him.

Mason slides his fingers around mine and brings my palm to his mouth giving me a small kiss.

"I'm sorry about earlier. Everything blew up with Callum right before we left. I guess I let it get the best of me."

"You're forgiven." I smile, rubbing my thumb along the back of his hand.

"God, I'm so fucking glad to have you here," he says, pulling me closer. Climbing on the bed next to him, I lean my head against his shoulder and lay my arm across his chest.

"I'm glad to be here. So glad," I sigh, letting my eyes drift closed.

"How did things go with your dad at lunch?"

I called Mason earlier as I panicked standing in my bathroom getting ready to meet up with him. Thankfully, despite the fact he was busy, he was there to calm me down.

I knew before even meeting up with him, I wasn't going to bring up the tuition issue. I'm done looking to him as a parent, as someone who I thought would always be there. I need to live on my own two feet, and I'm determined to do that now.

"It was painful..." I say, running my hand along his chest. "I told him how angry I still am for all the lies and secrets. He finally told me everything, or at least most of it. How they met, how it happened. As hard as it was to hear, I'm glad I've finally been given the chance to know the truth."

"Are you okay?" Mason asks, knowing how hard it was for me to hear.

"Yeah, well I will be. I just need a little bit of time. I told him I forgave him for what he did, but I wasn't ready to forget or if I'll ever be ready to meet them. I know it's not Kyla and Kaden's fault, but I feel like meeting them is still betraying my mom."

"Sometimes you have to let people heal on their own terms, right?" he says, repeating the same phrase I used earlier.

I don't say anything, instead, I nod my head again and squeeze him close.

"I got a call from my buddy, Brannon, from back home. He's planning on coming into the city in a couple of weeks to visit. I'm trying to figure out something for us to do. We were thinking of hanging out at Dean's house, grilling out and maybe lighting off some fireworks. You and Lissa could join us, if you're up for it."

Tilting my head up, Mason turns his head to peer over at me. Wrapping his hand in my hair, he waits for me to respond.

"Yeah, that sounds like fun. I'll talk to Lissa about coming, but either way I'll be there."

We continue to lay here in bed as Mason tells me stories of him and Brannon growing up. I find myself smiling as I think of a young Mason riding dirt bikes and playing football after school. It's like the stress we were both wearing earlier has lifted and, in the quietness of my bedroom, it's just the two of us.

I can't predict what tomorrow will bring, and I don't know what the future has in store. The only thing I do know is regardless of the feelings I have for Mason, it's much more important for me to have him in my life in some way than not at all.

I just hope I don't break my heart in the process.

chapter eighteen

MASON

It's after seven o'clock when Brea and Lissa pull up outside of Dean's house. As much as I've been looking forward to having Brannon visit, my body physically aches to have Brea near me. I feel like I just got her back.

The nice part about Dean and Seth's house is it's out in the middle of nowhere. As much as I like living in the city, coming out here reminds me a lot of being home.

My eyes track Brea as she climbs out of the driver's seat toward where I stand with Graham and Brannon.

"Damn." I hear Brannon grunt next to me. "Please tell me the redhead is not yours."

I can't help but chuckle at his appreciation of Lissa. You'd have to be blind not to see how beautiful Lissa is. She's all long legs and red hair, with a spitfire mouth to match.

"No, the brunette beauty next to her is mine. The redhead is Lissa, her best friend. I'm sorry to break it to ya, man, but she's already spoken for," I say, leaving him standing here as I saunter toward Brea. I can't wait any longer. As soon as she spots me, her eyes gleam. The smile on her face nearly knocks me on my ass.

"Hey." I smile, wrapping my arms around her. She melds into my body easily.

"Hi," she purrs.

"Before you maul my best friend, don't you think you should be a gentleman and introduce me to your friend?" Lissa asks over my shoulder, but I don't even bother to move much less turn around. "Where are your manners?"

See what I mean?

"I missed you," I whisper, ignoring Lissa, pressing my lips where her neck and shoulder meet.

I feel her body relax beneath my touch as I take a deep breath, inhaling the strawberry scent of her shampoo. Stepping back, I slide my hand into hers.

I want to laugh when I turn and see the annoyed look on Lissa's face as she stands there with her arms crossed in front of her, waiting.

"Since when have you ever needed help starting a conversation?" I ask with a wink, earning me an eye roll.

"It's okay, darlin', I have no problem introducing myself. My name's Kyle Brannon," he says, winking at her as he reaches to shake her hand. Lissa slides her hand in his as Brannon raises it to his mouth, kissing the back of it. We all watch in bated breath as Lissa's eyes widen before she snatches her hand away, rubbing the back over the denim of her jeans. Brea's shoulders shake with laughter as Graham smothers his smile behind his clenched fist.

"I have a boyfriend," she retorts.

"I know, firecracker," Brannon says as she turns and sashays to the backyard. Brannon's eyes track her movement as she goes, wearing the biggest grin on his face.

"Yeah, Brannon, you shouldn't have done that." I laugh, running my hand along Brea's shoulder.

"Something tells me I'll have a lot of fun convincing her it was an innocent gesture." He smiles, holding his hand against his heart. "I just wanted her to know not all of us have piss poor manners."

"You must be Brea," he says, holding his hand out to her.

"Don't even think about it," I threaten, which earns me a laugh of my own.

"I've heard a lot about you, Brea. It's great to finally meet you. Anyone who can tame the wild Mason Reid has my admiration," he says, winking at me.

"Shut the fuck up," I chide, pushing him on his shoulder as Brannon and Graham both laugh. "Yeah, laugh it up, fuckers."

With Brea's hand in mine, we follow along behind Lissa, finding Dean and Seth firing up the grill. They had started cooking not too long ago and by the way my stomach growls at the smell, the food is almost done.

Stepping onto the backyard patio, I let Brea walk in front of me as we take the stairs. Lissa is seated at the table with a bottle of beer in her hand.

"She even drinks beer," Brannon mumbles, running his hand over his chest. "A woman after my own heart."

"Don't let her hear you say that," Brea jokes back as Brannon chuckles.

We all sit at the table and eat. Brannon takes a seat next to Lissa, which has her rolling her eyes but I don't miss the small smile lining her mouth.

We sit relaxed and talk about how things have been going. Brannon shares with us some of the work he's been doing back home. Brannon was good friends with Callum and I growing up. He was a grade between us so he had made friends with Callum's friends, including Callum's best friend Wes. Wes and Brannon have been talking about going into business together, expanding the Motorsports Shop. This is something Brannon has been into since we were just kids, so it's great to hear their vision for where they want to take things.

Once we have all finished eating, we decide to light a fire. Dean and Seth are getting the shit together to set off fireworks. It's illegal in Illinois, but that's one of the perks about being out here in the middle of nowhere. There's no one around to call in and complain.

Spreading the blanket on the grass, I sit and pat the seat next to me, holding my hand out toward Brea.

"I'm cold," she says, running her hands along her forearms. The temperature has dropped since the sun has long since gone down. The heat from the bonfire next to us is not doing enough to warm us up.

"I'll keep you warm." I wink, standing, lifting the blanket up from the ground with me.

Taking a seat, I hold the blanket up for her to sit in front of me and say, "C'mere."

She comes to me easily, her back pressed against my chest as I pull the blanket over us.

No one is paying us any attention. Looking around the fire, I watch as Brannon and Graham shoot the shit with each other. The smile on Graham's face is one I haven't seen in a long time, and I know he's happy to have another familiar face from Arbor Creek here with us. Lissa's on the other side of Graham, curled up in the lawn chair with a blanket wrapped around her, texting on her phone.

Brea runs her fingers up and down my arm as she leans her head on my shoulder.

"Mm," I moan, leaning in close to Brea's neck. "I could get used to this."

Twisting her head toward me, she lifts her mouth up to mine and I don't hesitate. As soon as our mouths connect, I hear her whimper. Swallowing her cries, I open my mouth and my tongue meets hers.

"Get a room, will ya. Some of us don't want to see that," Brannon jokes.

I separate from Brea, pressing my forehead against hers, whispering a low, "asshole." That earns me a smile.

"If you don't want to see it, don't look," I retort, raising my hand from beneath the blanket to flip him off.

Brannon gives me the finger before turning his conversation about the four-wheeler he recently bought back to Graham.

I skate my fingers along the edge of Brea's shirt. As soon as they meet her creamy smooth skin, I feel her body tremble beneath me.

Pressing my palm against Brea's stomach, my hand raises higher fingering the edge of her bra. The blanket is pulled up beneath her neck, hiding the way my fingertips peruse her body.

As soon as my hand cups her breast, I let my finger pluck her pert nipple peeking through the thin material. The sudden inhale of breath is loud enough that if anyone were paying attention, they would've easily heard her.

I run my nose against the column of her neck and whisper in her ear, "Did that feel good?"

I feel her whimper again as I murmur a quiet "shh" in her ear.

Pulling the material of her bra beneath her breast, I roll her nipple between my thumb and finger. Angling her head back, she presses her mouth close to my ear.

"Mason," she moans. "That feels so good."

I feel her the rise and fall of her chest beneath the palm of my hand.

"You have to keep quiet or I'm going to take you out of here," I mutter. I'll be damned if I let anyone hear her cries, but at this point I don't want to get up and move us.

"Please," she whispers and I don't waste any time finding out what she means as I pull her shirt down, covering her stomach.

"Stand up, baby." Her body trembles beneath me as she moves to stand. "C'mon."

I see the smirk on Brannon's face. "Where are you two going?"

Lissa's head peeks up from her cell phone for the first time in twenty minutes. "Don't tell me you're going for a walk to your little secret hideout." Mention of the last time we were here has my mind filtering back to the way Brea rode me.

"She's cold. We're going to go grab some more blankets. We'll be right back."

I don't wait another second for their replies as I grab Brea's hand and pull her along behind me, up the patio stairs, and through the sliding glass door.

The only thing I care about is getting her into a room with a lock so we can be alone for a few minutes. The bathroom is located just off the kitchen by the pantry. I turn my head to look at Brea and I see the smile that takes over her face when our destination dawns on her.

"This isn't how I wanted our first time since I got you back to go, but I can't fuckin' wait."

"It's okay…" she whispers, although there is no one within earshot to hear her. "Hurry!"

Pulling her into the bathroom, I flick on the light before I slam the door behind us. Clenching my hands around her hips, I pick her up and press her against the wooden door.

My mouth is on hers in an instant, and all I can think about is more. More of her lips, more of her touch, more of her body against mine.

Grasping around her thighs, I place her so she's sitting on the edge of the bathroom sink. Brea doesn't leave an inch between us as her arms fold around my neck, bringing me closer to her.

Running my hands up her thighs, I finger the edge of her denim shorts, and her stomach clenches beneath my touch. Unhooking the button, I slowly ease the zipper down before slipping my hand in her underwear.

As soon as my finger meets her wet clit, I bite down on my bottom lip to smother my groan.

"Brea," I breathe out.

"Please. Don't stop," she whimpers.

I'm too far gone now, past the point of rational thought. All that pushes me forward is need. Raw need.

The tips of my fingers skim along the line of her lips before I rub small circles over her tight bud. I slip my finger inside her wet heat, causing my whole body to tense. My cock is like a steel rod, fighting to break free.

I slide my finger out before adding a second as I lean in close to Brea.

"Tell me how much you like my fingers," I command, earning me another moan.

Easing my fingers out of her wet pussy, I move my hand toward her breast once again. Rubbing my soaked fingers over her nipple, I hear her mutter out a quiet "fuck" as her body shutters with need.

She presses her hand against my aching cock, rubbing it up and down through the denim of my jeans. The friction is making it hard to concentrate.

Taking a step away from her, I let out a low groan when I see the look of desire on her face. "Ease up and lean back, baby," I say, grabbing the edge of her denim shorts and her underwear, sliding them down her legs.

She does exactly as I say, leaning against the mirror. I watch as she widens her legs, placing both of her feet on the countertop, leaving her middle on display.

"God damn," I grunt, pressing my thumb against her swollen clit. Her head rolls to the side as she squeezes her eyes shut.

"Oh my God," she whispers as I lean forward, gliding the tip of my tongue along her pussy, holding her legs apart as she squirms beneath my touch.

"You taste so fucking sweet," I groan. "I fucking missed you so much."

"Mason, I need you. I want to feel you inside of me. Please."

I unzip my pants and slide them off my hips. Reaching back, I grab my wallet and slip out the condom I stored in there after our last time. Tossing my wallet next to her, I use my teeth to tear open the wrapper and quickly slide the condom down my hard length.

Wrapping my hand around her thighs, I pull her closer to me. Rubbing the head of my cock through her wet folds, I line up my dick with her center before pressing in deeper.

With each inch, I feel the weight on my chest lessen feeling closer to her.

"So fucking perfect," I grunt, holding her hips and bending my head to meet her lips. As soon as I'm pressed to the hilt, I ease my way out before slamming home.

"Holy shit," I grit as Brea's head rolls back. "Does that feel good, baby?"

"So good," she sighs as I feel her body shake.

The only sounds that fill the small bathroom are from our heavy breathing mixed in with the loud slapping of our skin with each thrust.

"Take off your shirt," I urge.

Her body quivers with need, but she does what I ask, ripping the cotton material over her head and tossing it into the sink next to her. I keep a steady pace, never taking my eyes off her with each punishing thrust.

Sliding my hand along the lace of her bra, I pull the cup down beneath her breast. "You look so fucking beautiful." The sight of her tan smooth skin and her puckered nipple drive me wild. With one pluck of her nipple, I feel her body quiver as I pick up the pace. With one, two more thrusts I follow her over the edge, suppressing her moan with my mouth.

I don't move, enjoying the way her pussy twitches, clenching around me through the aftershocks of her release. With my hand pressed against her face, I pull her closer as her arms envelop my neck.

"I've never felt anything like that before. What are you doing to me, Brea?" I ask, kissing her forcefully before tilting back to meet her eyes. "You're going to fucking ruin me."

chapter nineteen

BREA

I t's been a couple of weeks since I got back to Chicago and I'm finally feeling settled in with school and work. Craig offered me the option of working at either Velvet or his new restaurant, Hard Stop. It's more of a laid-back bar.

I like the convenience of working on the weekend only, and the money at Velvet is great. He reassured me, if anything changed, to just let him know.

Mason and I have been spending more time together. We've yet to really discuss our relationship or even define what is going on between the two of us. Mason hasn't brought it up since our date when he referred to me as his girl, although I would love to hear those words fall from his lips again.

For now, I'm just enjoying having him around and our changing relationship from friends into something more.

When we are alone together, we can't keep our hands off each other. I find myself craving him more and more every day.

I've kept in touch with my mom, more than I did before the summer. Last night we spent nearly forty minutes on the phone, chatting about how things are going. She's already received an offer on the house and accepted, so things are finally happening. She is excited to move north to be closer to David, and hearing how happy she is, I am looking forward to it for her, too.

Before she let me go, she asked me if there was any chance I would be interested in coming home for the weekend. Some of our family were coming into town from out of state, and I know she would like for me to officially meet David. After spending the past three months there, I didn't have the heart to tell her I didn't want to so I told her I would think about it and call her tomorrow. I know how much she loved having me home during the summer and just wants me to feel included, especially after I told her how the conversation with my dad went.

Holding the curling iron up, I wrap the long strand of hair around the rod and stare at myself in the mirror. Music plays from the speaker on my phone as I hear our apartment door close.

"Lis!" I shout down the hallway.

"It's me!" she yells. She left about thirty minutes ago to stop by the convenience store a block away to pick up a few things. She had spent time this afternoon getting ready for work so she was well ahead of me.

Velvet is expected to be busy tonight. The first football game was today, which means college students are settling into the partying scene and looking to go out for the night.

"Hey, this was on the door," Lissa says, peeking her head into the bathroom handing me a large envelope. Based on the size, I'm going to guess it's a card. "I'm guessing it's from Mason by the looks of that chicken scratch on the front." She laughs as she turns and walks into her bedroom.

Setting the iron down on the vanity, I turn the card over and stare at my name written on the envelope. I would recognize the handwriting anywhere.

Slipping my finger under the seal, I tear it open and slide the card out. My eyes flutter over the words on the front about missing someone you love. With a roll of my eyes, I ease the card open and read the message written in black ink.

B,

It was one year ago today I met you. One year since you completely stole my heart. I know I've lost your trust and I don't deserve a second chance, but I'm a shell of a man without you. I love you. I will always love you.

I would do anything to prove to you how sorry I am for my mistakes. Please talk to me.

Love, Kaleb

"You okay?" I hear Lissa say, catching me off guard. I hadn't heard her approach with the music playing.

"Remember how I told you about Kaleb sending flowers when I was in Cleveland and how he texted me when I got here? This wasn't from Mason; it's from him."

"Oh, shit, really? I mean, you have to admire his perseverance. Have you talked to him at all?"

"Not since our fight at Velvet."

"Don't get me wrong, I don't think he deserves it one bit but maybe you should talk to him. It's clear he isn't taking the fucking hint or he would've given up a long time ago."

Rubbing my fingers over my eyes, I let out a slow breath.

"After the bull shit he pulled last time I tried talking to him, I really don't see the point."

"Oh, I get it completely. Like I said, he doesn't deserve for you to give him the time of day, but he needs to get it through his head that it's not going to happen."

"Yeah, you're right. I'll try to call him tomorrow sometime."

I was right when I said that Velvet was going to be busy tonight. It's a packed house. Walking out of the backroom, I saunter toward the bar to check on my drink orders. The sound of the music beats, feeling each thump pulsate through my body. Sometimes I wish I could clock out and head out to the dance floor.

"Can you make me a Jack and Coke?" I shout. Mason looks handsome dressed in his black fitted dress shirt and slacks. A white towel hanging from his waistband draws my attention to his ass. I let my eyes roam over his body as he turns toward the alcohol shelf.

He catches me staring at him when he turns to face me. I see the hint of desire in his eyes beneath the flashing lights. The look quickly changes to something I can't quite make out, but I know it's not good.

A hand slides around my forearm. Turning to peer over my shoulder, I'm surprised to see Kaleb standing behind me. Facing Mason, I can tell he doesn't like the idea of him approaching me, much less trying to talk to me.

"Can we talk for a few minutes?" Kaleb asks, nodding his head toward the club patio. The solemn look on his face is new, and for a second, I feel bad before I shove those thoughts aside.

"I can't right now, Kaleb. I'm busy," I say harshly. I know I said I would talk to him, but I wasn't prepared to do it now nor did I want to do it face to face.

"Please," he begs. "I promise I'll make it quick."

While I don't like the idea of being alone with him after our last conversation, I get the sense the Kaleb I saw that night is gone.

Running my hand over my forehead, I feel my resistance wearing thin.

"Um, yeah, that's fine," I say, nodding my head. I see Mason set the drink down on the counter. His movements are jerky, although I am not sure he heard us over the music.

"I just need to check in on my tables quick and we can head out for a few minutes. I can't be long though," I say. Accepting my answer, he nods his head as I pick up my tray and head toward my tables.

I make my rounds but as I do, I can't help but feel guilty for agreeing to listen to what Kaleb has to say. A part of me knows this is my opportunity to break it to him that we really are done. The flowers, the card, the text messages...they all just need to stop. After our fight during spring break, he was like a different person. The Kaleb I knew before was gone. A part of me still wants to know what changed, what I did that led him to fall into bed with someone else the second the waters got rough.

On my way, I stop Lissa. Most nights she helps tend the West bar with Mason and Farin. Occasionally, on nights we are busy, she will float between the bar and the tables serving drinks. She likes the extra tips that come from serving some of our VIP clientele.

"Lis, will you watch my tables for me? I need to take a fifteen-minute break."

"Yeah, I can. Everything alright?"

I nod my head. "Of course. Just want to take a break. Give me a few."

I can tell she's not buying it. The questions swirl behind her light green irises as she squints her eyes trying to decipher if she believes me or not.

"You're telling me later," she commands. Knowing I'm busted, I concede with a nod of my head just wanting to get this over with.

Rolling my eyes, I wave her off and mouth thanks. I don't doubt for a second that she's not watching me. I'm sure she'll piece it together soon.

Heading toward the bar, I see Kaleb standing off to the side. He is leaning against the wall, his legs and arms crossed in front of him. I feel Mason's eyes track my movement like a laser burning into my skin. It's as if he is silently begging me not to go through with talking with him.

Turning my head toward him, my eyes immediately find Mason's and I know I'm right. His nostrils flare as he works to disguise his frustration. Holding up my finger to him, I mouth I'll be back in a few minutes. He doesn't even let me finish when he shakes his head and walks away, tossing his hand towel against the counter as he goes.

"Let's make it quick."

Pressing his hand against my lower back, Kaleb ushers me through the crowd of people. I feel the heat of his body behind me as we push our way through. I don't know if he thinks I'll bail or what, but I can't ignore the uneasiness that fills my stomach.

Opening the door on the side of the building, we walk onto the patio. Several groups of people are standing outside. The temperature has dropped since earlier today, leaving the September night sky cool and breezy. The wind picks up, causing my hair to whip around in front of my face.

Walking to the corner, I move away from the doorway. I don't want anyone to overhear us, not to mention it's hard to hear with the sound of music filtering through the air as the door opens and closes.

Turning around, I face Kaleb and cross my arms in front of me. Rubbing my hands up and down my arms, I try to bring some heat to my goose pimpled flesh.

"What's going on? What did you want to talk about?"

"I wanted to say I'm sorry for everything, B. I made the biggest mistake of my life. Do you even remember what today is?"

Moving to stand closer to me, he wraps his fingers in mine. Immediately, I force a step back separating us. I know Mason and I haven't defined what this is between us. I don't even know what *this* is. What I do know is if I caught him holding hands with someone like Kaleb just did, I wouldn't be too happy.

"Yes, I know what today is, Kaleb. I got your card too. What exactly are you sorry for? Is it the fact that you got pissed at me for no reason when I got back from Cleveland or that you used it as an excuse to cheat on me? Or how about when you yelled at me the last time you showed up at Velvet?"

I feel the heat rising in my cheeks. The tone in my voice is not one Kaleb has ever heard. I see it in his eyes—the shock and the guilt.

"All of it. I made a mistake, alright? I just got sick of you choosing that fucking asshole over me. I missed you, B. I still fucking do. I miss the way you used to look at me. Seeing you now, seeing how that look is gone is fucking killing me."

"That is no excuse, Kaleb!" I fume. "You slept with someone else to get back at me. Who the hell does that?"

"Like you haven't slept with Mason since we broke up!" he roars, taking a step closer to me, searching my face for any clues.

"This isn't about me; we are no longer together so what I do is none of your business. This is about *you* and what *you* did."

"You did, didn't you? You slept with that piece of shit. I fucking knew it. I bet you were sleeping with him the whole time, weren't you?"

"Are you kidding me? If you honestly believe I would cheat on you, you clearly weren't paying attention at all."

Letting out a frustrated sigh, I run my hand along my forehead, massaging the skin. I feel my head pounding beneath the surface.

"I'm done talking to you about this. The flowers, the cards, all the text messages, Kaleb," I say, letting out a deep breath while pinching the bridge of my nose to lessen the throbbing. "They all need to stop! Do you understand? We are done." I shoulder past him, making sure not to touch him as I do. It happens instantly. His hand wraps around my forearm, whipping me back so I'm facing him.

"No, we're not done until I say we are! You wanted to talk about it before, so let's talk about it."

"I wanted to talk to you before you cheated on me. There's no point now, so let go of me."

I attempt to jerk my arm out of his hold in hopes he'll let go, but instead, his hand only grows tighter as he pulls me toward him. The movement causes me to twist my ankle, nearly falling as I let out a muffled cry.

"I suggest you let go of her right now!" Mason shouts. The anger in his tone causes me to jerk my head in his direction. The hold Kaleb has on me lessens, but he doesn't remove his hand.

"Or what?" he asks, pulling me closer to him, using me as a shield. I know Mason wouldn't let anything happen to me, but I still don't trust Kaleb. This isn't a side I've ever seen before.

"Or if you don't, I'm going to rip your fucking hand off and feed it to you."

"I can't fucking believe you chose this fucker over me. What, so he can go around getting his dick wet but I can't? Or are you willing to turn a blind eye to him like your mother did?" Kaleb seethes.

"You mother fucker!" Mason shouts, stalking toward him. Kaleb's grip on my arm loosens, his focus shifting to Mason. As soon as my arm is free, I rush to get out of the way.

Moving off to the side against the wood fence, I struggle to control my breathing as my heart beats rapidly beneath my chest. Forcing air into my lungs, I squeeze my eyes shut and run my hand over my arm, hoping to ease the pain.

"You'll be a lucky son of a bitch if I let you live to see the light of day. You're right about one thing. I've always wanted her before she was ever even with you, but unlike you I would never disrespect her by trying to interfere in your relationship."

Hearing Mason's words, my eyes widen as I watch him stalk toward me.

"Graham, will you remove this asshole from the premises before I do something I might regret?"

I spot Graham over Mason's shoulder. He looks to me, silently asking if I'm okay. I know he would never want anything to happen to me.

I give a discreet nod, reassuring him I'm fine as he escorts Kaleb out of the bar. I hear his muttered words under his breath as he passes by, but I force my eyes up to Mason. His eyes hold a wild look, a mix of worry and anger coursing beneath the surface.

"Are you okay? How's your arm?" he asks, rubbing it gently. Through the pain, I feel the pinpricks of desire from his touch.

I don't say anything as tears fill the brim of my eyes, threatening to spill. Wrapping me in a protective embrace, he brings me close to him, my hands still pressed against his chest.

"I won't let him put his hands on you again. I promise."

Emotion seeps through each broken word. I let the power of his strong body against mine and his clean scent wash over me.

He is always the one person who is here for me through everything.

"What were you talking about?"

"He just wanted to apologize to me for what happened, and I told him it was too late. I don't want to be with him anymore, but he still hasn't accepted it."

"That's not what I'm talking about, Brea. What flowers and cards are you talking about? Text messages?"

The guilt trickles in, not because I did anything wrong but because I kept it from him. I know how this looks on his end, but that's why I hid it from him. I wanted him to believe we had a clean break because I never talked to him since the last night he showed up at Velvet.

"When I was in Cleveland, Kaleb sent me flowers for my birthday. I got a card from him today."

"He did what?" Mason asks. The hurt in his eyes stabs me as his eyes fall to mine, his arm going slack at his side. I know he's not mad at me when Kaleb was the one sending them. He's hurt I never told him.

"I'm sorry, I should've told you but I didn't think it was a big deal. It wasn't a big deal to me, hell, it meant nothing to me. I didn't want you to get the wrong idea."

"Don't you think I could get the wrong idea finding out now?"

"Yes, but I thought he would get the fucking hint when I didn't respond. When I saw him today, I knew I had to be firm and end it with him. It's not anything for you to be concerned or mad about."

Mason edges away from me, sliding his hand into his pocket, pulling out his vibrating phone. Looking down at his screen, his brows furrow in concern.

"Mom?" Mason says, looking at me. It's close to midnight and his Mom is calling him.

"Is she going to be okay? How's Callum?"

"Yeah, I'll talk to Craig, but either way, I'll be there."

"It's not a problem. I'll figure it out."

"Yeah, okay. I'll call you tomorrow. Love you, too. Bye."

I watch as Mason holds the phone in front of him, swiping at the screen before slipping it back into his pocket.

"What's going on? Is everything okay?"

Mason's eyes have a far-away look, as if he's piecing together bits of his conversation with his mom. Bringing his eyes back to mine, he gives me a puzzled look.

"Hey, talk to me. Is everything alright?"

"I guess Callum's girlfriend, Ellie, is in the hospital. She wouldn't say a lot. All I know is she was assaulted and is unconscious. It's been over twenty-four hours and Callum is beside himself. I need to head back home and try to be there for him," Mason says, running his hand through his hair.

"Of course, I'll go with you," I reply without any hesitation.

"I'll be honest, I'm going to talk to Craig because I'll probably stay the week. My dad will be in Des Moines getting things sorted on the move. You think you can swing it?"

"We'll make it work," I promise as Mason pulls me closer.

"Thank you," he whispers against my ear. His words hit me hard, and I know there isn't a thing I wouldn't do for him.

MASON

"Brea, what's going on? Are you okay?" The sound of Lissa's panicked voice behind us has Brea peering over my shoulder. Lissa races toward us, folding her arms around Brea.

"Graham told me what happened. What the hell? Why would you come out here with him?"

I grunt at the question. It's the same one I have been dying to know. What is the point in talking to him now? Especially after all the bullshit that happened the last time he was here.

Running my hand over my face, I glance toward the entrance as Graham walks through the doorway. "Craig wants to see you," he says. I have no idea what this could be about, but at this point, I'm not in the mood to be here anymore.

"C'mon, let's get you inside. I need to talk to Graham to make sure Kaleb's gone and then talk to Craig about the next week."

"This week? What's going on?" Lissa asks, bouncing her eyes between Brea and me.

"I'll let you talk to her, inside though."

Brea barely smiles at me as Lissa pulls her inside. They head to the bathroom where I know she'll take a few well-needed minutes to herself. I give them the space as Graham and I continue into Craig's office.

It's not unusual for him to be at the club on a night like tonight, but considering the late hour, I'm wondering why he's sticking around.

"What's up?" I ask, stepping into his office. Rounding the two chairs facing his desk, I take a seat. Graham is behind me, taking a seat next to me.

"How's Brea doing?" he asks, wrinkling his brow in concern.

"She's alright."

"Good. Graham, I saw you got him out of here. Thank you for taking care of it," he says, nodding his appreciation to Graham.

"I told him he isn't allowed here again. This is the second time he's approached Brea and upset her during her shift. I'll keep an eye out for him from here and make sure the rest of the guys are aware he's banned."

"Thank you," Craig says, folding his hands in front of him.

Seeing this as my opportunity, I fill Craig in on what's happening.

"While I have you, I need to talk to you about this week. I know I've taken a step back at Hard Stop since school started, but I'm also going to need to take some time off from Velvet this week."

I see Graham's head swing toward mine.

"I received a phone call a few minutes ago from my mom. There are things back home I need to tend to, and Brea is going to come with me. We'll be leaving tomorrow afternoon and will likely be home next Sunday."

"Okay, no problem, son. You do what you need to do. I'll see about getting someone to replace you at the bar, and I'm sure I can get Farin to cover Brea's section. It will put us a little tight but we'll figure it out. Is everything okay?"

"Yeah, everything's alright. My brother has some tough things going on so I need to be there for him. My dad is also visiting Des Moines this upcoming weekend. It's probably for the best I head to Arbor Creek."

He nods his head, but doesn't ask anything further.

"Alright, well, I'll let you two get back out there. I'm heading home for the night. I know you two, along with Dean, have us covered."

We say our goodbyes as we walk out to the main floor.

"What's going on with Callum?" Graham asks as soon as we step out of Craig's office.

"I don't really know the extent of it, but I know his girlfriend was assaulted." Graham grunts and I know he's thinking the same thing I did. May God have mercy on the man who thought he'd fuck around on someone close to Callum.

"My mom is worried about him and asked me to come back. With the way our relationship is right now, I don't know if I'll be any help but she's right. I should probably make sure he's okay."

Graham gives me an appreciative slap on the back while saying, "He'll be happy to see you. I know he will."

"You know how I told you my dad has finally decided he's moving to Iowa? He's flying to Des Moines this week and is working to close on a house he's buying. He's transferring to the law office located there. I'm hoping I can see him while I'm home."

"That's probably a good idea."

"You sure you don't want to come back with us?" I know the question is pointless but I offer nonetheless.

"Nah, I will be seeing my mom in a couple of months when she's here for the holidays. There's nothing else left for me in Arbor Creek."

"You sure about that?" I ask, raising my eyebrow at him.

"Nothing." The words are spoken with conviction. He makes it clear this is the end of the conversation so I leave it alone.

Rounding the bar, I nod my head and apologize to Farin and Dean, who was covering for me, but they both wave it off.

My eyes search the crowd for any sight of Brea and I see her standing off to the side talking to a table of customers. I smile as I watch her head tilt back in laughter before she scribbles their order on her pad of paper.

The anger I felt watching Kaleb gripping his hand around her arm as she winced in pain was like liquid fire. I was ready and prepared to act on my threat when I told him I'd break his fucking hand if he didn't let her go.

It reminds me of the conversation I had with Callum and the anger and resentment he has toward our dad about having to watch him put his hands on our mom. I've never once said what he did was okay, but hearing about it and watching it happen to someone you love are two entirely different things.

Understanding Callum's perspective over why he is so infuriated by the way our dad treated Mom is a little easier now. While I know Dad is working to make changes from the man he once was, I sympathize with the feelings Callum has.

I watch as Brea approaches the server station ready to place her order.

"What can I get you?" I shout, leaning in close to her.

"I need two Budweiser bottles, a dirty martini, and a glass of ice water."

I nod my head to signal I heard her as I set out to grabbing the bottles from the cooler and slide them across the counter toward her.

"How are you doing?"

"I'm alright. I promise, I'll be fine. You can stop worrying."

I stop what I'm doing and tilt my head toward her, looking her dead in the eye. "I'll never stop worrying or looking out for you."

"I know. I love you for it, too." She smiles.

The words take me by surprise as I finish making the dirty martini and slide it onto the bar. I'm thankful for the dim lights as I'm afraid she might have seen how those words affected me.

Setting the drinks on her tray, she flashes me a wink before carefully weaving her way toward her tables. It isn't until she is a few feet away when I finally take a breath.

I know she didn't mean the words how she said them, but I can't ignore how they made my heart race.

We've never talked about what this is between us. Hell, before she left I tried putting some level of commitment on it and she practically told me no. As hard as it hurt to hear it, I know she was only doing it because she was scared. She was afraid if we put some label on us and things went south while she was gone, we would lose the friendship we had built before this began.

As much as I tried to explain to her how, no matter what, I'm not going anywhere, it didn't change what she felt, so I let it go. I knew I had to give her more time, and that's exactly what I've done.

Now I'm ready to move forward. I'm ready to show her how much she truly means to me. A huge part of me fears putting myself out there with her, only to be rejected. I'm not the type to jump into a relationship. Hell, this is the first time I've ever been with someone exclusively. She's already rejected me once; she could very well do it again.

Just hearing her say the words *love you* made my heart race.

Those thoughts play over in my mind for the rest of the night. It's not until after two in the morning when we finally leave.

We exit through the employee entrance and I hold the door open for Brea. It's cool out tonight and although the temperatures are always warm in the bar, I can tell the moment we step outside that Brea is already feeling the breeze. She slides her jacket on, picking up the pace as we walk to my SUV.

Hitting the unlock button, I open the door for her and watch as she climbs into the passenger seat. Shutting the door behind her, I walk around the front and slide into the driver's side.

"You tired?" I ask, hoping she's feeling more awake tonight. I know both of us need to be up early for class.

"A little bit," she sighs, using the lever on the side of the seat to recline her seat, turning her face in my direction.

"You up for coming to my place tonight?"

We've been staying over at each other's place more lately. Between the realization of how my feelings have developed to thinking about how hard it was seeing Kaleb put his hands on her, I just want to have her close to me tonight.

"That sounds good." She smiles, facing forward.

We pull into my apartment complex a few minutes later and I help Brea out of the car and inside. Walking into my bedroom, I slip my arms around her and pull her closer to me.

"I'm going to go take off my makeup and brush my teeth. I'll be back in a few minutes." She smiles, slipping her arm behind her, grabbing onto the door handle.

I toss her one of my t-shirts and a pair of boxers, as I lean forward to press a light kiss against her lips. Stepping back, I watch as she spins and slips into the hallway. My chest warms at the thought of her making herself at home.

I quickly shed my work clothes and slide on a pair of gym shorts. Walking into the hallway, I knock on the door and slip into the bathroom to brush my teeth next to her. We are in a comfortable silence as we stand side by side. A smile graces her face as she brushes her teeth.

Finishing up. I follow along behind her into my bedroom, flipping on the TV as we both crawl into bed. Brea curls up in my arms, running her hand along my bare chest as she watches the TV.

"I'm glad you're coming with me to Arbor Creek."

Lifting her head, she peers up at me beneath her long eyelashes. She runs her hand along my cheek as I lean forward to press a kiss against her soft lips. Her fingers slide into the hair at the base of my neck as she pulls me closer to her.

As soon as our mouths separate, she leans away far enough so she can look at me as she whispers, "I am, too."

Our kisses are deliberate as I push her against the bed and move so I'm settled between her legs. Her legs instinctively wind around my lower back, holding me close.

I want so badly to tell her how I feel; it's on the tip of my tongue. Her mouth opens and I feel her tongue skate along the line of my lips as I open to her. As soon as they connect, I find myself groaning as she tilts her pelvis up, grinding against my hard shaft.

The thin material between the two of us creates a friction, causing her chest to heave with each stroke against her pussy.

"God, you feel so fucking good."

Her body trembles as a whimper escapes her mouth as she pulls me down, our lips connecting once again. Twining my fingers in her hair, I run the pad of my thumb along the smooth skin of her cheek.

My heart pounds beneath my chest. Never in all my life have I felt the way I do now, being close to someone. It's the most terrifying thing to know someone has such power over you.

It's the little things about her that I crave. The way she tucks her hair behind her ear and the small smirk she makes when she thinks something funny, but doesn't want anyone else to know. It's not that I don't want to spend the rest of my life without her; it's that I can't.

When we first met, I knew she was going to ruin me. It wasn't one specific thing about her I fell in love with, but rather a million little things. It's how I know there will never be anyone else for me.

chapter twenty-one

BREA

The music is playing on low as the wind whips through the window, causing my hair to fly across my face. Leaning against the door, I let the sun beat down on my face as I sing along to the lyrics.

As soon as Mason told me about his phone call with his mom, I knew he wouldn't hesitate to go home to be there for his brother. After the argument with Kaleb showing up at Velvet, I didn't feel comfortable without him there so I offered to go with him.

We didn't have a lot of details on what had happened to Callum's girlfriend, Ellie. Something about the way Mason's mom, Connie, asked him to come home told him it was important. That regardless of their arguments and differences of opinions, his brother needed him more than anything. I knew Mason needed me, too, so here we are making the seven-hour drive.

Picking up my cell phone from my lap, I scroll through my Spotify playlist and click on J.Lo. Looking over at Mason, I grin as I turn up the volume.

Singing along to the lyrics, I slip my hand through my hair, holding it away from my face. Mason smiles, shaking his head at me. He always gives me crap for my love of old school rap.

He reaches over, sliding his hand along my leg and grabs my hand. Tangling his fingers with mine, he brings my palm to his mouth as he presses a light kiss before setting it back down in his lap.

"Thank you for coming with me." He flashes me a small grin. I wish I could see his eyes behind his shaded sunglasses.

Resting my head on his shoulder, I close my eyes and let the music playing through the speakers soothe me.

A little while later, we pull into a town outside of Arbor Creek named Everton where the hospital is located. Mason's face is stoic; his expression unreadable. I don't know if it's a good or bad thing as we walk toward the hospital entrance. Entering through the turnstile door, we approach the desk situated in the lobby.

"May I help you?" an older woman asks. It's hard to see her over the height of the desk, but her silver-gray hair curled to perfection and her big blue eyes make her hard to miss.

"Yes, I'm looking for my brother. His girlfriend, Ellie, has been brought here."

"Mason." The sound of a voice behind us has us turning. A petite woman with short blond hair smiles as she races toward Mason, throwing her arms around him.

"Halle, hey. It's great to see you."

My eyes track his movements, and I can't help but feel uncomfortable at how he reacts to seeing her. Folding my arms in front of my stomach, I cover myself in hopes of easing the roll in my stomach.

"It's great to see you. I bet you're looking for Callum. I can take you up to see him."

"How's he doing?" Mason asks, his eyebrows etched with worry.

"Not good. Ellie still hasn't woken up. We've been trying to get him to shower or even eat something. He isn't taking this very well. I think it will be good for him to see you."

Halle steps away from Mason, turning to show him to Ellie's room when she notices me standing beside them. I feel like I've intruded on their private moment, and I fight against the urge to look away.

As if suddenly remembering I'm standing here, Mason turns and runs his arm along my shoulder and I move to stand closer to him.

"Sorry, Brea, this is Halle. She's a friend of mine. Halle, this is Brea."

Halle reaches her hand out between us and I take hers in greeting. "It's nice meeting you." She smiles.

"Likewise." I smile back.

Mason rubs his hand over his mouth and down the back of his neck. I know he's unsure how his brother is going to take seeing him, but wants to be there for him all the same.

"Do you want me to go up with you? I mean, I can hang out in the waiting room, too."

I can tell Halle is trying to piece together who I am as her eyes travel between us. I fight against the urge to tell her to get lost, that we'll figure it out on our own. She must be a friend of Mason's so I don't want to be rude, but I also don't know what their relationship is with each other.

"Of course I want you to come up with me. C'mon," he says, holding his arm out to me. We thank the woman at the front desk for her help before heading toward the elevator.

Pushing the button for the third floor, we stand and wait. The only sound filling the silence is the beeping as the elevator passes each floor.

"Umm," Halle hesitates. "How's he doing?" I feel my eyebrows furrow at her question.

"He's good. I guess as good as he can be considering," Mason says, running his hand down the side of her arm reassuringly.

I'm not sure who she's referring to, but I can sense her uncertainty as she bites her lower lip, tucking her hair behind her ear.

"Is he," she sighs, letting out a shaky breath. "Is he seeing anyone?"

The emotion on her face nearly breaks my heart in two. Whoever she is talking about, she obviously cares about and I immediately feel like an asshole for assuming she could have something more with Mason.

"He's not dating anyone if that's what you're asking."

I am not sure if that's the answer she was looking for as a lone tear slips out of her eye and down her face. She doesn't move to wipe it away. Her head turns toward me and she flashes me a sad smile just as the elevator dings announcing our arrival.

"Halle, I thought you were taking off? Mason, is that you, man?"

The two guys greet each other as we exit the elevator. Another woman with long brown hair wraps her arms around Mason's waist.

"Hey, guys. Brea, this is Callum and my friends Wes and Kinsley. Guys, this is Brea."

Wes nods his head in greeting as Kinsley steps forward and wraps her arm around my shoulder. "I'm a hugger." She laughs in my ear. "I've never met any of Mason's girlfriends. It's nice meeting you."

My eyes find Mason over her shoulder and the smirk on his face says he wouldn't expect anything less from her.

"You, too," I mutter, forcing a smile on my face.

"How's she doing?" Mason asks.

"She hasn't woken up yet. Callum won't leave her side. It's been a couple of days and I know it has him worried. Kinsley just had to force him to take a shower and go eat. Until today, we had been bringing him food but even then, he was hardly touching it," Wes grumbles.

"Damn! What the fuck happened?" Mason asks the question I had been wondering myself.

"I know Callum wouldn't want me telling you all of the details out of respect for Ellie, but I can say she was abducted by some fucker who messed with her when she was a kid. She fought him hard, but she ended up sustaining a pretty bad head wound, which has left her unconscious. They're still searching for him."

I cover my mouth to hide the gasp hearing Wes explain what happened to Ellie. Tears stream down Kinsley and Halle's face, their grief and worry for their friend has my heart aching for this woman I don't even know.

"He'll be happy to see you. We just sent him to the cafeteria to eat. You should meet him down there." Kinsley smiles, adjusting the strap of her cross-body bag over her shoulder.

"That sounds good. We're gonna head that way now. I'll talk to you guys later," Mason says, turning toward Halle. "I'll catch up with you sometime before I leave, okay?"

"Okay," Halle replies. "Just send me a text or something."

After saying our goodbyes, Mason and I head to the elevators. Pressing the button to the main floor, we head out in search for the cafeteria.

"Damn, it's no wonder my mom wanted me here. I've never talked to Callum about Ellie with us not speaking, but Mom had mentioned her to me at one point. This has to be tearing him up right now."

Stepping across the small elevator, I give Mason a reassuring hug, resting my head against his shoulder. "He's going to be glad you came."

We follow the signs on the wall leading us to the cafeteria. Since my father was a doctor at the local Cleveland Hospital, I am used to being in and around places like this. Although there is one thing I've always stayed away from...hospital food.

Rounding the corner into the cafeteria, I hear Mason mutter "there he is" as my eyes search for Callum. The first night that I met him in Chicago, I had mistaken him for

Mason beneath the dim lights at Velvet. Now, in the well-lit room, he doesn't look like the same person I remember.

It takes me a second to collect myself when I see him. Although his hair is wet from his recent shower, the pale look on his face and the dark circles under his eyes show how worried he is and my heart breaks all over again. He picks up his tray and turns toward the table where he moves to take a seat when his eyes fall on Mason's.

As soon as they see each other, I watch as Mason takes the three hurried steps and wraps his arms around his brother. The strangled sob that comes from deep down in Callum's throat has me clamping my hand over my mouth to cover a sob of my own. I hear Callum's whispered words to Mason, "It's good to see you. I wasn't expecting you."

He claps him on the back. I watch as Callum runs his hand along his face, trying to contain the emotion after seeing his brother.

"Yeah, well as soon as Mom told me what had happened, I knew you could use some support. I know we never talked about her nor have I had the chance to meet her, but I know she's important to you," Mason says, taking a step back so he's next to me once again.

Callum's eyes find mine and I feel guilty for interrupting their private moment.

"Hey, Brea. Thanks to both of you for coming. It's... uh, it's really good to see both of you." I know what he really means is that he's happy to see his brother, but he really wishes it wasn't under these circumstances.

Mason claps him once again on the shoulder and says, "Of course, man."

Callum turns to take a seat at the table and Mason holds out his arm to me, allowing me to go before him. We take a seat opposite to Callum as he moves to crush his crackers before adding them to his bowl of chili.

"How is she doing?" Mason asks. I turn my head to peer up at him, and I see the concern on his face.

"She's okay. She hasn't woken up yet so there are still a lot of unknowns, but the doctor is optimistic," he sighs. "All the tests they've ran show signs she's responding. Right now, it's just a waiting game, just waiting for her to wake up."

"That's good to hear, man."

"How long are you in town for?" Callum takes a bite of his chili, his eyes bouncing between me and Mason. I see the question hidden beneath the surface. They are the same ones I saw in Kinsley and Halle's faces, too. They are surprised that Mason brought me with him and are wondering what we are to each other.

"Through the weekend. She was originally planning to head home to visit her family, but I convinced her to come along for a road trip. We'll probably head back to Chicago on Sunday morning."

Mason turns his head to me and gives me a side smirk. He knows it didn't take much to convince me to come with him.

We sit and talk with Callum for a little bit longer while he eats his bowl of chili. As much as he seems glad to see Mason, you can tell he is anxious to be with Ellie. I can't blame him.

Callum stands to take his tray over to the kitchen and comes back. "Thanks for coming today. It means a lot to have you here."

"Of course," Mason says, walking closer to him, giving him another brotherly hug.

"Listen, I'm not sure when I'll be leaving this place. God, I hope it's fucking soon because I can't take much more of this." Callum looks around, running his hand along his shoulder trying to ease the tension. "Before you head back though, will you get a hold of me?"

"Absolutely. I'll be around, I'm sure I'll stop by again at some point. I just wanted you to know I was here if you needed anything."

"I appreciate it," Callum says, hugging his brother once again.

With the promise of talking to each other later this week, Mason and I head out.

"How are you doing?" I ask as Mason steps in closer to me. He presses his mouth against the side of my head, and I hear his sudden inhale of breath.

"I'm really glad we came. I've never seen him so worried and crushed like this. He looks like he's a second away from falling apart."

I can only nod my head because even though I hardly know Callum, I understand what he means. He looks like a man who just had his world turned upside down.

"She'll be okay," I whisper, wrapping my arm around his waist, returning his embrace. "We just have to pray she'll be okay."

chapter twenty-two

MASON

The week has gone by fast. It's crazy how long it's been since I've been back, but damn it feels good to be here.

I know my momma is happy to have me, and even though Brea's a guest, she hasn't let me forget while I'm here I'm still responsible for helping with chores. I'm pretty sure she just wants to put me to work so Randy isn't out there all day.

Pulling my gloves off my hand, I use the sleeve of my t-shirt to wipe the sweat dripping from my brow as I take a drink of the water from my thermos.

"You talked to your brother today?" Randy asks.

"Yeah, I called him earlier and talked to him. I'm so glad to hear Ellie is doing better and is finally home with Callum. I know he was relieved, too. I mentioned to him Dad was in town. We're going over to his place tomorrow for dinner."

"Is that right?" Randy says. "That's good to hear, son. It's about time you all put this to rest."

"Yeah, I'm staying out of it from here on out, but I'm just looking forward to catching up with him."

"I think it's probably for the best, let the two of them handle it. You and Brea doin' anything tonight?"

"We are going to head into town to Brodie's. I want to meet up with the gang for a few beers while I'm still in town. We'll probably grab something to eat while we're there."

"Well, if you're wanting to head out soon, we should probably call it a day. It's about a quarter 'til five and I'm sure you'll want to clean up before you go."

Ready for a shower, we make our way out of the stables and across the property up to the house. I brought Brea down earlier this week and we went for a ride on the horses. She absolutely loved it, and I have to say, it made me incredibly happy to see how well she fit in with my life here.

My phone vibrates so I pull it out, checking the screen in hopes of seeing Brea's name, knowing she's just a few feet inside. My mom kicked me out the door earlier this morning, telling me to leave them be while she spent some time with Brea. I loved the way Brea smiled as she put on the apron my mom gave her and started helping her in the kitchen. I've been thinking a lot about the future and what life after college would look like. I can't lie, having Brea here with me sounds perfect.

I see Halle's name on my screen and I swipe to answer the call, raising it to my ear. Holding a finger up to Randy, I let him know I'll be inside in a minute before I answer.

"Halle, how are you?"

"You weren't going to leave town without saying bye, were ya?"

I chuckle. I wouldn't make it out of the county without her knowing and raising hell, I'm sure of it. "I wouldn't dare."

She laughs. "That's right. You're going out to Brodie's tonight, right? Kinsley mentioned Wes was meeting you and Brannon there."

"Yeah, Brea and I are going to stop there for dinner and a beer or two. You and Kins want to join us, too?"

"I was already planning on crashing your party, but I appreciate you offering. Such a gentleman," she jokes.

"I should've figured as much."

As soon as she hangs up, I slide my phone in my pocket and take the stairs up the deck. Swinging the screen door open, I smell the scent of my momma's homemade brownies and my stomach rolls in hunger. I regret telling the guys I'd meet them for dinner, and I immediately head over to the counter where they are arranged on the plate.

"Mason Thomas Reid, get your dirty hands out of there and go wash up."

Holding my hands up, I take a step back and flash her an innocent smile.

"You ain't foolin' me with your crooked grin. Get out of here. I'll have one for you when you get done."

"Yes, Momma," I say, turning on my heel and heading down the narrow hallway toward my bedroom. Brea has been sleeping in Callum's old bedroom this week. I told her it didn't matter, but she insisted it wasn't respectful. It's been killing me to have her so close, yet not close enough.

Stepping around the corner, I peek into the bedroom and watch her hands in the air as she runs the curling iron through her long brown hair. With a light knock, she puts the iron down and steps out of the way, watching as I walk into the room.

I haven't even looked in the mirror but by the look on her face, she likes what she sees.

"You sure law school is for you? I have to say, you make a damn fine-looking farm hand." She grins, looking me up and down with her grin taking over nearly half of her face.

"Oh, really?" I say, walking toward her, holding my hands out as if I'm asking her for a hug.

"Oh, no, no, you don't. I just finished getting ready. I'm not letting you get me all dirty."

"Mm, I'll be getting you dirty later, baby," I joke, raising my eyebrows suggestively. I love the way her cheeks flush a beautiful rosy color, complementing the color of her shirt perfectly

Truth be told, having Brea this close all week and not getting to touch her has me going out of my damn mind. I had to sit and watch her in her boxer shorts and t-shirt last night, looking fresh faced and gorgeous. I'm not letting another night go by without having her.

Flashing her a wink, I slowly walk backward out of the doorway and into the bathroom. After I strip out of my clothes, I make quick work about getting in and out of the shower. We don't have a lot of time before we are set to meet up with everyone.

I didn't bring any clothes with me into the bathroom so I wrap myself with a towel. I quickly brush my teeth and use my electric razor to trim the hair on my face before exiting the bathroom.

As soon as I open the bathroom door, I wasn't expecting to find Brea standing in the hallway. By the look on her face, she is taken a little off guard seeing me, too. I watch as her eyes roam over my bare chest, down my stomach to where the towel is knotted at my waist. The not-so-subtle way her throat moves as she swallows before tracing the path up to meet my eyes has me fighting off a huge grin of my own.

"Find what you were looking for?"

"Shut up." She narrows her eyes at me before looking away, making sure no one is coming.

"Is that a no? If so, you can come with me into my room and I'll help you find it."

Stepping forward, I twist my hand around hers and pull her closer to me. "I know I promised you dirty later, but I'm not as gentlemanly as you think. Come here," I say, drawing her closer, pressing a kiss against her lips.

The sudden inhale of her breath gives her away. I know she doesn't want to say no, so I don't give her a chance to try. With her hand clutched in mine, I pull her into my bedroom and shut the door behind her.

"You look so beautiful. I promise I won't mess it up before we go out, but you have had me going out of my fucking mind. Seeing the flushed look on your face, I can't wait any longer."

My voice comes out a low whisper as I lean in closer, running my nose along the column of her neck up toward her ear. "You have to be quiet though. I can't have Momma hearing you."

She lets out a low whimper and I quietly shush her in response. The towel wrapped around my waist is doing very little to hide how my body is reacting to all the little noises she makes.

"Unzip your pants, Brea."

The only light in the room is from the sun, casting a soft glow in through the bedroom window. Running my hand along her hip, I press my body closer to her so she can feel how much I want her. She presses her palm against my growing erection, and I bite down on my bottom lip to conceal a groan.

"Careful," I grunt.

Sliding my hand along her stomach, I gather the material of her shirt up around her chest and skim my fingers along the soft skin. As soon as my fingers line the lace of her underwear, I tilt my head closer and press the palm of my hand against her.

"Are you wet, Brea?"

It takes her a second to reply to my question as her head nods yes.

"I want to hear you say it."

"Y-yes," she whimpers.

"Let's see." I smile, whispering in her ear as my hand slides lower. Dipping my finger into her folds, I can't contain the grunt when I find her so fucking wet and waiting. I think she's been wanting this as bad as I have.

"Shit," I moan into her ear. My breath is coming out in heavy pants as I press my aching cock against where my hand is.

My fingers don't stop their appraisal as they slide lower and lower. She takes a step, widening her stance, which allows me more room to explore her.

When my finger dips into her wet heat, I know I'm screwed. I hold on tight to her, knowing I'm going to have to make this quick before we both blow our cover.

"Hang on, baby," I murmur, as I draw my finger out and add a second one.

"Damn, you're so fucking tight," I grunt, pressing the palm of my hand against her clit as my fingers set out to do what they were meant to do. Curling my fingers deep in her pussy, I hear as her breathing picks up and her body trembles. She's close; I can feel it.

"Does it feel good?" I groan.

Her muttered "yes" has me grinding my dick against the palm of her hand pressed between us.

"Come for me, Brea," I moan into her ear as I struggle to keep myself standing upright. Her fingers squeeze the shaft of my cock through the towel. The feel of her tight grip and the sound of her heavy breathing has me teetering on the edge.

"Mason," she whispers.

"That's it," I say, speeding up each thrust, matching the way my fingers ease in and out of her pussy. "Come, Brea. I'm coming."

Locking my knees, I press her further against the wall and use my weight to hold both of us up. Even in the muted lighting, I see the fireworks go off in front of my eyes as I follow her over the edge.

I'm thankful for the towel between us and the way her hand grips my dick because I'm certain had there been nothing, I would've made her a whole lot dirtier than I had originally promised.

Easing my hand out of her underwear, I slip the button back on her jeans and slide the zipper up. Raising my hand to my mouth, I slide the two fingers in. The sunlight streaming into the bedroom window highlights the soft skin on her face. I watch her eyes go wide as she takes in the way I suck all her juices from my fingers.

"I've been thinking about this all day," I grunt before leaning in closer, pressing a kiss against her soft lips.

Holding my hand out to Brea, I help her out of the Rover. I don't move to let go and neither does she as we make our way into Brodie's.

As soon as we enter, I spot the table toward the back of the bar. Wes and Brannon are seated at the high-top table with two tall-boy glasses of beer in front of them. Halle and Kinsley are standing near them, laughing at something, but with the two of them you never know what they are up to.

The worry I saw on their faces earlier this week is gone, knowing their friend is okay and is home with my brother.

I pull Brea along behind me as we navigate through the tables toward where everyone is seated.

"Ahh, there he is. For a second we were thinking you guys had run off and weren't going to show." Brannon smirks, remembering the night of the bonfire when Brea and I took off to be alone. He knew better.

Rolling my eyes, I turn to Wes. "Hey, man," I say, wrapping my hand around his and clap him on the back.

"Good to see you again," Wes replies before looking behind me to where Brea stands. "Hi, Brea. Here, you can have my seat. I'll grab another."

Wes moves down from the barstool and slides it over to Brea who mutters out a thank you before she climbs onto the seat. I pull a stool from an open nearby table, taking a seat next to her.

"How are you, Brea?"

"I'm good, how are you, Brannon?" Brea asks, giving him an amused smirk.

"I can't complain, although I'd be doing a lot better if that firecracker friend of yours was here. How's she doing?"

I watch as Brea bites on her bottom lip, smothering a grin. Despite the fact we all warned him she's taken, Brannon didn't let up getting to know Lissa that night.

"She's doing good. I'll tell her you said hey." Brea laughs.

"Yeah, you do that."

Halle and Kinsley approach and I extend my arm out for Halle as she slides up close, giving me a hug.

"Hey, Mason," Halle says, pressing her head against my chest.

"How ya doing?"

"A lot better now that Ellie's out and home with Callum."

"Yeah, I think we can all rest a little easier knowing she's doing okay."

The waitress walks past our table and I flag her down, ordering us two drinks and asking for her to bring us a menu.

"I talked to Sandy the other day and she wanted me to tell you to drop by if you can before you leave."

Turning my head, I peer down at Halle as she presses the palm of her hand against my chest. Hearing her mention Graham's mom has so many questions running through my mind.

I know Graham hasn't spoken to Halle since before we moved to Chicago. Anytime her name is mentioned, he does his best to change the subject entirely.

"How's she doing?"

"As good as either of us can, I guess. I go by and visit her every so often. I know she can get real lonely sometimes and it's getting harder for her to get around. I try to help her take care of her garden, pull weeds, things like that to help out."

Those are all things I know Graham would be helping her do if he was here, but he still refuses to come home. I know Sandy doesn't let on she needs the help. He can be so stubborn sometimes, I think he doesn't even see what's right in front of his face.

"I'll make sure I stop by on our way out of town on Sunday just to say hello."

Halle moves to the other side of the table. I turn my head to where Brea is sitting, and although she's lost in conversation with Kinsley, Wes, and Brannon, I can tell she was very much aware of the conversation I was having with Halle.

Running my hand along the back of her chair, I pull her closer to me and she eases her hand along my leg.

"When are you moving home?" Kinsley jokes. "It better be the next time I see you. I'm sick of all these people moving out of here. Don't even lie to me either; you know that you love living in Arbor Creek. You can even bring this little beauty with you when you do. Oh, and tow the Big Lug with you, too."

I know she is referring to Graham.

"I still have this year left before I start law school. I haven't even decided where I'm going yet for sure," I say, peering over to Brea. I see the question on her face. She's wondering the same thing.

"There is always Des Moines, you know. It's not far from here."

"Yeah, I'm sure I'll figure it out closer to when the time comes. I really enjoy living in Chicago though. I love the big city."

We spend the rest of the evening shooting the shit. Brannon and Wes announce they have decided to officially go into business together. He sold part of the company to Brannon and they are equal partners.

Hearing them talk about the next step has me excited for my two friends. Wes has always wanted to get deeper into the Motocross circuit and having the financial backing with the second partner will allow them to do the expanding he's always hoped to do. It also allows Brannon to focus on what he enjoys, which is working on dirt bikes and ATVs.

I watch as Halle, Kinsley, and Brea sit around the table talking together. I hear Kinsley quietly try to ask Brea if she would ever consider moving here to live in a small town. Brea's eyes look for mine, I notice from the corner of my eye, but I keep my attention focused on Wes as he talks while silently listening to what Brea says.

When she nods her head yes, I feel my chest expand and my heart warm. I feel like we are one step closer to each other. I would love more than anything to bring her back here.

The one thing I'm certain of is no matter where the future takes me, I hope Brea is always right here by my side.

chapter twenty-three

BREA

Turning down the long gravel drive, I lean my head on Mason's shoulder with our fingers clasped together. The sky is dark and the crickets chirping is mingling with the soft sound of the radio playing. Pulling up in front of the house, I'm surprised when Mason keeps driving toward the back of the property where the barn and the horses' stable sit.

He parks in front of the wooden building. There are two lantern lights hanging on the front of the barn and the lights cast a soft glow in through the window.

"Will you come into the barn with me?"

My eyes find Mason's and even in the muted lighting, I still see the look of want shining back at me.

Running the palm of my hand along the stubble lining his jaw, I tangle my fingers in his hair and pull him closer to me.

As soon as our lips connect, Mason unleashes a groan from somewhere deep inside his throat. When his tongue meets mine, I do my best to fight off a moan of my own.

With his forehead pressed against mine, he breaks our connection. Feeling his heavy breath against my wet lips leaves me with desire pooling deep in my core.

"Is that a yes, baby?"

Nodding my agreeance, I wait as he opens the door and jogs around to help me out. Gently taking my hand, he guides me to the side door leading into the barn.

As soon as we enter, I look around, taking in the several hay bales stacked against the wall. The saddles are lined up along the opposite side.

"You don't keep the horses in here at night?"

"No, they stay in the stables on the other side of the barn." Mason says, pointing toward the back. "We store the hay in here with all their equipment."

Grabbing onto his forearm, I lean in close as he pulls me along behind him.

"This way." He grins, leading me to the stairs along the side of the building. "There's actually a loft upstairs."

I feel the butterflies take flight in my stomach. It's been awhile since we've had a chance to be alone—no room-mates or parents. Just the two of us.

As soon as we take the last step, my eyes widen as they take in the space. For being a loft above a barn, this is nice. It's not big by any means, but the way it's set up would be enough for one person to live on their own. A small kitchen area with a table sits off to the side. On the other side of the room is a full-size bed with a small dresser.

"Does anyone ever stay up here? It's like a little apartment."

"No, not right now anyway. During the week, Randy has some farm hands who help him. When one of our horses was pregnant, one of the guys, Casey, stayed here to keep an eye on her."

"Wow, well, it's really nice. It's kind of cozy."

"Mm, very cozy," Mason hums, pulling me closer to him as he guides me backward until my legs hit the side of the bed.

Wrapping both of his hands around my waist, he runs his finger along the edge of my shirt. When I feel his fingertips against my skin, my body trembles with need.

"Lift your arms, Brea."

The words come out as a command. I raise my arms in the air as he pulls the lacy tank over my head, leaving me standing in front of him in my silk bra.

I watch as he bites down on his lip, his eyes grazing over every inch of my chest appreciatively. I'm turned on from the heat in his stare alone.

His fingers find their place on my hips once again as he traces a line up my side and beneath the edge of my bra. My breath starts to stutter as my heart pounds. He's slow in his inspection of my body, and each touch causes the need pulsating inside me to burn.

"You're so breathtaking," Mason murmurs just as his lips find mine, pulling me closer to him. I lose myself when our tongues connect. I'm grateful his arms are holding me tight or I'm certain my legs would buckle.

With my palms pressed against him, I appreciate the feel of his muscular chest as my fingers slide up and around his neck, working their way into his hair as our tongues twine together.

Before I know it, he's gone as he takes a step back and kneels on the floor in front of me. My eyes follow him, heavy with want. Slipping his fingers into the waistband of my denim jeans, he quickly unbuttons them and slowly slides them down my hips.

"Sit," he says. I do as I'm told as he yanks them the rest of the way off.

"Take off your bra and underwear."

"You're still dressed," I mutter, wanting to see him. It's not very often I get the delicious view of Mason without his shirt on.

"We'll get there, baby. I want to focus on you first."

"At least take off your shirt," I beg as I squeeze my legs together, needing the friction to ease the ache.

His eyes track my movement, and his nostrils flare as he watches me fight my arousal. My teeth dig into my bottom lip as he slides his hand to the front of his button-up shirt. Shrugging the sleeves down his arms, he adds it to the pile of clothes before pulling the white cotton undershirt over his head.

I've seen Mason without his shirt, but never on display like this for only me. Tattoos cover every inch of his chest and upper arms. He was intentional about their placement, never wanting them to be visible with his clothes on.

"Now take off your bra and underwear, Brea."

My body shudders as I force myself to stand on shaky legs. Reaching around, I unclasp my bra and let it slide down my arms, dropping it at my feet. Bending slightly, I slip off the matching silk underwear.

"Dear God," he moans, stepping closer as if there is a magnet pulling him. His tongue traces a line along his bottom lip. I don't even recognize the sound of my desperate whimper in my own ears.

Kneeling again before me, he grabs my hips and nudges me to sit on the edge of the bed.

"Lie back and open up for me, baby," he whispers. Doing as he says, I let my legs fall open. I feel the embarrassment heat my face. I've never felt this vulnerable for anyone before.

"So perfect," he mutters before his mouth is on me. Taking one long swipe of my clit, my back raises off the bed.

"Mason," I groan, sliding my fingers through his hair, tugging on the strands. The move causes him to unleash another moan, which only spurs him on further. He's like a starved man and I'm his feast. With each flick of his tongue, I feel my release rush to the surface.

He rubs the pad of his finger along the edge of my pussy up to my clit. With the combination of his heated breath and a light smack of his fingers, I am falling over the edge. His mouth is once again on me, drinking me in. His muffled groans vibrate against my sensitive skin, causing my body to shake with the aftershocks of my release.

He stands and I watch through heavy eyes as he unbuttons his pants and quickly discards them. Gripping his fist around his length, I am in awe as he uses his same fingers to spread the bead of pre-cum coating the head.

"I want you to fuck me," I state matter-of-factly, ready for more. He's made me wait long enough.

"Oh, baby, I fully plan to," he brags, fucking his tight fist. "Are you ready?"

Opening my legs for him, I slide two fingers through my wet folds. My body quivers as his eyes follow my movement.

"I'm ready," I rasp.

The hunger in his eyes staring back at me is unlike anything I've ever seen as he stalks toward me.

"Slide up the bed," he says as he crawls up the bed. With his body angled over mine, he leans forward, pressing a soft kiss against my lips. He doesn't stop there as he leaves a trail of kisses along my cheek and up toward my ear.

He leans forward, watching as he rubs the head of his cock against my wet heat. Easing his way in, my body trembles with each delicious inch. Mason clenches his teeth as his chest heaves, struggling to hold off his release.

"Fuck, you're so tight," he breathes. "Feels so good, baby."

With my legs draped over his forearms, he pulls me so I'm closer to him. Raising my butt of the bed, he eases out of me and quickly forces his way back in.

He squeezes his eyes closed as he thrusts his hips into me. The sound of his heavy pants combined with our skin smacking fills the air around us.

"Reach down and rub your clit," he breathes. His shoulders are wound tight as he fights to hold off his release. Running my hand along my stomach, my fingers ease down between us over the sensitive flesh. My fingers skate along my pussy lips as I rub my fingers around his aching cock with each thrust he makes.

"Shit, Brea," he breathes, gritting his teeth. "I want you to come with me."

I should tell him just watching the way his body reacts to me, to my touch, is enough to send me reeling, but I don't.

Instead, I do as I am told and rub my fingers against my swollen clit. The pressure against my tight bud causes my core to tighten. Mason unleashes a deep grunt and that's all I need to send my release racing through me.

Mason drops my legs to his side as he leans forward pressing his chest slick with sweat against my own. With my thighs pressed tight against his hips, I wrap my arms around his neck and pull him closer to me. As soon as we're a breath away, his mouth is once again on mine.

"You fit so perfectly around me, in my arms. It's like you were made for me."

His words come out hoarse and my heart beats out of control hearing him. Our chests heave as we both work to catch our breath and Mason rolls next to me.

"I could stay like this all night," I hum, closing my eyes as my body settles in next to him.

"This does feel perfect," he whispers. He tilts his head down toward me and presses as soft kiss against my forehead. "But we're not done. Turn onto your stomach and slide down to the end of the bed."

The look on my face must be one of surprise as he lets out a deep laugh.

Sitting up on my knees, I watch as Mason climbs out of the bed and pads his feet toward the foot of the bed. I do as he says and I follow him there.

"Turn around with your ass in the air and press your cheek against the bed."

I feel my face heat and I'm thankful I can't see him from this angle, although it would be sexy as hell to watch his perusal of my body.

"Mm, you look so fucking sexy like this."

Running his hands along the inside of my thighs, he moves my legs so they are spread further apart as butterflies take flight in my stomach.

The warmth of his breath against my backside causes my legs to tense as he runs his rough hands up toward my ass. Spreading my ass cheeks apart, he lets out a small groan before his mouth is on me.

My body jolts as his tongue slides, sucking on the sensitive bud before working his way up, fucking me.

"Holy shit," I moan, pressing my pussy against his face, riding him. This earns me a moan of my own.

He runs his tongue from my clit up toward my ass. The sensation new and unfamiliar, but feels so fucking good.

Raising up on my arms, I turn, looking over my shoulder. As soon as my eyes connect with Mason's, I watch as he inserts his finger in his mouth, wetting it. He draws it out slowly, knowing my curiosity of what he plans to do gets the best of me.

Pressing in close again, he runs his tongue from my clit up toward my ass once again, causing my arms to shake. Adding his finger, he lightly draws a circle around my heat, teasing my opening. My chest constricts with every strangled breath.

As soon as his finger enters me, I feel my pussy tighten around him.

"So wet and tight," he chokes out before adding a second finger.

As quick as he is there, he's gone and my body aches from the loss. Trailing his wet fingers up toward my hole, spreading the wetness around my ass, he presses his finger against my puckered skin as I take a deep breath preparing for the intrusion.

"Do you like that?" he asks.

I'm unable to form words or think rationally with the way his fingers rub around the tight ring.

"Someday, Brea, I'm going to fuck this hole." My body moves closer to him, as if reacting on its own.

"Is that what you want, baby? You want me to fuck you here?" he asks, running his tongue and finger against my ass. Every nerve ending comes alive from his touch, knowing it's exactly what I want.

He trails his finger down toward my pussy before inserting two of his skilled fingers.

"Mm, I think that's exactly what you want," he says, kissing along my ass cheek.

Peering over my shoulder once again, I see him wrapping his hand around his length. His fingers wet with my arousal are glistening as he fucks his hand.

"Fuck me," I moan, pushing back toward him as he takes a step closer, lining himself up. Gripping both of my ass cheeks, he holds me open as he enters me slowly, inch by delicious inch. My arms are shaking with need, unable to hold myself up anymore. Leaning forward, I press my face against the mattress of the bed. The change in the angle is forcing him in deeper with each thrust.

"Damn," he moans as he starts chanting my name. His hands are firm on my hips with each hard slap of his skin against the back of my thighs.

"I'm close," I moan. He slants his body over mine, gripping my waist. As soon as I feel his fingers rub along the tight bud of my clit, I'm catapulted into oblivion. Stars dance in front of me as I squeeze my eyes shut for one last thrust.

"I was right," he groans, kissing a line down the spine of my back. "You are perfect for me."

BREA

When I wake up the next morning, I stretch my arms over my head. The ache I feel from last night is a welcome soreness. Running my hand along my stomach, I let my mind drift back to how it felt having Mason in my bed the night before.

Don't get me wrong, I knew he was skilled in the sex department. His fingers were always capable of drawing out award winning orgasms. Sex with Kaleb had been good, but nothing in comparison to Mason.

I can't picture what life would be like if this was the type of performance I could expect every day. Sitting up, I move to climb out of bed. Even that small movement has me biting my lip from the aches.

Looking over to the nightstand, I see two small pills with a glass of water and a note saying, "take me." Picking the note up, I study the handwriting, recognizing it as Mason's chicken scratch.

"Really," I sigh, flipping the card over.

As soon I see what's written on the back, I choke out a laugh seeing the words "Yes, really" causing my stomach to clench. The movement triggering my body to tense once again.

With one hand pressed against my stomach, I lean forward and pick up the two Tylenol capsules, tossing them into my mouth. Taking a quick drink of water, I wash them down.

Smart ass.

After making a quick stop in the bathroom to relieve my bladder, I slide on my pullover and wander into the kitchen.

"There she is," Connie sings, standing at the stove. The smell of breakfast permeates the air, causing my stomach to instantly growl.

"Someone's hungry." She laughs, hearing my reaction to the delicious smells.

"Famished," I say, walking around the island to where she's standing.

"Can I help?" I ask, pulling up my sleeves, hoping to help her again. I enjoyed our time in the kitchen yesterday, helping her cook dinner for Callum and Ellie and bake brownies for the guys. My mom and I haven't baked together in years, but it made me want to do it more often.

"Nonsense, dear. I got this, it should be ready in just a few minutes," she reassures, looking up and flashing me a smile.

"You can help me grab the plates. There in that cabinet," she states, pointing to the cupboard on the other side of the sink.

Doing as she asks, I pull out the plates from the cabinet along with forks.

"How was your night out?" she asks, making small talk. The mention of last night causes the heat to rise in my cheeks as I turn focus my attention on setting the table. My body tingles thinking of the way Mason touched me.

Jesus, Brea. You shouldn't be thinking about this in front of his mother. Get a grip!

"It was a great time. It was fun to meet the people Mason has talked a lot about. It was also a nice change of pace," I say, setting the last plate down.

"Are you from a small town like Arbor Creek?"

"No, I actually grew up in a fairly big city compared to Arbor Creek. I'm from Cleveland."

"Is that right? I bet it's so much bigger in comparison to Arbor Creek. Could you see yourself living in a town this small?"

I can tell by the tone of her voice she's hinting at something here. Until I got here and Kinsley brought it up last night, I really hadn't given it much thought. I know I don't want to go back to Cleveland after graduation, and if moving here meant I could stay closer to Mason, I would do it in a heartbeat.

"My dream is to work with kids as a kindergarten teacher. I can do that just about anywhere. I would move if I knew being here would make me happy."

"You know, I've never seen my son as happy as he has been since being back here. Despite the issues going on between Mason and Callum, he seems to be quite head over heels. As a mother, nothing makes me happier than to see her sons in love."

The mention of love takes me by surprise and the sudden inhale of breath has me struggling to breathe. I hadn't even taken a drink, but I quite possibly may be the first person to choke on air. Holding my fist to my mouth, I cough, trying to force air into my lungs.

"Umm...I'm sorry, Mrs. Whitt, but Mason and I are just friends."

I don't even like the way it sounds and I find myself averting my eyes, knowing it's not the truth. We may have started out best friends, but the feelings I have for Mason are so much more than I am leading her to believe.

I'm quite certain that the way he worked my body over last night was unlike anything two friends would do for each other, but I'm not going to let myself think about it again in front of his mother.

Working up the courage, I turn my head and my eyes fall on hers. Her raised eyebrow and knowing smirk says she's not buying it, but I don't press any further.

As soon as I am finished with setting the table, I help her carry the dishes. We never ate family style at the table together where we dished our food while seated together.

As if on cue, I hear Mason's feet as he takes the stairs down into the kitchen. I sense something is bothering him the moment he walks to the room. The tired and worn out look on his face has me feeling terrible. I kept him up so late after he spent most of the day working outside with Randy.

"Morning, sweetie," Mrs. Whitt says, holding her arm out to Mason and he leans forward pressing a kiss to his mom's cheek.

"Morning," he mutters. "That smells really good."

I find myself standing here staring at the interaction between Mason and his mom, as if trying to decipher what could be bothering him. When he turns toward me, our eyes meet. My eyebrows furrow, as if trying to silently ask him what's wrong.

"I'll be right back. I'm going to go let Randy know breakfast is ready. You two have a seat."

Mason raises his closed fist in front of his mouth as he clears his throat, walking around me to take a seat at the table. My eyes follow him as I turn on my heel, pulling out the chair across from where Mason is now sitting.

"Good morning," I say, hoping he'll flash me his smile and reassure me everything's okay.

"Hi," he responds and I struggle against the urge to pull him with me out of the room so we can talk.

"Is everything... okay?"

"Why wouldn't it be?" His voice is clipped.

"I guess I don't know. Did you sleep okay?"

Picking up the pitcher of water, I pour some into my glass and take a drink.

"I slept fine."

The sound of Mrs. Whitt's laugh filters through the air as Randy follows along behind her into the kitchen. I hear Randy mutter something about smacking her ass and I can't help but laugh watching her swat his arm away.

"Alright, take a seat. It's time to eat," she chides, but he does what she says.

"Morning, son, Brea," Randy says. "You two got in late. Glad to see you up already."

The way he mentions us getting in late makes me think he is aware we didn't come inside right when we got home.

It was a little after two in the morning by the time Mason and I snuck into the house. Granted, they knew we were out so it's not like we really had to sneak around.

Once Connie sits down, taking a seat next to Randy and me, she grabs my hand. I follow her lead and reach across the table to Mason, folding my hand in his.

The heat of his touch warms my skin as I swallow down my worries. Looking up at him, I see his eyes soften as he bows his head and closes his eyes.

"Heavenly father, we thank you for this meal. Thank you for watching over our family through this rough week. Please use your healing hand and light as a reminder of the love we have around us. In your name we pray, amen!"

"Amen."

Opening my eyes, I find Mason staring at me as I move my hand back into my lap.

"Go ahead now, dig in. We don't want the food getting cold before we have a chance to enjoy it."

We begin plating our food and passing it to each other around the table. Each time my eyes find Mason's throughout the meal, he quickly diverts them from me. Most of the conversation is spent talking about how things are going at Whitt Construction and Mason's plans after graduation.

We already arranged to meet at Callum's house for dinner with Mason's dad, Steven, and Ellie. Mason was tight lipped when I mentioned it in the car on the way to Brodie's last night, but I know him enough to know he's nervous about how things will go.

I think it's time Callum knows the truth about his Dad going to rehab.

Mason and I don't talk for most of the afternoon. After breakfast, he goes out to help Randy in the stables again. I'm kind of frustrated if I'm being honest. I feel like he's running and I'm not sure why.

It left me feeling annoyed, so I hide out in my bedroom and take a nap for a little bit before relaxing on the front porch, reading what is left of my book I brought with me for the trip.

It's before dinner time when we make the trip to Callum's house. Mason mentioned to me awhile back that Callum had bought part of the property from Randy, specifically the area that had the pond he grew up loving. It was a quick drive.

The house sits far behind the trees and off the road, you wouldn't know someone lived here unless you were specifically looking for it. As soon as we near the house, I see the sleek black BMW sitting in front of the garage. Peering over, I see an older man who I would assume is Mason and Callum's dad.

Opening the door, I slide out of the front seat and round the back to where Mason and his dad are hugging.

"Good to see you!"

"It's good to see you, too. You look good," Mason says, clapping his dad on the back. Smiling down at his son and it brings out a smile on Mason's face.

"I feel good."

"You ready?"

I sense Mason's worry as he glances over at his father, climbing the front steps.

"You bet I am."

"Hi, Brea," he says, flashing his warm smile at me, too.

"Hello, Mr. Reid."

He looks incredibly handsome and dressed as I would expect for a lawyer in a suit and tie.

"Mr. Reid, do I look that old to you? Please call me Steven."

I agree as he holds his arm out for me to go in front of him. We take the steps toward the front door. Mason rings the doorbell as we all stand back, waiting.

Callum opens the door and my eyes immediately fall on the petite blonde standing next to him.

"Hello, son," Steven says, greeting Callum with a warm smile.

"Hello, father, Mason," Callum's voice is clipped. My eyes bounce between Callum and Mason before falling on Ellie's standing behind him.

Her eyes meet mine and it's as if we are communicating between the two of us how worried we are for how this could go.

"Brea, it's good to see you again," Callum's smile is less forced and I do my best to give him a reassuring smile in return.

Callum steps off to the side, holding his arm out to Ellie who stands next to him before waving us in.

"This is a nice place you have, man. I haven't seen it since I was home for Christmas but a lot has changed," Mason says, looking around the living room.

Ellie steps in close to me, holding her hand out for me to shake. "Hi, Ellie. It's nice to meet you, even though the circumstances that brought us here are very unfortunate."

I feel guilty for the mention of what happened to her.

"It's nice to meet you, too."

Despite the bruising on her face and her split lip that looks to be healing, she is so pretty. Her long blond hair falls over her shoulders, making her look almost angelic.

"Would you like something to drink? I can show you to the kitchen and leave them to talk for a bit," she asks as she looks over to Callum.

I sense the love between the two of them. The way their eyes find each other, as if connected to each other by some invisible force.

"That sounds wonderful." I smile, watching as Ellie looks to Callum. He nods reassuringly as we make our way into the kitchen.

"Your house is stunning," I say, looking around the kitchen to the oak cabinets that wrap-around the kitchen. The back of the house has French doors overlooking the pond Mason mentioned them visiting when he was young.

"Oh, this isn't my house. I'm just staying here for now," Ellie says. "It really is beautiful though. I don't want Callum to hear me say this but it's almost too pretty for me." She laughs as she opens the cabinet and takes out two glasses for the two of us.

"Would you like some water, lemonade, or I have some sweet tea I made earlier this afternoon so it's fresh?"

"I'll have some lemonade, please."

I watch as she pours a glass, handing it to me, before adding some to a glass of her own.

"Want to head out to the patio?" Ellie asks, peering her head around the corner to where the guys are standing in the living room talking. "I think they will be venturing that way in just a minute, I just don't want to interrupt them."

"Sure, it looks beautiful out there."

We walk out onto the patio and I can hear Ellie take an audible sigh of relief. I can't help but think, like me, being outside helps ease the stress of the situation.

"Are you as nervous as I am about how this night is going to go?" Ellie jokes, looking over at me.

"Yeah, I just hope they can all put aside their differences. I've talked to Mason more times than I can count about how he needs to understand that not everyone is going to see things from his perspective, but it doesn't make it wrong. I just hope things go well."

As if on cue, the sliding glass door opens as the three men step onto the patio. Having met Mason and Callum's mom, I see now they get a lot of their strong features from her, but their height and build are from their father.

"How did the two of you meet?" Ellie asks. "Callum mentioned he met you when he was in Chicago back in May."

"Mason and I have been best friends for a few years," I say. As soon as the words friends leaves my mouth, I see Mason's eyes look up from where he is standing at the grill and meet mine.

My eyes narrow at him, hoping to silently ask him if everything is okay. He doesn't give anything away, instead looks down at the grill as if I hadn't said anything at all.

"What about you?"

"Callum and I actually met at the bus station when he was coming home from Chicago. He had overslept that morning, apparently having drank a little too much. We were both in a hurry to get out of the rain and literally ran into each other."

I see a smile dancing on Ellie's lips, as if she is remembering the moment. Callum must've heard what she said, too, as his eyes divert away from the conversation with his dad to find hers.

She nods her head to him encouragingly as he flashes her a small smile before turning his attention to his father.

"What brings you back to town? Mason mentioned yesterday you were staying in Des Moines." We hear Callum ask.

"The same thing that brought me to town when you were visiting Chicago and the same reason why I've been trying to get in touch with you now."

The mention of what happened when Callum and Steven were both in Chicago has both Ellie and I freezing, as if holding our breath for how this could go.

"Son, I know I wasn't a good father to you growing up. Hell, I was an even shittier husband to your mother. I was lucky to have had her and I was a bastard who didn't value her like I should've. I had to own my problems, and I'm sorry you had to witness them and the burden was put on you. I understand why you feel the way you do about me and why you were upset with me back in Chicago."

"Well, I didn't expect to hear him say that," Ellie whispers low enough for only me to hear.

"What's changed? I don't get it," Callum barks.

"Oh no," Ellie whispers and for a second, I think she's talked to herself. "Let's head inside. You can help me get everything ready. I think Mason's almost done on the grill."

With a nod of my head, I follow along behind Ellie toward the patio door. Peering over my shoulder, I find Mason's eyes on me and I flash him a reassuring smile, too.

For the first time today, I see the somber look on his face as he shakes his head, and I'm starting to wonder if what is bothering him has nothing to do with our visit and more to do with us.

chapter twenty-five

MASON

That is the second time today I've had to listen to Brea refer to me as her friend. It's been nearly five months since we first hooked up, and although we may have initially meant for this to not go any further than the friend zone, things certainly progressed beyond that.

Watching as she follows Ellie inside the house, I feel the anger and frustration settle into the pit of my stomach. I'm so lost in my own thoughts I don't even pay attention as my dad and Callum hash out their problems in front of me.

Hearing my dad own up to his faults and how he almost lost it all, but made the step toward getting help, has me feeling relieved they're finally having this talk.

Flipping the burgers on the grill, I give them another minute before moving each of them over to the plate.

"I know how bad it sounds. I lost my family and moved to Florida but it took almost losing my job before I turned it around. It's fucked up and I know that, but I'm glad I finally did it. It's the first time in a long time I've had a clear head."

"You look good, healthy. I'm happy for you. Regardless of how we left things when you were in Chicago and everything happened between us, I'm glad you sought out help."

"Thanks, your approval means a lot. I got a job in Des Moines. I'll be moving up here in a couple of weeks. I'm here now wrapping up the closing on the house I just bought. I thought it would be good for me to come back home and be closer to family."

He pats his hand on my shoulder from behind. We've talked several times and up until he went through rehab, it was like my suggestions were falling on deaf ears.

I'm so relieved that for the first time in years, he is finally taking my advice and realizing that he needs the family support structure around here to help him continue this path in his recovery.

"I'd like that," Callum says, clapping him on the shoulder.

The sliding glass door opens as Brea and Ellie step onto the patio. They have glass dishes in their hands, walking over to the table to set it.

I sense both of their worry in how this conversation is going as Ellie searches out Callum. I feel Brea's eyes on me, but I don't bring myself to look her way.

We all sit down at the table and help ourselves to dinner.

"So, Ellie, how did you and Callum meet?"

I listen for the second time tonight as Ellie recounts how they ran into each other in Chicago after Callum was heading home. Our dad listens with genuine interest, as Ellie smiles, telling him about how she almost fell but Callum was the knight in shining armor who helped look after her on their trip.

I can't help but laugh when Callum makes a joke, implying that's one of a few times she's let him help her. She just raises her eyebrow at him, as if challenging him before telling her he's just kidding.

"How about you, Brea? I know you and Mason were friends for a while before you started dating. Where did you two first meet?"

Brea's eyes look to mine, as if she's trying to gauge how to answer the question. Her hesitation leaves me with another wave of frustration.

Pressing her lips together, she turns her attention back to my dad.

"We're just friends, actually. We met at school," she replies with a smile.

The sound of the doorbell ringing inside interrupts our conversation as Callum stands, excusing himself.

My eyes never leave Brea. I know I should drop it and let it all go but the hurt I feel takes over. As soon as the words leave my mouth, it's like I can't stop myself. "Just two friends who hook up and tell each other everything. Isn't that right, Brea?"

I hear my father clear his throat before he tosses the napkin from his lap down on the table.

"Mason," he commands. I see the tears form in Brea's eyes just before I pull my attention away from her, looking over to my dad.

"Excuse me," Brea says, moving to stand. I watch as Ellie follows her.

"I should go check on Callum. Brea, there is a bathroom right off the kitchen if you need a minute," Ellie says. Brea nods her head, picking up her plate and following Ellie into the house.

"What the hell was that about?"

"Nothing," I sigh, raking my hand along my face. "I shouldn't have said anything like that here. I'm sorry."

"I don't think it's me that you should be apologizing to, son. I think your apology is owed to Brea."

Tilting my head back, I look up toward the sky and squeeze my eyes shut. Things have changed so much in the past twenty-four hours. What I wouldn't give to rewind time to twenty-four hours ago when I was pressing Brea up against the wall in my bedroom.

"Yeah, I'm going to go check on her." I resign myself to say, moving to stand. Grabbing my plate with me, I enter through the sliding glass door and into the kitchen. I hear Callum and Ellie talking to two men, so I try to keep quiet as I walk over to the bathroom.

I hear Brea's subtle breaths and I feel like shit knowing she's crying. Raising my hand to the door, I tap on it lightly.

"It's me," I mutter close to the door.

The door handle jingles as the lock unclicks as she swings the door open to look at me. "Can I come in?" I ask, looking behind me, not wanting to draw attention to us.

"I don't want to talk about this right now," she says, running her finger under her red, puffy eyes. She looks down at her finger, seeing the mascara on her skin and moves to wash her hands.

"I'm ready to leave," she says, her eyes meeting mine in the mirror.

"Okay, I'll go tell my dad."

"No, I mean I'm ready to go back to Chicago. I don't want to be here anymore. I just want to go home."

My jaw clenches and my nostrils flare with everything I want to say to her. She is the only woman I've ever felt like with one look, I can read everything she's thinking and feeling.

Hearing her say we're just friends goes against everything I thought we had going between us. The night of the party at Dean's, she asked me to promise that nothing would change, but I never agreed.

The truth is, things had changed for me long before that night, I just wasn't given the opportunity to show her. Now I may never get the chance.

With a nod of my head, I move to stand away from her and hold my arm out for her to exit. I hear the door opening, as my dad enters through the patio and into the dining room. By the stern look in his eyes, he isn't happy I made Brea cry. He flashes her a small smile as I hear her let out an audible sigh.

"We're going to take off," I say.

He nods his head. "Yeah, I probably should, too. Let's go check and see where Callum and Ellie headed off to."

We follow along behind my dad through the dining room and into the living room where Callum and Ellie are standing near the entryway. Ellie's arms are wrapped around his neck, pulling him into a deep kiss.

My father clears his throat and I see Callum's body stiffen as he turns his head to look at us. I can't help the shit eating grin on my face, only because of all the shit he gave me when he was visiting Chicago between Brea and me.

He knows how much I hate pet names, yet he doesn't hesitate to give me shit when he heard Brea call me "Mase."

"Sorry about that, the detectives stopped by to give us an update on the case," Callum says and immediately I feel terrible for giving him shit.

"Everything okay?" my dad asks.

"He was found and locked away, which is all we can ask for right now," Callum says, pulling Ellie into his side.

"That's good to hear. I'm sure you're ready to put this behind you."

"More than you could ever know."

I give Callum a hug. "Thanks, man, for coming to town. For being here for me with everything at the hospital. For today," he says, and I know he's grateful that he had the opportunity to talk to Dad. I feel like he is finally understanding why I wanted him to just take a chance to hear him out.

"Of course, bro. You better start answering your phone now or I'll be back sooner than you expect." I laugh, turning to give Ellie a hug.

"It's really great to meet the woman who is finally keeping my brother in line," I joke. "Make sure he answers when I call him, will ya?" I laugh.

"I promise I will." She assures, patting him on the chest flashing him a wink.

After Brea and Ellie say their goodbyes, we all head outside. Brea is ten steps ahead of me, opening the door to the Rover, climbing inside before I even have a chance to open the door.

Standing in front of the SUV, I shake my head and run my hand along my mouth before I walk around to my side.

The tension in the cab hits me like a wall. Brea turns her head, facing the window, closing herself off to me completely the entire drive back to my parents' house. I don't bother pulling up to the house, hoping to give us a second to be alone as I continue down toward the stables. Parking out from of the barn, I turn the ignition off. The windows are down and the breeze from the September sky leaves the temperature comfortable.

"Mason, I really don't want to do this right now."

"No, Brea, you're not going to run away from this just because you don't want to talk about it. Sometimes when you care about someone, you need to put your pride aside and put everything out there on the table."

Her head whips over and her eyes narrow, looking at me. "You think that's what I'm doing? You think I'm running away?"

"Well, it wouldn't be the first time you've done it. You think I don't know the reason why you stopped talking to me after we hooked up?"

"Will you stop saying it like that? You made a promise to me nothing would change between us that night," she says, opening the door and stepping out.

"I didn't promise you anything because I knew it was a load of shit. You damn well know it so don't go pulling this shit with me!" I shout, opening the door and following her around to the back of the SUV.

"I'm sick of you always pushing people away when things get hard. You did it with your dad and now you're doing it with me."

"Pushing you away? You've got to be kidding me right now."

"You hide behind the whole 'It takes time to move on. People move at their own pace' bullshit for months. I've been patient. I let us take things slow because I didn't want to pressure you. Yet anytime the topic of us progressing into more is mentioned, we would conveniently go back to being friends."

I don't let her get away easily. I press my chest in close, evading her space as she tilts her head back to peer up at me.

"I want you to tell me something, Brea. Do you let all your friends touch you the way I do?" The words come out cold, emotionless. I know she can hear it, too, seeing the way her jaw clenches. "I had my mouth on every inch of your sweet body just last night. Is that something you share with all your friends or were those sexy as hell moans reserved only for me?" I command, looking at her dead in the eye.

I watch as her nostrils flare and her body tenses. If I was to reach out and touch her, I'm positive I would feel the heat radiating off her body and I don't mean that in a good way.

"I hate to break it to you, baby, but the places my tongue have been aren't usually reserved for friends."

I let the grin spread wide over my face. It was a low blow meant only to piss her off. I'll likely regret it later, but I'm sick of listening to her continue to throw our friendship in my face.

"It was just a hookup. You're familiar with those, aren't you, Mason? The one and done deals. You don't know the first thing about being in a committed relationship. How can anyone compete for you with all the women hanging all over you?" she retorts. "All I asked for was one night like they've all had. All I wanted was for you to make me forget."

The sound of her heavy breaths mixed with her angry words only infuriates me more.

"You know what, if that's what you want, then I'm glad you got what you wanted. Just admit it to me because I need to hear you say it. I'm not the guy you want to settle down with."

"You're not the kind of guy I want to settle down with," she replies. "I've known it all along, and it's time you finally hear it."

The words are hard, as if made of stone. If it weren't for the tears filling the brim of her eyes, I would think she was unaffected, but the moisture gives her away.

Nodding my head, I run my hand over my clenched jaw fighting back the hurt. All I want to do is reach out and shake her, beg her to stop this, and just see how much I fucking love her. I would do anything for her, anything in this world. With those words, she just went and sealed our fate, like the final nail in a coffin.

"I'm done chasing after you, Brea. I want you to hear me when I say it, I'm fucking done. You said it before, you can't make someone change how they feel. I'm not going to sit here and try to point out all the bullshit in everything you've just said. You want to go, then go!" I shout.

She stomps her feet, moving quickly toward the front of the house. My heart breaks watching her go. Running my hand through my hair, relishing in the pain.

The screen door slams shut as I look up, seeing Momma stand out on the front porch. I know by the look on her face she heard everything that was just said.

I hear Brea mutter a quiet apology to my mother as I follow behind her, marching up the steps as she walks inside the house.

"I'm sorry, Momma. We're going to head back to Chicago a little early. Some things came up and Brea needs to get home."

"Is everything alright?" she asks, her face full of concern. I've watched over the past week as she's worried about Callum and Ellie and hoped Callum and I could move past our differences. The last thing I want to put on her right now is worrying about me and Brea.

"Yeah, everything will be fine. I'm going to go get my stuff together and get it loaded." Leaning forward, I press a kiss against her cheek. "Thank you for letting us stay with you."

"You're both welcome here anytime, you know that, sweetie."

We are both packed and on the road less than an hour later. It's a quarter till eight and the sun has started to go down, and I know it's going to be a long drive to Chicago. I slept for shit last night; we didn't get in until after two in the morning. Looks like it's going to be another late night.

chapter twenty-six

BREA
december

"Well, aren't we just two peas in a pod," Lissa grumbles as she takes another heaping bite of her ice cream. Her red hair is pulled into a high bun on the top of her head, and every time she leans forward for another bite, it bounces around on her head.

I guess I don't have much room to talk. I haven't showered in two days, and I'm enjoying my night vegging on the couch. Things haven't been the same since I got home from Arbor Creek.

For one, I haven't spoken to Mason since he dropped me off outside of my apartment at two-thirty in the morning.

He tried contacting me a few times when we got back. In the beginning, I was upset that I told myself I needed time. It wasn't long before the calls and texts stopped and rumors started to circulate that he had been spending his time with Sierra.

I wasn't stupid enough to believe it was serious, but I can't lie and say it didn't bother me. Maybe I'm being a little stubborn, but after the way he embarrassed me in front of his dad and Ellie, it felt like it was the final straw. We promised nothing between us would change, but the truth is, my heart will never be the same. I was naive in thinking I could "hookup" with my best friend, as Mason likes to call it, and think feelings wouldn't develop.

What hurt the most was feeling like I was being treated like every other girl Mason has been with, then tossed to the side. After Kaleb cheated on me, I was humiliated I could let someone lie to me and break the trust we were building. Then things with Mason started to happen, and as much as I tried to pump the brakes, I couldn't stop the way my heart fell more in love with him with every passing day.

Now here I am again, with nothing left to show for myself but another embarrassing lesson to learn from at the hands of another man who took my trust and threw it away.

"This is the best way to spend our Friday night," I murmur, picking up the remote and selecting the next episode of *One Tree Hill.*

"Seriously though, why can't guys be as sweet as Lucas? I mean, the man is fucking perfect."

I can't help but nod in agreement because it's the truth. Chad Michael Murray is a slam dunk in my book.

"Amen! Let's make a pact to never settle for a season one Nathan Scott. We deserve us a season nine Nathan."

"Cheers to that," Lissa sings, holding up her spoon between the middle of us, taking my spoon and cheers to her.

If there is anything positive that has come out of the past three months, it's that Lissa and I have grown closer than ever. Shortly after I stopped talking to Mason, she went through a break-up of her own with Adam. I could sense things had changed between them after he graduated from college, going his own separate way in pursuit of his new career.

Three months after school started, he broke up with her through a text message. He even had the balls to pull the whole, "It's not you, it's me."

So, here we sit on a Friday, kicking off winter break much less, drowning our sorrows in a bowl of ice cream and binge-watching Netflix.

"What time are you leaving tomorrow to head to Cleveland?"

I promised my mom after I didn't go home for Thanksgiving I wouldn't miss Christmas. Things are different now. She finally sold the house and recently moved in with David.

I guess I just found it weird to stay with my mom and her boyfriend at their new house. I'm getting over my feelings about it though because I'm really looking forward to spending the holidays with my mom and family.

"I'll probably leave here a little after eight, that way I can make it for dinner."

"Sounds good, I won't be in town until Thursday so I can work my shifts starting on Friday night. Speaking of, are you sure you don't want to come to Velvet for New Year's?"

Glancing over to where she's sitting next to me, I raise my eyebrow at her as if she's out of her mind. I know Mason will be there, which is the very reason why I have steered clear. He's been doing the same since I started working at Hard Stop.

While the tips are great, they aren't as good as they were when I was working at Velvet. I just couldn't go back there and watch Mason's line of women parading in front of my face every night.

"No, I've decided I'm just going to stay in. I was thinking about going downtown and watching the fireworks."

Every year, fireworks are lit off downtown from the Navy Pier. Although it is usually freezing cold, it's always worth it to bundle up in your winter gear and watch the New Year's celebration.

"Okay, if you're sure. Although I'm pretty sure Mason's heading to Arbor Creek for the holidays so he may not even be there."

I know better than that, but I don't say a word. Mason wouldn't miss the opportunity to make a killing on New Year's. Not to mention, I know how much he loves a good party, and I wouldn't doubt he has plans to live it up on New Year's Eve.

"I'll think about it, okay?"

"Alright," she says, leaning back against the couch.

Getting up from the couch, I grab my empty bowl and walk into the kitchen where the bottle of wine we opened earlier is sitting. Pouring what is left into my glass, I meander over to the couch and plop down.

"You may want to chill on the wine, girlfriend. You won't want to be getting up at seven in the morning at the rate you're going."

She has a point, but I am not in the mood to be hearing it right now.

"I'll be fine. I'll set five alarms on my phone. If they don't wake me up, I know they'll drive you nuts until they do." I chuckle, which earns me an eye roll. Thankfully I was thinking about it earlier and packed all my bags so it's not like I have a lot to do before I leave.

"Holy shit, I feel like I just ate my body weight in ice cream," she groans, leaning back on the couch and pats her stomach.

"You never did tell me, how are you feeling about seeing your dad for Christmas?"

I told my dad the last time we spoke I didn't think I would ever be able to move on and accept his new family, and I've spent a lot of time thinking about it. In some ways, I feel guilty for how closed off I've been to the idea of meeting Kyla and Kaden. I know someday I will want to meet them because I know the divorce is not their fault. On the other hand, I know they may not understand why I've chosen to distance myself from their side of the family.

I'm just trying to get to the point where I'm able to put the past behind me. Although I'm trying to forgive, not being able to fully let go of the hurt my dad caused us is what is holding me back from truly doing so. I know I need to do that before I can move forward.

"I'm feeling okay about it. I mean, I know it was hard for him to hear all the things I said when we last saw each other, but I told him I was ready to forgive him and I'm doing my best to do that. I'm still not sure I'm ready to meet Patricia, Kyla, and Kaden, but I guess the way I see it is I can't jump all in with both feet. Sometimes you just have to take baby steps," I say, running my hand through my long hair. The strands are still damp from the shower I took earlier, feeling cold against my fingers.

"Just don't let him pressure you into doing something you're not ready to do. There is no right or wrong way, it's what is best for you."

She is right. I just need to make sure I am continuing to move forward and stop looking back. The past is in the past now.

"I was thinking when I get home, I might stop and talk to Sam at The Coffee House. I could really use the extra money to make up for the loss of tips I am making now at Hard Stop. Not to mention, school has been going a lot better this year, so I think I can manage the two of them, plus going to class."

"You know you don't have to do that, Brea. We only have a few more months left until we graduate. I have no problem covering more."

Lissa grew up a lot like I did, with two parents who were more than capable of providing for her. She has an expensive taste for clothes, which is why she even bothers working at Velvet. The tips are just too good for her to pass up.

"You know I don't want you to take care of me. I appreciate it but I need to know I'm contributing. I don't want a free ride."

"I'm going to pretend I didn't just hear you say that."

"Yeah, on that note, I'm going to head off to bed." I laugh, picking up my phone. "Goodnight," I say, walking into the kitchen and setting my empty wine glass in the sink before making my way down the hall to my bedroom.

Pulling back the comforter on my bed, I turn off the light and climb under the covers before pulling them up to my chin.

Sliding my phone out, I pull up Facebook and scroll through my newsfeed, checking to see what my friends are up to on winter break. I'm about to close out and head to bed when I see Mason's face on my screen.

My heart hammers nearly out of my chest as I take in the photo of him with Sierra. I think I rationalized the rumors that they were just that, rumors. Seeing him standing next to her in a picture though has a way of changing my perspective on things.

Her beautiful blond hair and legs for miles as she stands next to him. I can tell just looking at the dopey smile on Mason's face he's been drinking. He holds her close to him, so close her face is pressed against his cheek.

Tears fill my eyes seeing him with her again.

It's not like I haven't told myself he would move on eventually. If anything, I all but guaranteed it would after the way we ended things. He asked me to tell him if I saw a future with him, and I closed the book on us when I lied and told him he wasn't the guy I could see myself settling down with.

I've done everything I could to push him away and keep him away. I knew it wouldn't take much before he was back to his old ways. It still doesn't make my heart ache any less when I see it in front of me. I guess I just wish he felt like I did, so wrapped up in his heartbreak he can't even stand the thought of being with another woman.

Hitting the lock button on my phone, I slide my hand under the covers and reach out, setting my phone on my nightstand. I feel the alcohol induced haze pulling me under, as my eyes get heavy with sleep.

I just need one good night of sleep where my dreams don't plague me, making me think of all the things that could've been but I'll never have again.

chapter twenty-seven

MASON

The sunlight peering in through the window causes my eyes to squint against the brightness. Throwing an arm over my face, I grunt through the aches radiating through my forehead. Even my body is sore from moving my arm. *What the hell did I do last night?*

"If you're still planning on heading to Arbor Creek, you may want to wake your ass up." Graham yells before the pillow hits me in the face.

Grumbling, I chuck it back at him not bothering to pay attention to where I'm throwing it.

Rubbing the sleep away from my eyes, I peek an eye open but immediately squeeze them shut. The sunlight is blinding and it causes a sharp pain to shoot through my pounding head once again.

"What the fuck time is it?" I groan.

"It's after eleven. I thought you were going to leave an hour ago."

Shit! I was planning on being out the door and on the road already. I still need to get up and shower. At this rate, I'm not going to make it there until after eight o'clock tonight.

"Damn it. Why didn't you wake me up?" I grumble rubbing my eyes. My facial hair is longer than normal, but I quite honestly don't have the fucks to give where that's concerned.

"Am I your fucking mother now, too?" Graham spits. He's been giving me crap for the past week and I've about had it with his mood.

"No, but you're my fucking friend. Are you sure you don't want to come with me? I'm sure your mom would enjoy having you at her house this year."

I still feel bad for not stopping by to see her when I was in Arbor Creek before we left town.

"Naw, man. I'm planning on staying here. I'm helping Craig get shit ready for New Year's Eve. Mom is coming into the city tonight after she gets off work. We will spend Christmas Eve and Christmas morning together before she heads home on Monday morning."

"You're going to have to go back there someday," I say. Graham will do anything to avoid the topic.

Shaking his head at me, he turns and walks into the kitchen. Opening the fridge, he bends down and pulls out a bottle of water. Unscrewing the cap, he raises it to his mouth and downs half the bottle.

"We're going to do this now?" he breathes.

"I'm already going to be late, so why the hell not? Spit it out already. You know Gage wouldn't want you to avoid home like you have been. When are you going to accept his accident wasn't your fault?"

Picking my cell phone off the coffee table, I check for any missed messages.

"How long has it been since you've spoken to Brea?" Graham sneers. Hearing his question, I toss my phone down on the couch cushion. The force behind the throw causes the phone to bounce and fall onto the floor.

"What the fuck does she have to do with this?" I scoff.

"Are you blind? She has everything to do with this. You come back home after your trip and now you two are no longer talking. Don't tell me avoiding your trip home doesn't have anything to do with her."

"Actually, I hate to break it to you but it has nothing to do with her. I was up too late after a night out with Sierra. As much as you may like to think otherwise, I'm over this shit with Brea."

It's been three months and I've thought about her every single day, but I am not going to tell Graham that. I'm not going to tell my best friend how every day when I'm at school, I look for her. That my eyes survey the crowd of people hoping I may just catch a small glimpse of her. I purposely walk home from school and take the long way, passing by The Coffee House in hopes I'll see her sitting at one of the tables studying. I don't mention how whenever I see her, how she quickly averts her eyes and walks away from me, avoiding me altogether. Or how Lissa still gives me shit for what I did but tells me how she's doing or how I hang onto any piece of information like it's my lifeline.

I attempted to reach out to her when we got back from Arbor Creek. I knew she was hurt, and I didn't expect her to pick up. It didn't stop me from trying.

I tried every day for a week. The last time happened on a night that I had one too many beers. I wasn't angry, despite how hurt I have been, I could never be angry with her. I knew I needed to find a way to stop. If she wanted to talk to me, she would've answered. I just didn't know how to give it up. So, I did what any reasonable person would do, I threw my phone over the side of our balcony.

Okay, maybe it wasn't reasonable but it prevented me from contacting her. I told myself it was what I needed to do to give her the space she wanted.

"Sierra, really?!" he jeers, pulling me back to reality.

What he doesn't know is Sierra is the only person I've talked to about Brea. The week after we stopped talking, Sierra could tell something was wrong. I wanted someone to talk to, and despite the fact we have a history, we both know those days were in the past.

"She's my friend," I spit, picking up the t-shirt I tossed on the floor last night.

"Yeah, we all know how friendships with women work for you. You really are doing a fan-fucking-tastic job of doing exactly what Brea expected, you know that?"

"What's that supposed to mean?"

"She tells you she feels like she's just one of many in the long line of women, how she basically feels like you're only in this for the physical aspect, and when she stops talking to you, what do you do? You turn around and run to the person she always questioned you having feelings for?"

"Who? Sierra?!"

"You really are blind as hell." Graham laughs as he shakes his head.

"Do you remember the day in the locker room after she found out Kaleb cheated on her? You made a comment, most likely because you didn't want to say anything in front of Lissa and I about that night."

Squinting my eyes at him, I wonder how it is he knows. I never told him I knew they broke up.

I don't say anything because now I'm curious where this could be going, so instead I nod my head.

"I know you guys hooked up the night at the party." It takes everything in me to control my reaction. I don't want to know how he knows, and I also don't want to know why he never said anything until now.

Or why he's waiting until now to spill this.

"Okay," I say, letting it draw out, hoping he'll get to the fucking point.

"Brea doesn't open up and trust people like she does you. It's what drove a wedge between her and Kaleb. Then the night she finds out he was unfaithful, who does she run to? I don't know how it happened, man. I don't want to hear it, that shit stays between you two. All I'm saying is I've yet to see how you've shown her she's more than some quick lay. That girl is gold, man, pure fucking gold. You'd be a fucking idiot to lose her."

I don't say anything to him because as embarrassed as I am to admit it, he's right. Girls like Brea are hard to find.

Standing, I make my way down the hall leading toward my bedroom. Stopping, I turn around and face Graham, who's standing there with his arms crossed. I see the hint of pride at his assumption that he just put me in my place.

"You should really take your own advice. Halle isn't going to wait around for you forever. You'd be a fucking idiot to let her go, too."

The stone expression he wears regularly is locked back in place. If it wasn't for the slight twitch in his jaw giving him away, I would think he was unaffected by hearing her name.

"Yeah, that's what I thought." I chuckle, nodding my head before I turn and continue down the hall, effectively ending the conversation.

It was after nine o'clock when I pulled into the drive leading to my parents' house last night. Knowing tomorrow we would be getting up early to go out and cut down a tree, I opted to head to bed early. After spending seven hours in the car, I wasn't in the mood to stay up much longer.

Waking up the next morning, I jump in the shower and quickly get ready. Walking out into the kitchen, I am surprised to see Callum and Ellie sitting at the table with my mom and Randy. Ellie is drinking a cup of coffee as Callum and Randy are talking about a job they have coming up.

"Good morning, Princess!" Callum jokes.

I flash my middle finger to him in greeting. "Good morning," I grumble, shuffling toward the fridge, pulling out the container of orange juice. Opening the cabinet, I take a glass and pour before taking a big drink.

Callum stands up from where he's seated, approaching me. As much as he is a pain in the ass, it's great to see my brother.

"Good to see you, bro." I say, clapping his hand, pulling him in for a hug.

Looking over his shoulder, I see a smiling Ellie standing behind him. "I still don't know how you got lucky with this one." I laugh, leaning forward to slide my arms around Ellie's petite frame.

She looks a lot better since the last time I saw her; the bruises and cuts have long since healed. The smile she wears nearly takes over her face.

"Hi, Ellie," I whisper in her ear. "It's good to see you."

"You, too."

"I hear the trial wrapped up earlier this week," I say, looking between Ellie and Callum. The man who attacked Ellie happened to be her mother's boyfriend. Now that the news is out, I've since learned he had sexually abused her when she was younger. Ellie came to Arbor Creek trying to run away from that part of her life, only for him to turn up here and find her after he had been released from prison.

My brother later shared with me the hardest part; Ellie's mom didn't believe the abuse had taken place and up and left her when Ellie had him put away the first time.

Ellie nods her head as Callum moves closer to her, slipping his arm around her shoulder drawing her near.

"I'm glad to hear you'll finally get the peace you were searching for."

Taking a step back to give them some space. Callum leans down, pressing his mouth against her temple. Her eyes close, as if letting the words and his affection sink in.

When she opens her eyes, I see the tears fill her eyes and she struggles to fight them off.

"I finally know what it feels like to be happy, genuinely happy." she smiles as a lone tear streams down her face.

Callum doesn't waste a second before he pulls her into his arms, pressing his chin into her neck.

"Oh, honey," my mom says, coming up behind us wrapping her arms around Callum and Ellie.

I hear my mom whisper she loves Ellie as she lets out a choked sob. Randy comes up behind us, smacking me on the shoulder.

Turning around, I clap his hand, shaking it. "Good to see you, Randy."

"It's good to see ya, too. Glad to have ya home."

Randy, although he isn't my biological dad, raised me as if I were. I don't remember much from my parents' divorce. I was too young and my mom kept a lot of it from me. What I do remember is from the point I was in elementary school on, having both my father and Randy in my life.

Randy was the one who taught me how to fish and how to ride a horse. He took us camping and made sure we understood the importance of taking care of your family. When I think about the hard life Ellie was handed, I can't help but be grateful for having someone like Randy step in.

The sound of knocking on the door breaks us all from the seriousness of the moment. Heading to the door, I turn the knob, swinging it open. A cool breeze wafts through the air, hitting me in the face.

"Hi," Kinsley cheers. Her smile is bright and her nose is red from the cold temperatures. Peering over her shoulder, I see Halle standing behind her with a beanie on her head. The pompom on her head bobbing as her head shakes with her shivers.

"Can we come in?" Halle shouts. Her jaw is clenching as she raises her hands to her mouth blowing warm air.

Stepping out of the way, I nod my head ushering them in. As soon as the door closes, I have two arms around my waist. I would expect nothing less.

"What are you two doing here?" I ask, looking between them.

"What, no 'glad to see you'. Good grief, did you lose your manners in the big city, too?" Halle retorts with her eyebrow raised.

"It's great to see you." I laugh, scooping her up in a hug. The sass she throws my way is what I could expect seeing come from her.

"Yeah, yeah," she grumbles, slinging her arm around my neck. Kinsley laughs behind me as she chats it up with Ellie.

"We're just here to pick up Ellie. We're heading to Everton to do the last of our Christmas shopping," Kinsley announces. "Are you ready?" she asks Ellie.

Ellie's face is a little red around her eyes from the tears a moment ago.

"Yeah, give me a minute to freshen up and then I'll be ready." Ellie excuses herself to the bathroom as Callum follows along behind her. I want to shout behind him she's capable of using the bathroom without his assistance, but I know he wants to make sure she's alright.

"Where's your girl?" Halle asks, looking around the room for Brea. "She can come with us, too, if she wants."

Running my hand along my jaw, I look over at my mom who has her eyebrow raised in question. We haven't talked about the fact I'm here, minus one guest.

"Mason, honey, I was surprised to see you didn't have Brea with you when you got in last night. Is she in Cleveland with her family?"

The mention of Brea causes a weight to settle in the pit of my stomach. I knew this conversation was coming, but I wasn't prepared to answer the questions.

"Brea's not here," I clarify, looking at Halle. "I haven't talked to her actually, so I'm not sure what her plans are. I'm sure she's spending it with her family," I reply dejectedly, looking at my mother.

I sense her concern as she studies my face.

Callum and Ellie enter the kitchen and I'm glad to see Ellie's smile is back on her face.

"Alright, I want you to make sure she treats herself to something while you guys are out," Callum says, looking between Halle and Kinsley. I'm thankful for the change in conversation, steering it away to lighter topics.

"Are you giving us permission to spend your money because, honey, I can promise you that will never be a problem for me," Kinsley promises as Halle barks out a laugh. Halle walks over and eases her arms around Ellie's waist.

Callum and I put on our coats and head outside to walk the girls out. As soon as they are backing down the driveway, we head to the stables wanting to check on the horses.

The cold air bitter makes it hard to breathe much less talk. That doesn't seem to deter Callum though.

"How are things going with you? Where's Brea?" Callum asks. He wasn't in the room when she was brought up earlier and I should've known he would ask about her, too.

"Honestly, I haven't talked to her since the last time we were here. Other than that, things aren't too bad."

"Just friends, huh?" he asks, picking up on the topic from the last time we were here. I thought we did a decent job of acting like everything was fine, but he has always been good at knowing when something is wrong with me.

"We were never just friends, at least not to me. I guess she saw things differently."

"I'm sorry to hear that," Callum says, looking genuinely sorry. Opening the side door, we enter the stables. It's heated in here; I rub my hands together, working to add warmth to my skin getting my blood flowing again.

"Yeah, I guess I shouldn't have expected any different. She deserves better than I could ever give her. What about you and Ellie? How is she taking things now that the trial is over?"

"That girl is a rock, man. Don't get me wrong, the trial was rough, especially having to go through the testimony and resurface a lot of the memories she's worked to bury. Thankfully, Dad really helped make sure she was prepared for what to expect," he says, and I'm so glad to hear that he's been able to turn to our dad during all of this. Although he's a defense attorney, he knows what it's like in the courtroom, and I know it helped ease some of the stress weighing down on them.

"Ever since she heard the verdict, it's like she's been able to breathe. He'll spend the rest of his life in jail. There is the possibility of parole after twenty-five years, but I'll make it my life's mission to ensure he will never see the free light of day as long as I'm still walking this earth."

I hear the relief in his voice. Leaning against the gate, I rub the palm of my hand on Trixie's nose. She has been my mom's horse for the past ten years. It's kind of fitting considering she tends to mother to all the other horses.

As if sensing Callum's tension, Trixie runs her nose along his forearm asking him to pet her and he does.

"I think I'm going to ask her to marry me," he says, catching me off guard.

"Really? That's amazing, man!"

"Yeah, I don't want to do anything over the top. She's so low key she'd probably kill me if I did." He laughs. "I don't want to wait though either. I was thinking maybe I'll do it sometime this week like on New Year's Eve morning, so we can celebrate with everyone when we get up. Maybe we could make a trip to Chicago in a couple of weeks to visit."

"That's awesome. Let me know when and I'll try to get some time off from Velvet. If not, you two can always stop by and see me there."

"Awesome, we'll do that. I'm going to surprise her so don't mention it. I wouldn't mind taking her to Velvet. I know she'll be excited to see Brea again."

"No, uh… Brea actually isn't working at Velvet anymore. Remember the restaurant I mentioned I was working at during the summer? She's working there. I guess she really didn't want to be around me anymore."

"I'm sorry, man. You know, when Ellie and I first started talking to each other, she kept me at arm's length for quite a while. She did everything she could to stay away from me, but I was persistent as hell. I knew there was something between us and, for whatever reason, she was determined to stay away. I never gave up though. I knew she was worth it."

The truth is since I got back to Chicago, I haven't spoken to Brea once, although it's killed me. I knew she was worth it though and, if I was going to get her back, I had to prove it to her.

chapter twenty-eight

BREA

"**B**rea, get your sexy ass out here right now!"

Standing in front of the mirror, I take two steps back toward my bed and sit on the side of the mattress.

I've been dreading this night all week. When Lissa called me earlier this week to tell me that Mason took time off for winter break to head home to Arbor Creek, I knew what was coming next. She was trying to convince me to work at Velvet for New Year's.

I had fully planned to stay in for the night and become one with the couch while consuming unhealthy amounts of ice cream, watching the ball drop on TV.

When I told her what I had planned, she told me I was depressing and it was time we got off our ass and move the hell on.

Watching how happy my mom was with David this past week made me realize she was right. Mason hadn't even attempted to reach out to me, and by the looks of his pictures on Facebook, it's clear he wasn't drowning in his sorrows like I was.

It's time for me to put on my heels and get ready for a night out. Brushing the hair behind my ear, I pick up my clutch from my bed and open it, pulling out my lip gloss. Running the nude gloss along my lips, I rub them together.

My hair and makeup is on point tonight. It had been a while since I've put in the extra bit of effort to get ready. Hell, I can't even remember the last time I wore heels.

Standing up, I look at the black strappy sandals wrapped around my foot and ankle. The dress I am wearing is sexy, a champagne color with a black lace overlay. It is shorter than I normally like to wear but not too revealing.

Standing up, I run my hands along my stomach and turn to check my appearance in the mirror.

"You look smokin' hot, B! Seriously, what the hell does Mason think he's doing?" Lissa says, fanning herself.

Rolling my eyes, I turn to face her. "You don't look too bad yourself. I can't believe Craig said I could work tonight!"

"Are you kidding? Do you realize how busy Velvet is going to be? We need all the help we can get. Not to mention, you have experience and the customers love you."

"If that's the case, I'm surprised he let Mason off knowing how busy they are supposed to be," I say, turning to look at Lissa.

She runs her hand through her hair, checking herself out in the mirror, trying to ignore the way her cheeks turn a rosy color as she rubs her lips together. As soon as she catches me looking at her, she turns to pick up my lip gloss and runs it along her lips.

Narrowing my eyes at her, I say, "He did let him off for the night, right?"

Lissa acts like she's surprised by the question out of my mouth. "What? Do you think I'm lying?"

"Yes, I do. You're acting weird, and I can tell something is up."

Letting out a heavy sigh, she spins around to face me and grabs me by both of my hands so I can't run. "Alright, so I may have fibbed just a little bit. He did get time off to go to Arbor Creek, but according to Graham he got into town on Thursday. He'll be working the bar tonight."

Yanking my hands out of Lissa's grasp, I let out a frustrated groan. "Are you frickin' kidding me? Why would you do that?"

"I know you have it in your head he's all partying it up and moving on, but the truth is that's a load of shit. He hardly will talk to me now, but from what I've heard, you two are about as depressing as they come. I knew if you thought Mason was going to be there, you would never agree to help Craig and work tonight. I also think it's time for you and Mason to put aside your shit and stop avoiding each other."

"I would've thought you would understand, considering your ex-boyfriend just broke up with you in an equally shitty way."

"Maybe that's true, but I know for a fact he isn't thinking about me. Mason, on the other hand, is. You seriously look hot as hell right now. I can't wait to see that struck stupid look on his face when he sees you, too." Lissa laughs.

Rolling my eyes at her, I pick up my clutch before taking a second look in the mirror. As annoyed as I am with her, I can't say I disagree with her. The way the dress hugs my body, accentuates my curves, and the color looks great against my olive skin. The heels make me taller and more confident. Despite how bad my feet are going to hurt tomorrow, I know they make my legs look killer, too.

I don't talk to Lissa for the entire way to Velvet. I'm so annoyed she lied to me I don't even bother waiting for her as we get out of the car. Walking toward the employee entrance, I watch as Graham takes a step outside and watches as we both approach. He has his arms crossed in front of his chest.

Taking the steps up to the side door, I flash a small smile at Graham.

"Hey, B! How are you doing?"

"Hi," I say. "I'm alright. Just ready to get this night over with."

"She told you, huh?" he asks, the side of his mouth curving up slightly.

"You knew about this, too?" I say, peering up at him, letting him see how annoyed I am.

He lightly chuckles as he looks past me to where I'm sure Lissa is before his eyes fall on mine. "Yeah, she did. It was my idea. You two are just so stubborn about things I knew you wouldn't put yourselves in the same place without a little shove."

"It will be okay, I promise," Graham says, running his hand along my shoulder reassuringly. "You look beautiful tonight, B. Something tells me he isn't going to get any work done tonight because I have a feeling he won't be able to take his eyes off you."

I let out a subtle laugh as I shake my head, letting out a slow breath.

"Do me a favor though…make him work for it. He deserves it!"

"Oh, don't you worry. I fully plan on it."

Graham laughs as he turns to grab the door handle and swings the door open, holding it for us to enter.

Walking down the narrow hallway toward the employee locker room, I'm relieved when I enter to find it empty. We are a few minutes late so it appears everyone must already be out on the main floor as people start entering through the door. Lissa and I quickly stuff our purses into the locker and slide the lock back on it.

The sound of the locker room door swinging open has us both turning our heads to see who it is, as Sierra struts in. She's dressed in high heels and a black halter dress. Her high heels make her legs look even longer as her platinum blond hair drapes over her shoulder.

I can tell she's surprised when she sees me. What I didn't expect to see was the smile lining her face. It's not the sinister smile I expected to see, but a genuine smile and it's immediately setting off warning alarms in my head.

"Brea, I didn't expect to see you around here."

Standing up tall, I turn toward her and say, "Yeah, Sierra, I'm sure you didn't. Now that Mason and I are done, I'm sure you thought you could weasel your little way in and take my place. How's that going for you?" I give her a sarcastic smile, knowing full well if she's taken my place in Mason's bed, there's no way he feels the same for her as he did about me.

The smile on her face grows wide as she laughs, which only pisses me off.

"Ah, there she is," she says, looking over at Lissa who is standing next to me doing her best to smother her laughter.

It takes a second for it to click that she isn't laughing at Sierra, but at me. I feel my cheeks heat up as I turn my head toward my best friend and raise my eye brow at her, challengingly. As soon as Lissa sees the anger on my face, her expression falls and she mutters a quiet apology.

"I'm sorry, Brea," Sierra starts. "I swear I'm not here to make you mad. I don't know what you think is going on between Mason and I, but I can promise you I'm not trying to replace you. I just meant it's good to see that you're still there and you still care. It means he hasn't lost you for good."

I feel the tautness ease hearing her explanation as I work to cover the look of annoyance on my face. I still don't trust her; hearing her just now makes me want to believe her.

"Listen, I know you're not my biggest fan and I understand," as if reading my thoughts. "Hell, if I were in your shoes I'd probably hate me, too. Mason and I have a history that doesn't exactly make me look like I'm someone you can trust. What you need to know is the friendship he and I have now is very different than it once was. He's not the same person he used to be. I guess love will do that to you." She chuckles, as if she knows a secret she's dying to share with me.

"He misses you, too, you know. More than he would ever want me to admit to you."

She smiles as she turns to grab the handle on the door. She pauses for a second and tilts her head over her shoulder, meeting my eyes. The smile she wore when she first walked in is back on her face, and I realize in that moment, she really means what she said.

"Oh, and, Brea, it's good to see you back."

She doesn't say anything else as she opens the door and makes her way out into the hallway.

"What the hell was that?" I ask, confused.

"No clue," Lissa says, pasting a reassuring smile on her face. I knew Lissa and Graham were in cahoots, getting me here tonight. I'm starting to wonder if Sierra didn't play a part in it, too.

The lights are already drawn low, but as soon as I step out of the hallway and onto the main floor, I feel his eyes on me before I see him. The connection we've always had to each other is still here. The warmth I feel from his stare radiates through my body.

Standing tall, I roll my shoulders back and head toward the tables with my notepad in tow. I make my rounds, serving customers and taking their drink orders. The feel of the club tonight is unlike anything I remember from my time working at Velvet. It almost feels electric. The energy so thick, it's pulsating. Just knowing Mason is here and watching me has a confidence pouring out of me. I want him to know what he's been missing since he hasn't bothered to reach out to me.

Once I make my rounds, I head to the server station to put in my drink orders. The West bar is already busy with customers waiting in line. I'm not surprised to find Craig has four bartenders working the bar, with Mason strategically covering the end closest to our tables.

Stepping up to the server station, Mason turns his head toward me. When his eyes fall on mine, I feel like everything I worked hard to conceal is laid open in front of him. He always could read me like a book, and I know with just one look, he can see how heartbreaking the last three months have been for me.

Leaning in close, Mason yells over the music, "What can I get you?"

The stubble lining his jaw is longer, and his hair has a disheveled look about it, but God, he looks so handsome. I find myself staring at him and forgetting what was even said.

"What?" I shout back.

Flashing me a smile, he repeats himself, "Did you need something?"

Nodding my head, I rattle off my order to him before tearing my eyes away from him. I let my eyes roam over the busy club, to the packed crowd moving to the beat of the music.

I feel Mason's eyes on me once again, taking in the way my body moves. Turning my head toward him, I find him staring at me as he continues to mix the martini in the tumbler. I rub my lips together, checking my lip gloss as I smooth my skirt down.

"I'm surprised you're working here again," Mason points out. He looks so handsome in his black dress shirt and black slacks. He's wearing a silver tie tonight. The sleeves of his dress shirt are rolled up to his elbows, showcasing how incredible his forearms look.

"Craig asked me to help knowing it was going to be a busy night. The tips were tough to pass up," I say. I don't tell him I was also promised he wasn't going to be here because what's the point?

"You look beautiful," he says. Peering up at him, for a second I think he regrets saying it but he doesn't take it back.

"Thanks," I mutter. "You look good, too."

I feel like our conversation is awkward and forced, skating around all the things we want to say but don't know how.

He slides the drinks onto my tray. I move to slide the tray off the counter, but Mason reaches his hand out to stop me.

"Will you talk to me before you leave tonight?" he asks. I see the hope on his face, and for a second, I find myself struggling with how to respond.

Then I push the thought out of my mind as I peer up at him.

"After all this time, do you really think it's worth it? It's been three months, Mason."

His nostrils flare as he looks behind me. I watch as his jaw clenches, before looking down to me once again. The emotion I see on his face makes me regret everything I just said.

"It's worth it to me, but I guess if you think it's a waste of time, then I understand," he says, pulling the towel out of his waistband and wiping off his hands.

"Hey," I say, covering the top of his hand with mine. "I'm sorry, I didn't mean it. You're right, after the way we ended things in Arbor Creek, I think it's time we sit down and talk about everything."

His eyes soften as he nods his head.

"Can I give you a ride home when we get off? Maybe we can talk then?"

"Yeah, I'll let Lissa know. We rode here together."

Flashing him a small smile, I slide my tray onto my arm and turn to walk toward my tables.

The night flies by like a blur. I'm thankful we are busy because it leaves little time for me to think about Mason and our impending conversation. It also helps me avoid thinking about how sore my feet are going to be tomorrow when I take my morning walk.

The DJ comes on the microphone announcing we are five minutes away from the clock hitting midnight.

"Will you ring in the new year with me?" Lissa shouts, laughing as she throws her arms around my neck, pulling me into a hug. I can't help but laugh at her exuberance.

Looking over her shoulder, I see Mason working at the bar. He leans forward to slide a beer on the counter, and when he stands back up, his eyes fall on mine. He flashes me a small smile and a wink before helping another customer.

Pulling back from Lissa, I shout over the music to her. "Hey, before I forget, I don't need a ride home tonight. Mason is going to take me home."

I see the smile growing on her face, but she bites her lip to conceal it.

"I knew you two wouldn't be able to stay away from each other if I got you in the same room together. You're both miserable without the other." She laughs.

"Alright, ladies and gentlemen. We are a minute away from the clock striking midnight. If you don't have your special someone next to you, you better find one now," the DJ shouts.

Wrapping my arm around Lissa's, we look up at the wall to where the big screen is displaying Times Square and the ball dropping.

Everyone starts to cheer as the countdown begins.

"Happy New Year!" we yell as Lissa throws her arms around my neck in a big hug. My eyes once again look behind her, hoping to find Mason but the disappointment sinks low in the pit of my stomach when I don't see him standing behind the bar.

I can't hear anything over the cheers from the crowd. Taking a step back from Lissa, her smile nearly splits her face in half at something behind me.

"I think someone wants to wish you a Happy New Year, too," she yells before tossing me a wink, turning around and leaving me standing here.

Mason's hand wraps around mine, pulling me to turn around.

His arm finds its way around my waist, pulling me closer to his chest. Tilting his head close to my ear, I feel his heated breath on my face as he says, "I know we said we'd talk about everything and we will, but the thought of not kissing you on New Year's was killing me. Especially seeing you in this fucking dress."

His chest is pressed against mine and I can feel it heave with every deep inhale. The look of longing I see chips away at any resolve I had left. His eyes search mine, as if searching for any indication I may push him away just before he leans forward and presses a soft kiss against my cheek.

"Happy New Year, Brea," he whispers close to my ear.

The feel of his warm lips against my skin and his clean scent is a heady mix.

He pulls his head back and I can't help but feel disappointed.

"A kiss on the cheek, Mason? Is that really how you think I want to be kissed on New Year's?"

The startled look on his face confirms he wasn't expecting that question.

"You just kissed me like I was your friend, Mason Reid. I thought we made it clear when we were in Arbor Creek there's nothing friendly about the way you kiss me."

The corner of his mouth curls up in a grin as I wrap my hand around the base of his neck, crushing his lips against mine. I feel all the tension leave our bodies as we relax into each other. Mason's grip on my hips tightens as he pulls me in closer to him. A deep groan vibrates against my lips as I open my mouth to him.

It's as if we forget where we are and it's only the two of us.

Sliding my fingers through the hair at the base of his neck, deepening the kiss. His hands are all over my body, running along my hips to cover the swell of my ass.

With his forehead pressed against mine, he breaks the kiss and runs his soft lips along my cheek toward my ear.

"I've missed you so much. I've thought about how much I love kissing you a thousand times. The memories are nothing compared to the real thing," he sighs, pressing another kiss against my lips.

chapter twenty-nine

MASON

Being away from Brea for three months was hard enough as it is, but watching her in that short as fuck dress was enough to bring me to my knees. She looks incredible tonight, and it's a reminder of everything I've been missing for the past three months. Her toned legs looked tan against the champagne and black lace of her dress. The strappy heels she was wearing will be the star of many of my nightly dreams to come.

When she approached me at the bar and said she didn't think it was worth talking about what happened, I was ready to throw in the towel and leave. Remembering my conversation with Callum at the stables, I was reminded of how Ellie had kept him at arm's length. Despite her best attempts, he didn't give up and eventually broke down her walls.

Brea and I had a lot of catching up to do, and I knew I owed her an apology for what I said the night we had dinner at Callum's, but I also had questions I needed answers to, too.

When the clock approached midnight, I couldn't stop myself of being close to her. I was watching her and Lissa together, hugging and sharing their excitement. When she flashed me her beautiful smile, it was like my legs moved on their own accord, needing to be closer to her again.

I knew I was skating the line when I kissed her. I was running the risk from upsetting her and having her push me out completely, but when she kissed me back, I knew I was all in. I was ready to do whatever I had to do to prove to her everything between us is more than friendship. I was ready to tell her I loved her and I would stop at nothing until she was mine.

"Well, look at you. I think that's the first smile I've seen on your face in… oh, I'd say three months." Sierra laughs, smacking me on the shoulder.

"I'm going to go out on a limb and say our attempt at getting Brea here tonight was a success, huh?"

Wiping the towel along the bar, I get everything wrapped up for closing. Peering over my shoulder, I narrow my eyes at Sierra. "What are you talking about?"

"Oh, you don't know? Well, it looks like it worked. Lissa, Graham, and I were talking the other night about how sad and depressing you both have been lately. I mean, c'mon. It's true! That girl has your balls in a vise grip." Sierra chuckles.

"Seriously," I grunt, tossing the towel along the bar.

"Whoa, it's okay. You know how much I like you two together; you were happy with her. Be honest, you've been all broody and mopey while she's been gone, which goes back to what I was saying. That smile on your face I just saw before I pissed you off is the first smile I've seen since before you left for Arbor Creek."

"Yeah, I guess you're right. I just didn't realize this whole plan had been orchestrated by the three fucking musketeers."

Hell, most of the time Brea and I were dating, if we can even call it that, Lissa rode my ass about how I wasn't good enough for her friend and needed to grow up. I know she came from a good place, but it was like she was expecting things to fail. Like she wanted to remind me when I would break Brea's heart, like it was inevitable, she would be there to knock me on my ass.

"Don't act like this isn't exactly what you've been wanting. Hell, how many times have you told me you wish you could see her? All the times we would walk by The Coffee House were obvious, too, by the way. Are you going to talk to her?"

"Yeah, once I finish this up I'm going to give her a ride home and we're going to talk."

"Well, then what the hell are you hanging around here for? I'll take care of this for you, get out of here."

"Really, are you sure?"

"Yes, I'm sure. Get out of here. Oh, and do me a favor, don't say anything stupid again like how it's only hooking up. Women don't like to hear that kind of shit."

Raising my eyebrow at Sierra, I want to laugh. Mostly because I think she is the exception to that statement. "Don't give me that look. I just didn't want it with you, and you didn't either so put a cork in it. Oh, also, make sure she knows that, too."

"Thanks for finishing up for me. I owe you one," I say, winking at her as I move to the employee locker rooms where I saw Lissa and Brea take off to.

"You're damn right you do." She grins, as she starts shutting down the register.

Before I leave, I quickly check the locker room in case they are still in there. After I come up empty, I head outside only to find Lissa's car pulled up right by the door. It's the middle of winter in Chicago, which means the temperatures are in the negative degrees. The dresses they were wearing would likely have them freezing to death.

Holding up the remote to my Range Rover, I click the remote start before the engine roars to life. I hold the keys up as I signal to Brea I'm letting the car warm up a bit. Walking over to the passenger side, I open the door for her and hold my hand out.

"Hi, Lissa," I say, smiling at her.

Brea looks at me and my hand, smiles, and places her palm in mine. Her hand feels so small and it dawns on me how much I've forgotten how this has felt.

"Hi, Mason," Lissa replies, flashing a wink at me. I know now she had been responsible for getting Brea here tonight. As soon as she knows I know, she throws her head back against the headrest and laughs.

"You don't keep her out too late, you hear me?" She giggles, knowing it's already past two in the morning.

"You have my word." I chuckle before shutting the door.

Walking Brea toward my SUV, I help her in before jogging around the front of the card to slide in.

My hands feel stiff from the cool air. Rubbing them together, I work to add some warmth to them.

"It's freezing out tonight," she sighs. I lean forward and turn the heat up on the seat warmers.

"Where should we go?" I ask, peering over to Brea.

"I'll be honest, I want to talk but I'm feeling exhausted after the long night. My feet hurt and I just want to put on my pajamas. Would you mind if we went to my place and just talked there?"

"No, that sounds perfect."

We don't talk on the way to her house. The entire drive there I feel like my thoughts are plaguing me. I've had so many things built up in my mind I've wanted to say and now none of it seems relevant having her next to me.

When we pull up outside her apartment, we park right next to Lissa. She left just a few minutes before we did so she couldn't have been here for long. I can tell Brea is tired by watching how slow she takes the stairs in her high heels.

As soon as we push the door open to her apartment, she is quick to bend down and unstrap her heels.

"I'm going to go change quickly. If you want to just hang out here, I'll be back in just a minute."

It doesn't take her long before she changes her clothes. I am surprised to find her with her hair pulled up on the top of her head and her makeup removed from her face. This is the Brea I fell in love with. The woman I loved watching get dressed up for a night out, but was also ready to strip it all off and just relax for a night in. She's the calm to my crazy at times when my mind would get too loud. She always knows how to keep me level headed.

She tucks her leg beneath her as she crawls next to me on the couch. Pulling the blanket over her lap, she faces me on the other end of the couch and I recline back on the sofa.

"You look so beautiful when you're like this. Stripped down, showing me who you are beneath it all. You let me see the real you instead of the version the rest of the world gets to see."

She gives me a sad smile before looking at her hands. I sense she isn't sure what to say, or how to even start, so I decide to do that for her.

"Listen, I know things went down terribly when we were in Arbor Creek, and I'm sorry for what I said at Callum's. I was hurt and it was uncalled for. I'm sorry for not only saying that in front of my father, but for how it made you feel. I hope you know what happened between us was more than just a hook-up for me."

She tilts her head up to look at mine, and her eyes search my face like she's trying to gauge whether I'm being truthful or not.

"Why?"

I narrow my eyes at her. "I heard you talking to my mom in the kitchen that morning. Hearing her tell you how I was feeling about you and for you to say we were just friends felt like a punch to the gut."

I can tell when she realizes what I had heard. "We never talked about what we were after I got home from Cleveland."

"I told you before you left I wasn't going anywhere. I didn't. You're the only person I want to be with. Since that night at Dean's when you gave yourself to me, I've only been with you. Hell, Brea, it's always only been you."

"Mason," she says, and I can tell I broke through to her. The tears well up in her eyes as she runs her fingers beneath them, wiping away the errant tears.

"Do you still trust me?"

She seems to think about it for a moment and it worries me, knowing how much trust means to Brea.

"Yes," she says with absolute conviction.

"You asked me to promise you that night nothing would change and I couldn't, B. I couldn't. If I'm being honest with you, I've been in love with you since before that night. All I've ever wanted was you. I know I've done a shit job of showing you through my actions. Yeah, I might not always get it right but I'm trying. You can't tell me when you think about all the times we were together, you didn't feel it."

She moves the blanket from her lap and crawls across the couch to where I'm sitting, climbing up on my lap so she's straddling me. Easing her hand down beside us, she pulls the lever to the recliner, pushing it backward.

"Do you really mean that?" she asks, looking down at me. A strand of her hair falling forward is pressed against the side of her cheek.

Using my hand, I push back the strands so that I can see her face and look her straight in the eye.

"Brea, I love you. I swear to you it will only ever be you. You're my best friend. I love how when you're cold, you curl up next to me. I love how you are so outgoing with everyone, but you only show who you truly are to a select few people. You've been guarded, and I understand why, because of the lies you've had to face. I promise you though, you don't have to lock up your heart anymore. I will always be here to take care of you."

Running her hand along my cheek, I relish in the feel of her warm skin against my mine. She traces the pad of her thumb along my lower lip before leaning forward, pressing a soft kiss against my lips.

Skating both of my hands along her hips and up her back, I pull her in closer, deepening the kiss. The salty mix of her tears combined with the taste on her lips that is uniquely Brea. I will never get enough of her.

Keeping her head pressed against mine, she leans back far enough so we can see each other. The love I see shining hits me like a slam to the chest.

"I love you, too," she breathes as another tear streams down her face.

I can't help but smile. Running my thumbs underneath her eyes, I wipe away the moisture. "Why are you crying, baby?"

"I'm just happy," she says, smiling at me. "I've waited for you to tell me those words for so long."

"Good," I say, pulling her closer and pressing another kiss against her lips, "because so have I."

Rolling over, my hand meets the silky-smooth hair draped over the pillow next to me. My mind registers the soft sound of Brea's breathing next to me.

Memories of last night filter through my mind, remembering how we made up after we got back to her place. Then, when we were done, we made up for lost time after that.

Brea's warm body curls against my side as I slide my arm over my face, using it to shield my eyes from the bright sunlight. I'm careful not to wake her as I turn my head toward her.

Her long eyelashes feather out across her skin as her hand presses against her cheek. I take in the small pout of her lips and the light freckles that pepper her nose. I've always loved how she has shown me all the layers of her.

I lose track of how long I lie here watching her, appreciating the feel of having her close to me. She's felt so far away for too long. I'm almost scared when she wakes up, it'll all be a dream.

"You're staring," she mumbles quietly.

My chest vibrates beneath my quiet chuckle I hadn't realized she was awake. Although I can't find it in me to care that I've been caught looking.

"You're breathtaking."

She peeks one eye open before slowly opening the other. Blinking slowly, she adjusts her eyes to the rays of sunshine peeking in through the window.

Running my thumb along the curve of her cheek, I press my mouth against hers. She groans quietly before I swallow them down. I know she doesn't like how I'm kissing her when she hasn't brushed her teeth but I don't care. I've been without her for too long, watching her from a distance. Now that I have her back, I'm going to take advantage of it.

At least until I wake up and this all goes away.

I roll back onto my pillow and pull her over with me, so she's resting her chin on my chest.

"Good morning." I grin, taking in her sleepy face. I can see the thoughts and questions swirling in her eyes.

"What's on your mind?"

We've spent so much time apart. We've always been so open and honest with each other, except where our feelings are concerned. I'm not going to let that happen again.

"I guess I'm just curious what you were up to while we were... apart."

"I was a miserable fucking mess." I laugh, but the truth is it doesn't even begin to say it.

I can see the hurt on her face before she quickly covers it up with a sad smile.

"It's still surreal, having you here, in my bed. It wasn't easy being apart, seeing pictures of you online, hearing from other people what you've been up to. It felt like everyone knew more about my best friend than I did and I hated it."

"I don't know what you heard or what people were saying, but I was someone no one wanted to be around. You can ask Graham. I don't know if we've ever fought so much in all our years as friends. I think he helped Lissa get us together again only so he wouldn't have to put up with me."

"You want to know what I was up to?" I ask, going back to her earlier question.

She nods her head from where her it's resting on her fist, looking down at me waiting for me to answer.

"I didn't do much of anything, if I'm honest. If I wasn't at school, I was at Velvet or here. No one wanted to be around me, not Graham or Dean. After you quit working at Velvet, I couldn't bring myself to be there. I felt like shit because I knew Craig counted on me but I told him I needed more time off."

"I ended up missing my shift back at work. He apparently blew up my phone but, uh…I accidentally broke it trying to keep myself from calling you. I wanted to give you your space and that's the only way I knew how. Anyway, Sierra showed up over here looking for me and found me halfway through a bottle of whiskey."

"I know you don't like her and I don't blame you. If you don't want me to be friends with her, I won't. I guess I just felt alone so I opened up to her and told her what happened. You should know when I was done, she actually told me I deserved it and called me an asshole."

Brea's mouth curves up a little hearing that last tidbit.

"I guess she's not so bad," she jokes.

"Mhm," I hum, shaking my head at her.

Brea's face turns serious and I wait for what she is going to say next. Whatever it is, I know it's important.

"It's not fair though, for you to take all the blame. I lied to you and I hate myself for it. After you stopped calling, I told myself I deserved for you to give up on me. On us. Why wouldn't you after what I said? It was a lie, Mason. I didn't mean it for a second. You're all I've ever wanted."

"Don't," I command, hating the way she's being hard on herself. "I knew you didn't mean it. We may have avoided our feelings by not admitting them out loud, but that doesn't mean I didn't feel it. I have always felt your love, B."

Hearing me use the nickname people close to Brea have used has a smile stretching across her face.

"Say it again."

I pause for a second. My brows furrow as I tilt my head in question.

"I have always felt your love…"

"That's not what I meant," she says, scooting closer, pressing her hands against my face, holding my attention.

"What part?" I ask, playing stupid.

Her face turns stone cold as she squints her eyes at me, not impressed. The subtle smirk on her face proves although she is not liking my game, she is playing along.

"I've always felt your love, B."

I barely have a chance to finish when her lips crash against mine. Sliding her leg over my hip, she climbs on top of me.

Having her heat pressed against my dick has me turning hard in an instant. I know she feels it, too, as she rubs herself over my cock letting out a whimper.

Those moans, I swear to God those moans.

She's ruined me.

epilogue

MASON
june

Moving the box to my left hand, I do my best to keep it balanced against my chest as I reach my other hand out to close the trunk of Brea's car. Squinting my eyes against the sunlight, I make my way into my building and up to my second-floor apartment.

The box in my hands is the last of our things. It's been a week since Brea and I graduated from college. It didn't take much to convince her to move home with me.

After we've spent so much time apart, I think we both knew we didn't want to be without the other and were willing to make it work.

In a few short weeks, I will be starting my internship at the law firm my dad works at in Des Moines. We wanted to move to Arbor Creek, but with the distance it would take every day, we felt it only made sense for us to move to Everton.

Not only would it be closer to where I'm interning, but there were more job opportunities available for Brea. She has been submitting applications to a few of the local schools, although there are still not many to choose from. Everton is bigger than Arbor Creek, but not by too much. Until school starts, she was thinking about applying at a couple of the daycare centers in town until something becomes available.

I move the box to my left arm and reach out my right to try and open the door to our apartment, only for the door to swing open before I get the chance.

"Sorry, we got distracted unpacking."

"Brea, I think I got your dresser put together. I didn't know where you wanted it so I let Mason arrange it to how you like it," Brea's dad says, as he steps out of our bedroom and into the hallway.

Brea is still working on repairing her relationship with her dad. Although it took some time and encouragement from both her mom and me, she has put the past behind her and is working on moving forward.

I was with her when she finally met Kyla and Kaden. They took the trip to Chicago with their dad when we graduated. It didn't take her long to warm up to them, and I know now how happy she was to finally meet them. While she has admitted she will never have a close relationship with their mom, I think it took seeing how happy her mom is with David for her to accept the place Patricia will have in her life.

"That sounds perfect. Thank you so much for making the trip here and helping us get everything put together and in order."

You can see the sparkle in Nathan's eyes, knowing how much being here with her has meant to him. We went out to dinner after our graduation ceremony and he pulled me aside, wanting to tell me thank you for being there for his daughter. He admitted he's aware that her giving him a second chance and allowing them to be at our graduation was because of me encouraging her. I know now how much that has meant to him.

"I had to see where Mason was whisking you off to. Your dad needs to know you'll be safe after all." He chuckles, flashing me a wink. "I know Mason will always make sure you're well taken care of though."

Brea moves in closer to me, sliding her arm around my waist as she peers up at me, flashing me a big smile. Looking at her, I give her a wink of my own, letting my eyes travel to her lips. I wish her dad wasn't standing in front of us because I want nothing more than to have them pressed against mine.

"Well, listen, Brea, I should probably take off. It's going to be a long trip to Ohio. Come here and give your old man a hug before I go."

Brea drops her arm from around me and walks over to where her dad stands, wrapping her arms around him and rests her head against his chest. He doesn't take his eyes off me. I see the emotion on his face as he mouths "thank you." With a nod, I head toward our bedroom and give them a moment to say their goodbyes.

Once I hear the door shut, I walk down the hallway to where she's standing at the table, unpacking a box.

"Is this the last of it?"

She turns to face me, dressed in a tank top and a pair of my gym shorts, rolled up around her waist. Her hair is piled high on her head, bouncing with every move that she makes.

"This is it. It's official; you're my roomie. How does it make you feel, babe?" I ask, pulling her closer.

"Just your roomie, huh?"

"Oh, you're more than just my roomie, babe," I say, pulling her closer and tangling my hand into her hair, kissing her deeply. Her arms slip around my waist as she presses the front of her body against mine. I feel the steady beat of her heart beneath me.

She opens her mouth and runs her tongue along my lips. Letting out a deep growl, I open my mouth to her.

"Yeah, that kiss certainly feels a hell of a lot more than a roomie," I say, pressing my lips against her forehead.

She flashes me a smirk before stepping back to open the box.

"Have you talked to your brother today?"

"Yeah, he had to make a trip this morning to Des Moines to take some materials to my dad. They are starting on the house remodel this week. I guess he and Ellie are going to drop by later this evening though."

The relationship between Callum, my dad and I has been a lot better since our visit last fall. A lot of it has to do with how well our father has been doing in his recovery. I know how much it means to Callum to have him around now, especially knowing his wedding is coming up.

"Two more months until they officially tie the knot. It's crazy how fast time has flown by."

Callum proposed to Ellie on New Year's Eve and, of course, she said yes. Ellie made him promise the wedding would be small and intimate between the two of them and their close friends and family.

Callum just wants her to be his wife, which mean he happily agreed with whatever she was proposing.

Raps are heard against the door as I turn my head looking out the window. I spot Graham's souped up pick-up parked out front.

Swinging the door open, I find him standing there holding two boxes in his hands and an annoyed look on his face.

"A little help," he grumbles as I open the door further letting him enter.

"You could've called me and told me you were here. I would have helped you bring shit in."

"I got it," he grunts as he walks down the hall.

"It's the one on the left," Brea yells, shouting out directions to Graham's room.

As soon as he's out of the room, Brea swings her head up with her eyebrow raised expectantly.

"I thought he wasn't supposed to be here until tomorrow?"

"Yeah, I thought so, too."

I'm still shocked to hell that I could convince him to move here with us. It damn sure wasn't easy. When Graham got the call three months ago that his mom's health wasn't going so well, he put his stubborn pride aside and finally agreed it was time to go back to Arbor Creek.

Since then, he and Dean have decided to open a security business together. Their plans are well under way. Craig has agreed to help them both, as a silent partner, under the condition that they open locations in Des Moines and Chicago. He certainly has the experience with overseeing the security at Velvet and Hard Stop. Craig even agreed to hire them on as their first client.

The sound of his heavy booted feet down the hallway ceases the conversation as Brea turns back to the box and begins unloading items onto the table.

"Will you help me carry in the big stuff? There's not much. We should be able to get it in a few trips."

"Yeah, I'll be right down," I confirm as Graham stalks past me out the door.

"You still think it was a good idea he moved with us?" Brea asks, looking up at me.

"Of course, I do. Sandy needs him home right now. He may not want to be here, but give it time and he'll come around. Sometimes you have to let people heal on their own terms, right?" I say, leaning back, winking at her. She laughs as she tilts her head up to me.

"Yeah, you're right."

"Of course, I'm right, baby." I lean my head forward and press my lips against hers.

Moving to head out the door, "Mase," Brea says, stopping me as she grabs me by the hand and pulls me closer to her.

"Promise me it will always feel like this between us," she says, holding her hand between us as her fingers curl around mine. "Promise me nothing will change."

I run my eyes over her face, the soft tan skin and the way her hair is falling out, framing her face. The smile on her lips begs for me to lean in and kiss her.

"I can't promise you nothing will change," I say, and I see her throat move as she swallows. "Because I know with every passing day we're together, I fall more in love with you. I do promise I won't ever let a day go by where you don't know it."

The smile that breaks out across her face nearly knocks me on my ass. Using her hand, I pull her closer to me as I press a kiss against her lips. "Mm, I love you, Brea Wade."

I don't take my eyes off her as I take steps backward, moving toward the door. She bites her lip between her teeth as she shakes her head.

"I love you, too, Mason Reid, and I always will."

Thank you for reading **LOST BEFORE YOU**! I hope you love Mason and Brea as much as I do.

You can continue the Heart's Compass series with Until I Found You, Graham and Halle's story. It's a second chance romance with an edge of suspense.

If you loved Lost Before You, I appreciate your help in spreading the word, including telling a friend. Reviews help readers find books! Please leave a review on your favorite site.

You can sign up for my newsletter to learn more about my

new releases. You can also join my Facebook group, Brooke O'Brien's Rebel Reader Group, for exclusive giveaways and sneak peeks of future books. To join, visit:

www.authorbrookeobrien.com/follow

Now, turn the page for a sneak peek of Until I Found You…

UNTIL I *found you*

A HEART'S COMPASS
BOOK THREE

USA TODAY BESTSELLING AUTHOR
BROOKE O'BRIEN

chapter one

HALLE

"Woah, we're half-way there," I sing, as I furiously massage the conditioner into my hair. "Woah, livin' on a prayer."

I'm not quite sure why I'm singing this song, but it's fitting for this morning. I'm the type of person who sings when I'm trying to focus or when I'm in a hurry. Although I can't sing when I'm trying to read a street sign. I'm one of those people who turns down the radio to see what's fifteen feet in front of me. That's neither here nor there right now.

The point is, I'm running late, and I need all the help I can get. It would come to the surprise of no one that I'm running behind schedule. In fact, if there's one thing you could ever count on, it's that I'm usually two or ten steps behind everyone else.

I get distracted easily, get caught up staring off at whatever shiny object has stolen my attention, like right now. Which is why I'm singing to myself as I stand in the shower, rushing through the process of washing my hair.

I have twenty minutes in which to make it to the Hopeful's Bridal Boutique on the other side of our small town of Arbor Creek. Today is a big day for Ellie, one of my best friends, as she'll hopefully find the dress she's been searching for.

In all honesty, it's not Ellie I'm worried about who will be ticked at me for arriving fifteen minutes past the time I was supposed to be there. No, not at all. It's my roommate and other best friend, Kinsley. She's the yin to my yang. It's what makes our friendship balance out—everything I'm not, she makes up for by pushing me to be.

Kinsley would never be caught dead arriving late for anything. It's more likely she would arrive fifteen to twenty minutes early, with a checklist of everything she needs to do. I'm more of a fly-by-the-seat-of-my-pants kind of girl. I don't have much of my life planned out. I don't even know what I'm going to wear today, let alone have I thought ahead on where I see myself in five years.

I keep Kinsley young and she reminds me to never take life too seriously because, let's face it, we're all going to end up at the same place. I can't take any of this shit with me anyway. I just hope I arrive late when I go too.

Leaning my head back, I let the suds wash away before I run my hand over my long hair, wringing out the water before reaching down to turn off the faucet.

Reaching outside the shower, I blindly pat around for the towel I set on the rack. Grabbing it, I pull it toward me and use it to pat dry my face as the sound of hard knocking pounds against the door.

"Shit. Shit," I groan to myself, realizing I had spent far too much time in the shower. Along with Ellie and Kinsley, our good friend, Brea, who rounds out our little biker gang of badassery is joining us for today. Brea's dating the brother of Ellie's fiancé, so really, she's her sister-in-law for all intents and purposes.

There's a pounding at the door that comes for a second time, spurring me into action. Brea was supposed to be here any minute now, so we could ride together.

Wrapping the towel around my body, I tiptoe my way out of the bathroom and down the hallway. I can imagine the look Kinsley would have on her face if she were to witness this moment, knowing I'm leaving drops of water on the hardwood floor behind me.

This is why we're friends. She needs to learn not to sweat the little things, like water on your floor. It will dry on its own.

Clutching the towel to my chest, I don't bother even looking out the window as I swing the door open and turn back around.

"Hey Brea," I call out over my shoulder, "give me just a second to get dressed, and we'll head out."

Moving quickly, I'm mindful to step around my little puddles of water, careful not to slip and fall, as I head back down the hall toward my bedroom when the sound of his deep voice hits me.

We're usually not prepared for the moments that change our lives. I didn't see it coming the day Graham Shaw broke my heart, shattering it into a million pieces. I thought he was going to be in my life forever, but it turns out forever came sooner than I had expected.

Which brings me to this moment. For a second, I question if this is a cruel version of déjà vu, only now I don't want to believe my ears. Jolting myself into place, I squeeze my eyes shut hoping that what I just heard was all in my head and not at all what I thought it was.

"Do you always open the door to strangers and invite them in, without even checking to see who it is?"

Turning slowly, I wish I would've prepared myself better for what, or rather whom, I was about to see.

My eyes narrow and it takes me a second to collect myself, getting over the shock of seeing Graham Shaw standing before me in all his handsome glory.

"I didn't realize you were a stranger," I bite back, realizing the way he had left me with so many unanswered questions still hits like a hard slap to the face, even after all this time.

My eyes stare intently, as I hold the towel wrapped around me tight. It feels like all the air has been sucked out of the room and of me, reflecting on how much weight is carried in one sentence alone.

If I didn't know any better, I'd say there was a look of guilt that passes over his face, but before I can analyze it further, it's gone. His jaw flexes, as his eyebrows furrow, looking back at me.

I never had expected to be a stranger to Graham, yet now it seems like that's who we are.

It's a weird feeling staring back at the man you loved more than anything. Remembering all the things you knew about him, like the way he used to bite his lip when he was deep in thought or how he'd crack his knuckles when he was nervous.

Looking at the man in front of me, I can't help but feel as though I don't know anything about him. It was hard to get through every day after he left. It almost feels like a lifetime since I last saw him.

Damn, he looks good though. I used to love running my hand over his pecs down to his abs. He always worked out, but when he was younger, he was lean despite years of football and lifting weights. He's filled out more and it pains me to say it, but time was so good to him.

It makes me even more angry to think about all the women he's attracted since then.

"I know you better than you know yourself, Halle. Don't be fooled. I don't understand why the hell you'd open the door and let someone in, not realizing who's on the other side. It's not safe. I could've been anyone."

"First of all, it's been five years. You knew who I was then, but I'm not that girl anymore, Graham. You don't know me at all. Second, if you weren't paying attention when I answered the door, I thought you were my friend, Brea. I didn't think you were just anyone."

His eyebrows raise higher and I realize then if he hadn't felt guilty before, he does now. Maybe even a little shocked too.

"You always were a pain in my ass," he mutters to himself, running a hand over his face and down over his jaw.

In doing so, I watch as he stares back at me and for the first time since walking into my apartment, he lets his eyes roam over my face to my neck and down over the rest of my body. When he finds his way back up, I meet his stare with my eyes narrowed into slits. His stare is so blatant, his eyes burning into every inch of me.

"You used to love that about me," I retort.

A small smile curves at his lips. The mention of the past and what we used to be stings, like a zap to the heart. I had closed all roads to my heart where Graham was concerned a long time ago.

I'm not going down this same road with him again. Not anymore. He had his chance.

"Well, listen, this little reunion has been fun and all, but I have to get going. My friend is gonna be here any minute. So, if you don't mind telling me what the hell you're doing here, that'd be great. That way I can send you back on your way."

The curve of Graham's smile grows, and I want to roll my eyes and demand him to leave.

"Mm, there's the fire," he smirks.

I kid you not, the fucker has the gall to smirk at me. He always loved getting me riled up. I want to smack him upside the head, he makes me so angry.

"Tick, tock. I don't have all day."

"Are you talking back to me right now, Halle?"

"Yes, Graham, that's how conversations with me work. Now get to the point."

Chuckling, he crosses his arms, which leaves me momentarily distracted as my eyes roam over him, taking in the way his muscles bulge when he flexes.

"Kinsley sent me here. Something about helping her roommate load up some things for her for Callum and Ellie's wedding. Do you know anything about that?"

"Kinsley." I pause, feeling the edge of irritation seep into my tone. "I'm sorry, you said Kinsley sent you over here?"

Of course, she did. If there's anyone in my life who hoped Graham and I would end up together, it was Kinsley. In fact, she had our whole wedding planned out for us, knowing exactly every detail we'd want for our big day.

She really missed her calling as an event planner because I swear, the woman is as organized as she is frustrating right now.

"Yeah, I was down at the salon a little bit ago. She helped get me in for a haircut under short notice, so I was doing her this favor in return."

I want to ask him what he's even doing here. Why he's in Arbor Creek when he made it clear when he left that he was never going to return, at least not this soon. As much as it's killing me to ask, I leave it alone.

It's a dead end road and, quite frankly, I don't have it in me to care anymore.

"That's funny, considering Kinsley helped me load everything up last night," I deadpan, looking at Graham unamused.

"Is that right?" He laughs, just as my phone pings with a text message.

Turning on my heel, I continue down the hallway toward my bedroom to grab my phone.

Brea: I'm stuck in traffic on the highway. I'm sorry, I'll have to meet you there.

Ugh! Locking my phone, I toss it absentmindedly somewhere on my bed. Opening my drawer to my dresser, I grab my black lace bra and matching panties. Dropping my towel, I make quick work of putting them on while sauntering across my room toward my closet to figure out what to wear.

Looking in the corner mirror, I see Graham eyeing me from where he still stands rooted in place in our entryway. There's a fire in his gaze, one that's been a long time since I've seen, but remember from all those years ago.

I let him drink me in standing before him, reminding him of everything he let go of when he chose to run away rather than face his problems head on.

It's terrible of me to say, knowing the series of events which led him to leaving, but it doesn't change the fact he hurt me when he did.

Seeing him look at me the same way he did all those years ago lights something within me that's been burned out, withering away for a long time. I've tried to move on, used meaningless relationships with nameless guys as a way of burying my feelings for him.

Staring back at him, I wonder if he's having the same thoughts I am, about how time and distance has changed things between us but the connection between us is still there.

I feel confident and sexy, watching the way his eyes eat up every inch of my body, down to my painted red toes back up over my chest and to my face.

"If that's all, don't let the door hit you on the way out, Graham. Travel safe when you head back to Chicago," I say, opening the closet to search for something to wear.

Peeking my head out from behind the door, I spot Graham reaching down to adjust himself. Biting my lip, I clear my throat as his eyes dart over meeting mine.

"Oh, and do me a favor, will ya?" I smile, loving how wound up he looks, waiting for what I'm about to say.

My smile widens, knowing I have him right where I want him. "Lock the door for me when you go. I wouldn't want anymore strangers showing up at my door and inviting themselves inside."

Leaving him with a wink, I force myself to focus on what I'm doing. I'm glad he can't see me now because my cover would be blown.

I'm so spaced out, thinking about the way he looked at me, that I can't even think straight.

My ears perk, listening for any signs of him leaving. I hear him mutter something about me being a pain in his ass followed by shuffling feet before the door opens. The sounds from outside filter into the apartment and down the hall, then a moment later the door closes once again.

Stepping out from behind the closet door, I take a seat on the edge of the bed and fall back, looking up at the ceiling fan spinning around.

Graham is the only man who's ever made my heart beat out of my chest.

What he's doing back in Arbor Creek, I have no idea, but I'm glad to see him again.

HALLE

Leaning over into the trunk of my car, I carefully stack the third box onto the pile before slowly lifting them into my hands. Feeling shaky, I pause and let out a slow breath. I probably should save myself the stress of carrying three boxes of breakables inside, but my momma didn't raise no bitch. Why make two trips when I can get this done in one?

Slowly and carefully, I make my way toward the front of the Hopeful's carrying the boxes of wine glasses and the vases that I ordered on Amazon. The clock is starting to wind down, we're just a couple months away from when Callum and Ellie walk down the aisle.

Taking the step on the curb, I peer into the front of the boutique window and see my girlfriends huddled in a circle. My eyes widen, flashing them with a hard look that says, "one of you pay attention to me and help me open the damn door." As if picking up on my laser focus, Kinsley turns and sees me. Her eyes widen, taking in the stack of boxes in my arms before rushing toward the door to help usher me in.

"What the heck are you doing? You could drop those! And what took you so long to get here?" she mutters, holding the door open for me.

"What are you talking about?" I ask, playing coy. I know she's aware of the fact I'm late. Twenty minutes according to the clock in my car, but I'm playing it off like I'm early. I like to give her hell, it's one of my favorite things to do. Considering she's the reason why Graham showed up at my door this morning, I feel like she deserves it. I'm still not sure if I should be annoyed or mad at her for it yet.

It's why she's my soul mate. She helps balance me out, keep me in line. Most days I love her for it, but days like today when I'm stressed to the max and feeling the error of my ways, I don't want to hear her obvious disapproval.

"We were supposed to be here at nine thirty. It's nine fifty-two, Halle. What took you so long?"

Setting the boxes onto the small table, I turn and face Kinsley.

"What took me so long?" I reply sarcastically. "Well, let's start with the visitor who showed up at my door the moment I was getting out of the shower. Let's start there."

Kinsley looks at me and there's a small grin that stretches across her face.

"I don't know what you're talking about, but I'm glad to see you got the wine glasses and vases here for Ellie to see."

Looking over her shoulder, I see Ellie and Brea standing near a rack of dresses. Kinsley's grandma, June, is sitting in a chair off to the side. She smiles as she watches Ellie hold out each dress she browses.

With an annoyed smile on my face I nod my head. "Wouldn't want to ruin your plans," I retort, waving my hands at her and her notebook. She's been using that thing to call out orders to all of us for the past week. Strolling past Kinsley, I wrap my friend in a hug.

"You look so pretty, Ells. Are you excited to find the perfect dress?"

"Honestly, some of these dresses are so intimidating," she sighs. "I just want something simple. Callum promised me simple."

Ellie doesn't ask for a lot, but the one thing she did say was she wanted a small wedding. She wanted a day filled with all the people she loved as she tied the knot of forever with the only man she's ever loved. Callum, being Callum, promised to give her everything she ever wanted and more. He just wanted to know she was his.

I'm so happy to see someone who deserves it more than anyone finally get her day.

I can't deny the small part of me that feels my heart ache in my chest after seeing Graham today. Five years ago, I thought I found my forever. We were young but were so in love. The two of us together, I thought there was nothing in the world that could tear us apart.

Moments like this, the memories come crashing over me in waves. I find myself doing what I've always done to bury the pain, I find ways of coping, distracting me from the way my heart aches with missing him.

Bringing myself back to the present, I run my hand along Ellie's back before I whisper in her ear, "I promise it will be everything you want and more."

Standing back, I flash Ellie my best smile hoping that it hides my sadness and gives her the reassurance she needs.

"Why don't you show us one of the dresses you have your eye on? Do you have a style you had in mind?"

Kinsley start clapping her hands excitedly.

"Ells, I promise you're going to look stunning." Kinsley walks toward her, reaching over her shoulder to pull a dress off the rack. "I saw you looking at this one. I think you should try it on. Who knows, maybe this is THE dress!"

I take a seat next to June and she reaches over, patting my forearm. "Hi, sweetie, you doin' alright?"

Running my thumb over my fingernail, my mind wanders elsewhere. As soon as I hear the lock on the dressing room door, my eyes shoot up to find Ellie looking stunning in a gorgeous white dress.

It's simple and form-fitting, molding to her body like it was meant for her. Blush highlights her cheeks. She's never liked being the center of attention, but the sparkle in her eye shows just how happy she truly is.

Kinsley lifts the train behind her, using her other hand to help Ellie step onto the platform. We all turn to look in the mirror, searching for any sight of what Ellie may be thinking, but the subtle way she bites her lip shows she's trying to fight back the smile that wants to let loose on her face.

"Ellie, oh my God," Kinsley mutters, pressing her hand to her mouth as tears form in her eyes. I force down the emotion rising in my throat. She looks beautiful.

Ellie's had an incredibly hard life, facing more tragedy and heartbreak than any one person should ever have to endure. Nearly nine months ago, we almost lost her when she was assaulted and abducted. She's fought her way out of that life, and she continues to fight with every ounce of determination in her. No one in this world deserves the happiness she has been given more and seeing how happy she looks in that dress has tears silently streaming down my face.

"What do you think?" Brea asks. Looking around the room, I notice there isn't a dry eye in sight.

"I love it! It's pretty and so perfect. Do you think Callum would like it?"

Ellie bites the inside of her cheek, looking uncertain. There's a hesitancy in her voice, before Kinsley interrupts the seriousness of the moment bursting out laughing.

"Are you kidding? He's going to lose his shit when he sees you walking down the aisle and I can't wait to see it happen."

June laughs softly and I know she, along with the rest of us, agrees with Kinsley's statement. Although I'm positive Callum would be tripping over her no matter what dress she picked.

Ellie quickly swipes away the tear that threatens to fall before she subtlety nods her head agreeing. "I think this is the one then." She smiles. "Oh, God, I'm getting married."

She says the statement with shock underlying her tone, as if she can't believe it's about to happen either.

"You and Callum are going to live a happy life, Ells."

We snap a few pictures of her in the dress, being sure to capture different angles. Holding out my hand, I help her back to the fitting room to change.

Kinsley is back to work looking over the rack of brides-maid's dresses, so I reassure her I'll help Ellie as she gets the rest of the dresses in order.

I feel her eyes are burning into me, as if she, too, is sensing something is wrong.

"You've been pretty quiet today. It's like your mind is somewhere else. How are you handling everything?" Ellie asks quietly.

"What do you mean?" I question, as she slides the dress down over her hips.

"Brea told us about Graham moving back to town. I fig-ured the news would be hard on you. You don't have to pretend with me though, Halle. I'm here if you ever need to talk."

This is what I love most about Ellie. She's been through so much in her life that she understands the hard. When you need someone to be there for you, not necessarily with the right words to heal you, but just be there for you—it's her.

"I'm sorry, it seems selfish of me. I don't want today to be about me. This is such an incredibly exciting time for you. I promise I'll pull out of my funk. Seeing him earlier was unexpected and more difficult than I ever thought it would be."

"You don't have to worry about that with me, Halle. If there is anyone who understands how you're feeling, it's me. You don't have to pretend around me. Like I said, I'm here for you. You just let me know when you're ready."

I nod. "Thanks, babe." I give her a reassuring smile. She reaches out to grab my hand, squeezing it.

"Now seriously, let's talk about how Callum's going to react when he sees you in this dress. You'd look great in a potato sack, that's why I hate you. He's going to be crying, stumbling over his words. It's going to be adorable." I laugh.

She blushes, her smile growing a mile wide. "That's my plan."

I'd always hoped I'd see Graham again, but having it become reality has me lost in my head. Lost in the past, but I'm doing my best to pull myself out of it. I've been forcing a smile on my face for a long time. I've gotten somewhat good at it by now.

We all have that one person our hearts will always go running back to and, for me, that person will always be Graham. I only wish I were his reason to stay.

Do you want more Graham and Halle?

Check out Until I Found You today at:
www.authorbrookeobrien.com/untilifoundyou

BOOKS BY BROOKE

A Rebels Havoc Series

Brix
Sins of a Rebel
Tysin
Trey
Madden

Men of Blaze Series

Personal Foul
Reckless Rebound (Cocky Hero Club)

Tattered Heart Duet

Torn
Tattered

A Heart's Compass Series

Where I Found You
Lost Before You
Until I Found You
Now That I Found You
Where You Belong

Standalones (In order of publication)

Wild Irish

Learn more and purchase your copy at:
www.authorbrookeobrien.com/booksbybrooke

PLAYLIST

Love Triangle by RaeLynn
Unsteady by X Ambassadors
Every Little Thing by Carly Pearce
Raise Up by Petey Pablo
Different for Girls by Dierks Bentley & Elle King
Yours by Russell Dickerson
Come Over by Sam Hunt
Hurricane by Luke Combs
Shoop by Salt-N-Pepa
Don't Ya by Brett Eldredge
How Not to by Dan + Shay
Tin Man by Miranda Lambert
In Case You Didn't Know by Brett Young
Any 'Ol Barstool by Jason Aldean
I'm Real by J.Lo feat. Ja Rule
Stay A Little Longer by Brothers Osborne
She Got the Best of Me by Luke Combs
No Scrubs by TLC

Listen to the playlist on Spotify at:
www.authorbrookeobrien.com/lostbeforeyou

ABOUT BROOKE

Brooke believes a love worth having is worth fighting for, and she brings this into her stories where her characters risk it all for love.

When she isn't writing or falling in love with a new book boyfriend, you can find her spending time with her family, cheering on her favorite sports teams, listening to ASMR, or binge-watching the latest true crime documentary. She loves rockin' a comfy hoodie with leggings and believes the best days include a good nap.

Brooke loves connecting with readers and hopes you'll join her on her social pages or reader group to stay in touch. To follow Brooke and join her newsletter, visit authorbrookeobrien.com/follow.

ACKNOWLEDGMENTS

My Boys – I love you more than anything on this earth. Everything I do is for our family.

Mom, Gram, & Ash – Thanks for always being supportive of this journey. You've pushed me to go after everything I want in life. Love you! Special thanks to my Momma for being my second set of eyes.

To my AMAZING beta readers – Giovanna, Julia, Erin, and Barb. Thank you for reading Mason & Brea's story before anyone else, for your honest feedback, and helping me make their story better. I'm so grateful for you! <3

Kate & Kelsey – What would I do without you two? I don't want to find out. Thank you for being there for me when I need to brainstorm an idea or tell me it's going to be okay when I need to hear it.

My editor, Roxane LeBlanc. I enjoy working with you. Thank you for being honest and patient with me. I've learned so much from you!

My proofreader, Julie Deaton. You have a fantastic eye for detail, and I appreciate all your help in getting this book polished off. Thank you for everything!

Najla and Nada with Najla Qamber Designs, you are so incredibly talented and blow me away with your work. Thank you for designing the most beautiful cover, complete with matching the interior.

To Stacey, Natalie and the crew over at Wit & Wonder PR, thank you for your support and helping me promote my work. I'm forever grateful!

Lastly, to all the fantastic bloggers and authors who have shown me support throughout this journey. I hope you know how grateful I am for every one of you. A special thank you to Jenn with My Slanted Bookish Ramblings, Andrea with Just a Girl a Book and a Blog, KayCee with Double Decker Books, Aurora with Whoo Gives a Hoot, Angie Hallock, Laurie Breitsprecher, Kayla Ries, Brooke May, Katie Fox, Abigail Davies, Danielle Dickson, Tiffany Carby, Bella Emy, and Ember-Raine Winters.

COPYRIGHT

Qamber Designs
Cover Photo © iStock
Edited by Rox LeBlanc, Roxs Reads
Proofread by Julie Deaton, Deaton Author Services
Version: BMO08042023

www.ingramcontent.com/pod-product-compliance
Lightning Source LLC
Chambersburg PA
CBHW060858210726
48293CB00006B/1856